A
PERFECT
DISGUISE

CHRISTOPHER AND DEBRA DATTA

1

Zooey Krause crushed a mouthful of ice chips between her teeth while waiting for Joe Quigley to arrive, a man she'd never met but was preparing to dislike. He'd called her detective agency that afternoon asking that they meet in the evening at some place other than her office, and he was late. She didn't mind working on a Friday night, but she'd expected better manners from the smooth-talking voice on the other end of the phone.

The air-conditioning in Mark's Soft Shoulder Bar was on the fritz again, and the steamy August air made it hard to breathe; it lingered in Zooey's nose, making her clothes, her red hair and even her third gin and tonic smell like a damp basement.

Mark, the bar's owner and a husky middle-aged Philippine American with close-cut hair and a mustache, spun the dial of his prized black antique art deco radio, and it came to life with an ominous buzz on the counter beside her. A large, flat-screen television hung high above the bar, the display dark. Mark preferred listening to his radio.

"Hey, Mark," slurred a drunk at the bar, "turn the damned TV on. I wanna watch Fox News."

"Oh, for Christ's sake, Joey, why you wanna watch that cable trash? I'll tell you what's on. Fox is saying the Dems hate America and cheated with illegal immigrant votes to win the last election, and CNN says the Republicans hate democracy and are racist pigs, and they all of them talk trash about the Mexicans on the border. Good luck and goodnight."

"Well, them Dems is Communists is what it is, and the country's headed for a fight, like that shootout we seen in Alabama when them FBI thugs tried taking them guns from them militia patriots. Them sissy libtards is gonna shit their pants. See if they ain't. I tell you, there's gonna be trouble and plenty of it."

"Have another Jack Daniels, Joey, and shut the hell up."

"Hell of a way to treat a customer."

"Hell of a way to run a country."

"I'll drink to that," said Joey, as Mark poured him a Jack, neat. The TV stayed off and the radio came alive playing a jazz station, Mark's favorite.

Zooey looked around the bar, thinly scattered with the usual Friday night crowd of misfits and drunks.

Propped up in the booth behind her, three old men wearing identical red Washington Nationals baseball shirts and caps traded slurred comments about a ballgame.

At the end of the counter to her left, an unremarkable and fat surrealist poet, sometimes Zooey's drinking partner, drew a comic strip with a black pen. She watched for a while, and then turned away, combed her long red hair with her fingers, straightened the collar of her black cotton blouse and examined her smudged reflection in the beveled mirror behind the bar.

Part of Mark's job as the silent partner in her detective business was to read her moods, and he floated over.

"Mix you another? It's on the house," he said, flashing his professional bartender smile. When she just shrugged, he wiped the counter with a dirty rag, his lazy circles expanding until he bumped her hand.

"Hey, come on Zooey, come alive! What's wrong?"

"Nothing. It's just that a client, or rather a potential client, stood me up."

"Yeah? Who is he?"

"Some corporate hack named Joe Quigley. He insisted he couldn't come to my office, so I suggested we meet here. Now I'm thinking maybe he got one look at this place from the outside and decided to spend the evening alone with a beer."

"So how about that gin and tonic?"

"Sure, thanks. Hit me again, Mark." She laughed grimly.

Zooey heard a gusty wind slam shut a neighbor's door and it suddenly smelled like rain.

"But if I don't get more business," she said, "I'll have to rob a bank to pay Jason this month."

"So I'll float you a loan if you need it," said Mark. "But you won't, so what's got you down?"

Zooey opened her mouth to reply when a young kid stumbled out of the men's room. As Zooey watched, the kid wavered, and then collapsed backwards against the bathroom door. He wore faded jeans and a sleeveless, threadbare T-shirt stretched over his skinny chest, and had long frizzy black hair and a faint mustache that hadn't seen soap for days. Mark walked over to collect his bar tab, and then put an arm around the kid's shoulders as he directed him out to the street.

Lightning lit the stained-glass windows that circled the domed ceiling of the barroom, throwing clear, strong colors across the room. Zooey turned back to her still-empty glass and decided to leave before the rain started, since the idea of watching this storm from her apartment balcony with a glass of brandy seemed better than hanging around the bar. When Mark returned, she slipped a ten-dollar bill across the counter.

He pushed it back to her.

"Hold on, girlfriend, I think your man's arrived. A three-piece suit is hanging out, inspecting the place." Mark nodded to the door. "Behind you. Now don't turn around too fast; you might scare him off."

Zooey glanced up into the mirror to see a dark, thin, sharp-featured man studying her. She swiveled around on her barstool and stared back at him for a moment before waving him over. After holding her gaze, he scanned her body from head to toe slowly, scrutinizing Zooey's face, her clothes and her style.

She waved him over again. He mimed a startled reaction, smiling, throwing up his hands, and then approached her.

A real London Fog and Bacardi type, Zooey thought. He wore a perfectly tailored three-piece suit, black wool with a pinstripe, a white shirt, and a red silk tie.

"Zooey Krause?" he asked when he closed the distance between them. He straightened his tie and looked around the room. The building housing Mark's Bar had once been a church, and later attempts to hide that fact hadn't hidden that fact. Located in Adams Morgan, a seedy but gentrifying Washington, D.C., neighborhood, Joe Quigley's stockbroker uniform looked out of place.

"I'm Zooey, and you're Joe Quigley. Well, sit down, Joe. Have a Salem?" She offered him the silver case she'd inherited from her father. She no longer smoked, but carried the case for clients, still dented where her dad had fallen on it when he died.

"No thanks," he said, sitting down.

"What's your pleasure?" Mark asked Joe from behind the bar.

"A draft. No, make that a scotch, please. Neat."

"I'll have the same," said Zooey.

Joe's handsome face included a small, narrow nose, heavy-lidded eyes and a thin and neatly formed mouth. His hair was dark and left long in back.

"Sorry I'm late," he said as his drink arrived. "I just couldn't decide whether to go through with this. My story is complicated, and I need someone I can trust, who can keep my affairs confidential. But I didn't have any idea how to go about hiring a detective, so I just picked your name off the computer directory. Seems like a silly way to hire someone, but then I've never needed a private investigator before."

Joe delicately sniffed and then sipped his scotch. The twist of his nose indicated to Zooey he was either an inexperienced drinker, or more likely the opposite and he was reacting to the quality of the house scotch.

Joe looked up with a grim smile. "I guess I will have one of those Salems. I'm always trying to quit."

"Sure thing."

Zooey sat up straighter and offered her case again, and then lit his cigarette, noticing his trembling hands. They were smooth and delicate: a technician's hands. She wondered whether he was always this high-strung. She observed he had no wedding ring, but maybe his girlfriend was cheating and he wanted photographs to prove it. Infidelity was the bread and butter of her business. Either that, she guessed, or he had some other low-class job for her that didn't fit his white-collar corporate image.

"You're not what I pictured," Joe said, exhaling. "You're young. How long have you been in the detective business? If you don't mind my asking."

"Hey," interrupted Mark. "No smoking. City ordinance."

"So arrest him," said Zooey with a shrug. Turning back to Joe, she said, "I don't mind you asking. Three years. But it's a long story, really, and not very interesting. Why don't you tell me why you want to hire a me?"

Joe swirled the whisky in his glass as Zooey pulled a notebook from her pocket. Loose papers spilled out, forcing her to climb down from her stool to gather them up off the floor. She hid a smile; something was always happening to screw up her professional pose.

"This story is going to sound crazy," Joe said into his drink.

"Don't worry how it sounds. I listen to crazy stories seven days a week; it's my job."

Zooey pretended to sip her whisky. She knew she didn't sound sympathetic, but then she found that Joe didn't need encouragement to begin.

"Well, you know that my name is Joe Quigley, and I grew up here in the suburbs of D.C. I'm an engineer at the experimental nuclear power plant project north of Washington in Maryland. The Blackstone Plant. You must have heard of it."

Zooey shrugged.

"I'm an associate engineer. As I was saying, the Blackstone project is experimental and highly controversial after all the problems with nuclear energy we keep hearing about. It's called a breeder reactor, technically a fission-fusion hybrid. After I got my degree at M. I. T. fifteen years ago, I was hired as part of a research team to study the feasibility of using fission to power fusion reactions. Do you know anything about this field?"

"Not really."

"Well, let's just say that it's been an exciting project. If we succeed, we'll provide cheap energy for the world with zero carbon emissions, and if you're an idealist like I once was, you'll understand why this work has been my life's dream. The United States can afford fossil fuels because we're rich, but Third World countries are the ones who really suffer. The price of fuel drains their budgets. If they could have this cheap source of clean electricity, they'd have a better chance to develop and global warming would be a thing of the past. And then they could even afford more imported goods, so the world economy would benefit. It was a wild dream of my youth, perhaps, but I've always considered myself fortunate to have this job, and that's just about all there was to tell about my life until six months ago."

Zooey didn't understand much of what Joe had said, but his enthusiasm for the work came through clearly.

He gulped at his whisky, and his nose twitched again, with definite distaste this time. "But to explain about why I called you, I should tell you about the Blackstone annual Christmas party last December. One of the worst things about working for any company is the annual Christmas party, which I've fortunately managed to avoid until last year."

Joe shook his head. "I'm sure you know what those parties are like. Some guy you normally hate gets drunk, puts his arm around you and calls you 'son' or 'buddy.' And then you can't tell him to shove off, of course, because 'it's Christmas.' I hate the holidays."

He smiled as Zooey laughed, nodding.

"I usually try to get away for a vacation during December, but this year it didn't work out. Last summer I wrote to request brochures about a cruise to Bermuda, but then I got a job promotion back in September and I had too many projects on my desk to get away, and that's why I was in my office on December 24th last year when my boss caught me trying to sneak out the back door early. He grabbed me by the arm and dragged me to the annual Christmas extravaganza. He said it was good for morale."

Joe eyed her, judging her reaction as he continued to talk.

"These parties are a big deal—I mean, they hire a band, put up streamers and wreaths and a twenty-foot Christmas tree. There are cookies and hot hors d'oeuvres, but mostly an unlimited supply of booze. Open bar. Everyone drinks and dances for hours, and every year there's at least one office affair that leads to a divorce. Ho, ho, ho. So there I was, holding a glass of champagne punch and standing behind the giant tree hoping no one would notice me, planning to sneak out the minute my boss turned his back. While I was standing there, I noticed a woman from the system operations crew named Mary Gentry. Mary was telling a joke to a group of people, and everybody was laughing. She was so beautiful I couldn't take my eyes off her. She wore this tight-fitting, low-cut black velvet dress; every man there watched when she crossed the room. Her hair was long and black, a red ribbon pulling it back from her forehead. Her skin was pale and creamy, a color that reminded me of candlelight. I also noticed that she blushed often when she talked. She was absolutely charming."

Joe sat silent for a moment. Zooey sensed from his expression that Mary was now a former part of his life, and that they had drifted apart. Or else she was dead.

"What happened then?" Zooey prompted.

"I asked her to dance. You wouldn't believe it, but she turned that lovely face to me and I froze; I mean, I couldn't breathe. Then, to my surprise, she laughed. She said I looked like a stuffy bigwig who wouldn't know how to dance."

He laughed, thinking about it. "And boy, was she right. There was rock music playing, but I put my arm around her waist as if we were starting a waltz. I wanted her to stay with me all evening, but she had plenty of other men waiting to dance with her. Still, I could tell she liked me. And she's the reason I want to hire you."

"She's disappeared?"

Joe's downed his drink. "Yes, she's gone. But I should tell you some other things, first. I've always been pretty shy with women, but I never felt shy with Mary. After the Christmas party, we started going out; you know, to movies, restaurants—it hardly mattered, because we always had a good time, no matter what we did. But what surprised me was her intelligence; nothing important ever slipped past her. And she understood me better than anyone else ever has."

Joe waved for another round of drinks and Mark stepped up with the scotch.

"We fell in love right away," Joe continued. "Or maybe not right away, but after four months I asked her to marry me, and she said yes. No hesitations. We didn't tell anyone about our engagement, we didn't want the office to gossip, but I was busy making plans for our future when everything fell apart. It started when Mary told me that some of her friends were afraid the plant was cutting corners on safety regulations.

"Anyway, Mary started getting ideas—she thought these safety procedures at our plant were being ignored to save money, and that there were problems with the way the Union pension fund was being managed. Then she got some wild idea that the Union leadership was being paid off by our management to ignore the danger. She was obviously wrong, as I explained to her many times, but she didn't believe me. The next thing I knew, she'd called a newspaper reporter for the *Washington Spirit*, without telling me until later, of course. The reporter's name was Virgil Fitts. Do you know him?"

"I've heard the name."

"Well, she told Fitts her story, and he got interested. I've heard about this Fitts; they say he's a womanizer. With all his experience, I'm sure he knew right away that Mary was an excitable dreamer, and that her story was nothing more than a loose collection of rumors. But Fitts saw the chance to create a scandal; big headlines for the paper because everyone loves to pick on nuclear power. Naturally, he convinced Mary to push it further.

"As time went on, Mary got more and more obsessed about this safety and pension thing, and we argued all the time about it. It was bad, because I'm in a position at the plant to have known whether her accusations were true or not, and I absolutely knew she was wrong. The safety standards at the Blackstone Plant are rigidly adhered to. I'm mainly responsible for seeing that they are, and I thought Mary should have taken my word about that. But she saw my objections as an attack on her."

Joe shook his head and sipped his drink. "I wish I could tell you exactly what she was like. She always got involved in everyone else's problems, was always helping somebody, and she always cried at the sad parts of movies. I know that sounds silly, but she wasn't silly. She really cared about problems at the plant, and that's why she was so stubborn about it with me.

"And the way it ended, that's the worst part of it."

Joe looked away.

Feeling embarrassed, Zooey reached for her glass and found it empty again.

"One Tuesday a month ago," he finally continued, "Mary left the plant at eleven o'clock in the morning. I didn't know about it at the time, but a friend of hers said she was in a hurry, and that she mentioned having an appointment with a newspaper reporter. Wherever she was going, she had an accident on County Road 5 on her way into town. Someone found her car flipped over in a ditch at the bottom of a hill. The police said she must have been doing ninety miles an hour to jump the guardrail like that. It broke her neck. She died right away. Never had a chance."

Joe jumped off his stool and headed for the men's room, and Zooey felt sorry for him. His carefully constructed world of pinstripe suits and silk ties, complete with this new love, had come apart quickly.

There was something odd, however: when Joe described himself as shy with women, Zooey had almost laughed. It was hard to believe that a man as successful and attractive as Joe Quigley could have avoided the attention of women. Yet there was a kind of desperation behind his manner that made Zooey want to help him.

Outside, the storm had broken, and the room echoed with the drumming of rain against stained-glass windows. Joe didn't reappear for ten minutes, so Zooey listened to a breaking news report on Mark's radio about a left-wing terrorist group threatening to attack some red-state city in the Midwest to make "fascist cops and their supporters" pay for the murder of innocent black men. Zooey just shook her head. Politics. None of it made any sense to her.

When he sat down beside her again, Zooey asked, "Are you all right?"

Joe's face was pale; he gave her a tight smile. "I don't know. I guess so. I'd rather get this whole thing over with."

14

Zooey picked up her notebook again. "When did Mary have the car accident, exactly?"

"It was a month ago."

"And what did the police say?"

"They did an autopsy because of all the publicity, but in the end, they said that she'd simply been driving recklessly. There wasn't any evidence of foul play, booze or drugs, if that's what you mean."

"And you don't agree with their verdict?"

"I think the verdict was fair. I just want to talk to Virgil Fitts."

"That reporter from the *Spirit*?"

"Yes. He's disappeared, and I want you to find him."

Zooey was surprised at that and tapped her pen on the bar. "And what will you gain by talking to him?"

"Let's just say that after Mary died, he did a 180-degree turn in what he'd been reporting about her. He wrote a follow-up story that her death on County Road 5 was a suicide caused by a cheating boyfriend. None of it made any sense given how he'd treated her story before. Now there's a rumor circulating around the plant that I was screwing somebody else's wife and Mary had found out about it.

"Look, someone or something got Fitts to change his story, and I want to know what."

Zooey picked up her refreshed drink. She'd expected some kind of cheating to enter Joe's love story, and she was almost disappointed.

Joe caught the involuntary twist of Zooey's mouth.

"You believe his story, don't you?" Joe said, and then continued bitterly, "Well, sure, why not, everyone else does. And it's ruining me. Can you imagine what life is like for me now? All Mary's friends blame me for her death, wondering whose wife I screwed. Listen, Zooey, Mary was high-strung sometimes in her idealism, and she was always emotional in her approach to things. She got upset when I didn't support her suspicions about Union tampering at the plant. But I swear to you, she still loved me, and if her friends at the plant saw that she was upset at work, it was only because... well, that's just the way Mary was sometimes. She didn't try to hide her feelings, and even if she tried, she wasn't any good at it."

Zooey pursed her lips thoughtfully and turned to look for Mark. He was talking to the cartoonist, who was still drawing at the end of the counter.

"Mark!"

"Yes, Zooey?"

"Would you pour me a cup of coffee? Anything more for you, Joe?"

Joe examined his empty glass. "More of the same."

He sighed. "I don't drink very often, but this rail scotch starts tasting good after you've had a couple."

Zooey considered what Joe wanted her to do. "Are you sure that you only want to *talk* to Virgil Fitts?"

"I want to know what happened. Why? Do you think I'll go after him with a sawed-off shotgun?"

"It happens. Maybe I've only been in the detective business three years, but I know payback is everyone's favorite motive for murder."

Joe twirled his glass impatiently. "Look, all I want you to do is find Virgil Fitts. I've called his office every day for two weeks, and nobody knows where he is. His paper says that he's out on a drinking spree. It fits right in with his character, and it's not the first time, from what I've heard. I don't want to hurt the guy, but I want to find out why he changed his tune and printed that suicide story when he knew better. The rumors are ruining my life."

"Right. Well, I'll find Fitts so you can talk to him. You give me a sendoff, say $500 for coffee and doughnuts, and I'll subtract it from my $500 a day plus expenses. When I learn something, I'll call. Meanwhile, call my office if you need to talk to me and leave a message with Jason, my secretary. I'll get back to you."

"You don't have a cellphone?"

"I do, but I don't give out that number. If it's important, Jason will call me and forward the message."

She downed her coffee, noticing that the rain had stopped. As Joe wrote a check, his hand looked steadier.

"Here's your sendoff," he said.

She slid the check into the left front pocket of her black cotton pants and pulled her leather file from the counter. "Mark?"

Mark stood at the front door of the bar, surveying the street. "How much do I owe?" Zooey called out to him.

"I'll cover that," Joe said. "I'm not ready to go home yet."

"Thanks," Zooey said. "Goodnight."

Joe hesitated. "There is one more thing I should tell you."

"What's that?"

"I think Mary was pregnant."

"Ah," said Zooey. "I'm sorry."

"Me too," said Joe.

She slid carefully off her barstool and extended her hand. Joe shook it delicately.

"Goodnight, Zooey."

Zooey orbited toward the door, the scotch rendering her unsteady on her feet, as the radio news still carried on about that crazy threat to attack the police in some Midwest city. It sounded like a big story, but she wasn't interested. She gave a sidelong look at Joe, who was ordering another scotch and no longer looked so out of place in Mark's Bar.

Zooey followed the cracked sidewalk up Biltmore Street to her apartment. The city was damp and dark, except for a hundred street signs blinking like votive candles up and down the avenue.

2

Zooey didn't wake until noon on Saturday morning, roused by a sultry breeze drifting in like steam through her open bedroom window. As she peeled the sheets from her skin and stretched her arms, she felt the first wave of her hangover. She gently rose from the bed, closed the window and turned on the air-conditioning, cursing herself for forgetting to do that the night before.

Heading straight for the shower, she decided again that drinking with clients was a bad idea. An almost unavoidable hazard of the profession, however, since her mostly male clients talked more openly and spent more freely after they'd both had a few.

Evidently everyone in her building was getting the same late start, and the water pressure in her shower thinned to a trickle just as she rinsed the soap from her skin. She dried herself quickly and pulled on a thin blue dress. Then, after a breakfast of coffee and aspirin, she began making phone calls.

She'd half-expected to reach Fitts at home, but got no answer. Nor would the other ten Fittses in the phonebook admit to being related. Next, she tried the offices of the *Washington Spirit*, where she connected with a reporter.

"Hey, babe," answered a young male voice, "do you look as good as you sound?"

"No, I'm a humpback with a club foot. Is Virgil Fitts there?"

"Naw, but let's talk about us."

"I'm his niece, and Mother asked me to look him up while I'm in Washington. We haven't heard from him in years, and she'll never forgive me if I don't say hi. Do you know where I can find him?"

"We haven't seen his shadow for a few days, sugar. He may be drunk or he may be on a story, I don't know. But hey, I know how you can contact me."

With a heavy sigh, she said. "Oh, I'd so hoped to see Uncle Virgil before I leave." She forced herself to sound girlish. "Isn't his wife around?" she asked, taking a chance.

"He's been divorced for years now; she blew town with the kids, I hear. But there is one guy who might know where Virgil is."

"Good. Who's that?"

"Give me your number and I'll give you his name."

She gave him the number of a local female cop she knew.

"Wallace Durnam, the editor of this rag, might know where he is. Every Saturday you'll find him at a place called the Westerner's Bar. It's just down the street from here. Now, how about dinner at my place?"

"Give me a call and we'll arrange something."

She hung up and walked into her small kitchen to pour a second cup of coffee.

She lived on the second floor of a red brick townhouse that had once been as elegant on the inside as it still looked from the street. The interior nevertheless retained a certain dignity, though it now housed four tiny apartments, two on each floor. An old photo of the foyer hung just inside the front entryway, showing a crystal chandelier glittering above a Persian carpet. The chandelier was long gone, and green linoleum now replaced the carpet. A coin-operated washer and dryer sat under the stairs, and at least one bicycle was usually chained to the upstairs bannister.

Zooey's apartment had four rooms. Her landlady, whom she hadn't seen since she'd rented the apartment three years before, had made a point of proudly directing her attention to the antique claw-footed tub in the bathroom, original to the house, and in which Zooey had managed to rig up a decent shower. The other rooms included a bedroom, barely large enough to fit a double bed and dresser, a small kitchen and a living room/study. Her kitchen's main drawback was its pint-sized refrigerator, stowed under the counter next to the sink; it could hold little more than a quart of milk and a jug of wine. The kitchen walls were brick, the same ruddy color as the walls outside, and she had a window which, though it faced another building, managed to grab enough sunlight to please her only plant, a wilted African violet gifted to her by Mark. There was a small balcony, accessed by a door in the living room, with a single black iron chair and tiny table.

Zooey finished her coffee and stacked the empty cup on a pile of dirty dishes in the sink.

A half hour later she was driving past the *Spirit* offices in the Chevy Chase neighborhood of northern Washington, a neighborhood where an eclectic mix of old stores and private residences had been demolished and replaced by towering corporate office buildings.

The bar was surrounded by a few surviving small neighborhood shops set among the modern grey edifices. She parked her old Mustang in front of a delicatessen. It was hot again, but Zooey could feel a shift in the air that suggested a repeat of yesterday's thunderstorm. A few kids hung out around the curb, but they ignored her as she crossed the street.

Zooey couldn't see anything when she pushed open the door into the Westerner's Bar, so she stood for a moment letting her eyes adjust to the dim light. The bar air was a cloud of stale cigar haze that was like sandpaper on her corneas. Apparently, this bar's management also considered city ordinances against smoking optional. She squinted as she walked to the counter to order a beer.

The room was larger than it appeared at first glance, though there were surprisingly few tables and chairs. Zooey suspected the reporters who kept this joint in business probably stood at the bar for quick shots between assignments. The only cowboy-themed decorations in the Westerner's Bar were nylon lariats hanging limply on the dark green walls. A Schlitz malt liquor bull blinked overhead, and she could smell the toilets from across the room. The bartender was an ex-boxer, she guessed, from the battered look of his nose. He wore a yellow T-shirt with the sleeves cut off and a portrait of Daffy Duck on the front.

"A beer?" she asked, and then watched as he pulled a frosted mug from a freezer under the counter. He filled the glass, scraped the foam off the top and handed it to her.

Thirsty, she took a fast gulp.

"Good beer," she said conversationally.

"Thanks. And we got some lunch specials. You should try my ribs," he suggested, pointing with one finger of a well-muscled hand to the wall menu written in chalk above the front door.

"Sure you can spare some of yours?"

"I got plenty," he said with a grin.

"Maybe later. Right now, I'm looking for Wallace Durnam. I hear he spends his Saturdays here."

"That's right. He's over there, against the wall."

The far side of the room flickered in the ruby glow of pint-sized table candles set in red glass lanterns. In the center, directly underneath one of the lariats, sat a large man slouched forward in a straight-back chair. Zooey felt a stab of panic. Oversized men intimidated her; they reminded her of her dead father. A few young men—reporters, she guessed—approached and lingered at the far side of Durnam's table. As she watched, he pulled his cigar from his mouth and spat out a few words in their direction. When he finished, they shuffled away and out the door.

Zooey took a deep breath.

"Send him another drink, whatever he's having," she said to the bartender. "He looks like he could use it."

Zooey knew that Durnam had edited the *Spirit* for more than twenty-five years, and while it wasn't *The Washington Post*, it catered to and was popular with the African American community, had a reputation for controversy and was influential in city politics to a degree out of proportion to its size. The word was that Durnam was a dictatorial dinosaur, the stereotype of a dying newspaper breed. He would probably soon be replaced by some young intellectual with a Ph.D. in journalism, and the paper would die in short order.

The bartender set a drink on Durnam's table, nodding back in her direction.

She decided politeness was the proper tact as she walked over to him. "Hello, Mr. Durnam. My name is Zooey Krause. Can I talk to you for a minute?"

Durnam snickered, then yelled over her head to the retreating bartender. "Hey, Gerber, when in the hell did you start serving teenage girls?"

"Since they started paying," Gerber shot back.

Zooey sat down before Durnam could ask her to leave.

"Someone from the *Spirit* told me you spend your Saturdays here. Classy place." She looked up at a lariat.

Durnam frowned, his mouth pursed in annoyance. "Hey little lady, you from the Salvation Army? Well, I gave at the office, so you can take your trumpet to the park." He blew smoke at her, chuckling male approval to himself.

Zooey strained to maintain her composure. She'd expected this sort of crusty abuse. "Listen, Mr. Durnam, I don't want to ruin your day, but I'm a niece of Virgil Fitts. I happened to be in Washington on business, and I promised my mother I'd look him up. He's my dead father's half-brother, but nobody in my family has seen him for years. I tried calling his office at the newspaper, but I guess he's on vacation or something. Anyway, I wondered if you could tell me where to find him. I don't want to bother him or anything, just say 'Hi' from my mom."

"Hi from mom? I'm sure Virgil won't want to miss that." Durnam looked over her shoulder at the door.

"Mr. Durnam, can you help me find Uncle Virgil? I mean, I'm leaving town tomorrow and…"

"No, I can't." Durnam tossed down half his drink.

"Could you just pass on a message for me?"

"Look, sweet cakes, he hasn't been at work all week. If you find him, tell him he's fired. I prefer my reporters to at least pretend to do their jobs."

"Do you think he's in trouble? I know that he drinks and…"

Durnam slammed his glass on the table. "Why not try the library?"

Zooey decided to drop the polite act before she ground her teeth to stubs. "Look, I'm not here for some burlesque audition."

"Shove off then, because you're no niece of Virgil's. I know his family, see, so who are you really? Virgil is African American, sweet cakes, and you don't look the part, even light skinned as Virgil is. Maybe you're working for his ex, or maybe he owes his bookie money." Durnam glanced past her to a man entering the bar.

Durnam laughed and then coughed, spewing a brown speckle of chewed cigar leaf the size of a .22 caliber bullet on her dress. She stared at it in disgust. Durnam leaned forward, jabbing his chubby fingers at her face, and Zooey forced herself not to cringe.

"Sounds damn hokey," he said. "You're new, aren't you? My guess is you're some bargain-basement P.I. pushing for back payments on his alimony. You can tell his ex to forget it, sis."

Zooey realized she was blowing it. She really wasn't much of a detective, mostly taking on cheating spouses, insurance fraud and lost animal cases. She wasn't good at cross-examination, and what was worse, Durnam obviously saw right through her. The truth, she decided, was her best last chance to salvage anything from this mess.

"Okay, Mr. Durnam." The "Mr." stuck in her throat like a raw oyster. "My name really is Zooey Krause, and like you said, I'm a one-woman detective agency. But I don't want to get Virgil Fitts into any kind of trouble and I've never met his ex-wife. I've just been hired by someone who wants to talk to him."

Durnam laughed. "Lady, I've watched you in action here and I doubt whether you could bail water out of a bathtub." He swilled down the last of his drink and shrugged. "The business makes you a whore. I know the really good detectives in this town by heart; they're friends. You don't even come up in our conversations."

Though a lot of what he said was true, and probably because of it, Zooey's temper burst like a firecracker.

"Goddammit, Durnam! Yeah, I'm no Sherlock Holmes, but your newspaper is a flimsy scandal sheet and your big stories are backed up by nothing but rumor, useless speculation and pics of half-naked women. Anyway, I don't have to sit here and take this crap from a mud-slinging son of a bitch like you!"

She stood straight up and stormed to the door.

Durnam half-rose from his chair and almost knocked the table over with his barn-sized chest. "Krause, come back and sit down."

Every head in the bar turned.

Zooey stopped, and after a moment a smile unavoidably flickered across her face. So the monster missed her already. Let him wait, she thought. She wasn't about to be pushed around again.

"Sit down," he repeated, this time in a softer tone forced out through clenched teeth. He settled back into his chair with a grunt.

"Why?"

"Just sit down, for Christ's sake. Come on, I'll buy you a drink."

Zooey shook her head with exasperation, and then caught a glimpse of the Daffy Duck bartender laughing silently behind the counter.

Durnam was quite a character; she wondered how many similar scenes the bartender had witnessed. Slowly, she changed direction and headed back to her chair. As she sat, Durnam fixed his eyes on her, his face twitching. Then he raised his arm, shook the ice in his empty glass and yelled at the bartender, "Hey Gerber! Bring Krause here another milk, or whatever she's drinking, and refill mine."

Zooey folded her arms across her chest. "Beer."

Durnam shrugged. "Hell, it ain't often I get to view such a show of self-righteous indignation," he said. "I usually hear it from hucksters trying to sell me a bundle of goods, but you aren't a huckster. They always sound like farts in church when they try that self-righteous shit."

"You thought I was a con artist?"

"Maybe, or maybe not. But you come barging in here with some bullshit story about being Virgil Fitts's relative, and I got a staff to protect, or at least that's what I tell them."

Durnam relit his cigar.

"So why do you want to find Virgil?" he asked.

Zooey couldn't see any reason not to mention Joe's dead girlfriend. "Someone wants to talk to him about a woman named Mary Gentry. She died in a car accident about a month ago just north of D.C. Do you remember her? I've heard that the *Spirit* printed a story about it."

"Mary Gentry. Yeah, I remember her. Virgil brought her in on some story having to do with Union tampering. She wasn't too clear on her facts, but Virgil thought she was on to something. I can't say as I agreed with him, but I told him to go ahead and investigate it when he'd finished helping Joe Rodgers research his series on corruption in city hall.

"But I didn't want him putting too much time in on it. I mean, it was clear that this girl Mary was a political nut. But I figured that we could use some filler for a Sunday feature we were planning about the safety of nuclear reactors."

"When did this happen?"

"Somewhere around the beginning of July; I can't remember exactly. But the girl was scared, I'll say that. She thought maybe the newspapers could help her out of a jam. Believe it or not, plenty of people see newspapers as dedicated to comforting the afflicted and afflicting the comfortable, as was so famously said."

Durnam contemplated his cigar, turning it over and over between his fingers. "Still, she talked straight, if you know what I mean. So I gave Virg the green light on it. I guess I made a mistake about that."

"Why is that?"

"You saw the papers. When Mary died, and suspecting foul play, I printed a lead story: 'What Happened to Mary Gentry?' So then Virgil drove out to the Blackstone Plant where she worked and talked to a few people. He found out that she'd had some mental problems that he wasn't aware of. I mean, he'd never bothered to talk to her friends or the people she worked with about these wild ideas she had. Meanwhile, he spent the paper's time and money failing to substantiate the paranoid delusions this girl had about the Union at her plant. In the end, we had to print a retraction because her death was probably a suicide."

"Didn't you think there was something a little funny about that?"

"Funny? Not really. Look, I'm just lucky that the paper didn't go ahead and print a series of stories about Union corruption at the Blackstone Plant, which is what Virg wanted us to do in the beginning. There could have been a big lawsuit. I don't want to smear the reputation of Mr. Fitts. I mean, there was a time when there wasn't anyone better. But the guy's had a lifelong fight with the bottle, and for the last few years the bottle's been winning.

"Besides, he really took a fall this time. I ain't seen him in two weeks."

"Do you have any idea where he might be?"

"Well, Virg disappears from time to time. I don't really know where, and don't really care, to tell the truth. I've known him for years, and I know what his problems are. He'll just spend another year's worth of vacation time using a bottle to do battle with his conscience."

"What do you mean, conscience?"

"Taking advantage of that crazy woman and then screwing things up with the paper. Something like that, I would guess. But I'll tell you something else: you're not the first person to inquire about his health. There've been others before you. Virg never had so many friends."

"Were the police involved?" Zooey said, surprised.

Durnam crushed his cigar out in an ashtray and sat back, massaging his jowls. "Yeah, one cop visited. The other guy was a thug, a Russian. Said he was a friend of Virgil's and owed him some cash. Your story was better. He smelled rough so I threw him out."

"How about Virgil? Where is he?"

Durnam frowned and lit a new cigar, his eyes two dark slits watching her. "I'll tell you, Krause, I can't tell you where to go. But if Virg is in trouble, there's one friend he trusts. Her name's Francesca Darmini. Runs a high-class cathouse called the Orchid, and it's not the sweet smell that draws the crowd. Strictly top-notch politicians and high-class crooks hang out there. Strange stories seep through the cracks of the walls of that place."

"I've heard rumors. On Hopkins Street near Dupont Circle. It's advertised as a spa, isn't it?"

"Pay enough and you may get some info there. At least they'll listen until your client's money dries up."

She nodded and stood up. "Thanks, Durnam. For an SOB, you're not a bad guy."

Durnam half laughed, half choked as a nervous young reporter immediately sank into her chair.

She walked up to the counter to settle her bill with the bartender.

"Forget it," he said. "Now how about some lunch? It sounds like you've earned it."

"Durnam chased away my appetite. Maybe next time."

"Any time. Just ask for Gerber. And no cracks about baby food."

Outside, she was blinded by the midday sun.

Next stop, she decided, was Google, to read that story Virgil had written about Mary Gentry and the nuclear plant.

The encounter with Durnam had chased away the last remnants of her hangover, and she walked over to the delicatessen to buy a sesame bagel with cream cheese.

3

At seven o'clock that evening it rained again, and Zooey grabbed her umbrella for the walk to Mark's Bar. Instead of walking along Biltmore Street, where she'd have to dodge the umbrellas of Saturday shoppers, she took a series of back streets through a rundown, crowded neighborhood that started behind her apartment.

She gazed at the windows of the townhouses lining the streets. Some were freshly painted, their windows shining with the silver reflection of the rain-wet streets, the stoops swept clean in front of heavy and securely locked front doors. But most had yellowed shades pulled down behind smeared windows, or broken windows patched with plywood. On the corner of the next street was a house she'd noticed before, built of massive mauve-colored stones. It had two tall, arched entryways and a row of curved balconies on the second floor. All the windows were knocked out, and the inside walls were charred from an old fire.

Ahead on the sidewalk, a red-striped tomcat strode gracefully up the steps of one of the better-kept homes.

As usual, Zooey found Mark tending bar, relaxed and eyeing his customers like a sea captain surveying his ship. She spotted two or three minor racket men and an odd assortment of common street bums in the shiny, varnished, light-brown booths that hugged the walls around the bar. She shook out her umbrella and left it leaning against the wall by the door, a small pool of rainwater gathering beneath it.

Mark was always happy to see her, a fact that pleased her. It hadn't been easy finding friends in Washington.

"Zooey! How's it going? You look like you need something hot to drink," he said.

"Yeah, I'm a little chilly considering the time of year. I took a tour of the neighborhood before I came here."

She sat down at her usual place next to the radio. "How about asking the cook to fix me a hamburger and fries?"

"Sure thing." He wandered back to the kitchen.

Mark was stocky and moved behind the counter like a farmer plowing his field. His thick black hair was cut short, and although he looked like a kid from a high school yearbook photo, Zooey had seen him shut down some truly dangerous creeps with what she called his "umpire voice." He'd left Iowa at age thirty after his Philippine immigrant parents died, using his inheritance to fulfill a farm boy's dream of romantic decadence by running a bar in the big city. The bar he bought was the oddest Zooey had ever seen.

It had started as a church built by the Reverend Roger Pasce after his return from World War II. Dazed by the experience of combat but inspired by religious visions, Pasce had founded the Charity and New Hope Community Church and constructed the building that now housed Mark's Bar. Pasce spent five years shouting to empty pews, repeating an incoherent sermon about the angel of peace he'd seen flying above the streets of a small German town. An accident ended his fervor; he'd darted in front of a speeding taxi as he left the church one late night in January of 1962.

Pasce's son, a worldlier type, transformed the church into Pasce's Bar and Grill, making the building far more popular with the borderline neighborhood than the Reverend had dreamed possible. When Pasce's son made the money he needed, he sold the bar and headed to California, intending to sell whisky, beer and grilled cheese sandwiches from a beach bar to a new and sunnier geography of customers.

Mark, who eventually bought the business years later, met and helped propel Zooey into the detective profession. Four years ago, she'd been granted a divorce in North Carolina, finally ending a marriage that she'd known was a mistake after the first year. It had, unfortunately, taken another nine years for her to gather the courage to leave her husband Alec.

She ended up with half their savings as a divorce settlement, but all she'd really wanted was release from Alec and the monotony of his expectations of a wife.

She decided at a North Carolina train station to buy a ticket to Washington because she didn't know anyone there. Want ads in *The Washington Post* had directed her to a pay-by-the-week boarding house with kitchen privileges, where she'd shared a bathroom with two other tenants. Her life settled into the solitude she'd always craved, where she could spend most of her days reading detective novels.

She drank a glass of cheap white wine with breakfast if she felt like it, and ate pizza from a Greek takeout dive around the corner. Often, in the evenings, she went to movies, seeing them four or five times if she liked them, a pleasure she'd missed during her marriage. Alec had never liked to go out at night and wouldn't let her go alone without a nasty argument.

Late at night, after the movies, she'd visited a succession of rundown bars, which was how she discovered Mark's Soft Shoulder Bar two months after arriving in Washington. Mark was friendly, but understood that she didn't really want to talk to anyone. Yet after a month of drinking in silence, Zooey's curiosity pushed her reticence aside, and she began looking forward to conversations with Mark.

When he got to know her, Mark discovered her interest in detective novels, and he offered to set her up in the detective business with himself as a behind-the-scenes partner. She thought it was a joke.

"Look," she'd said, "why don't you buy yourself a girlfriend instead? I'm not looking for any romantic entanglements."

"No!" Mark had protested. "Just business! I mean it! After owning this bar, a detective agency is my greatest ambition."

Zooey had laughed him off, but the idea stuck in the back of her mind until the end of her first year in Washington, when her money began to run short. On a whim, she looked into what it would take to open a P.I. office, and found it surprisingly easy.

The city website informed her:

The Metropolitan Police Department of the District of Columbia, which is the agency responsible for licensure and regulation of private detectives in the district, does not require private detective applicants to have education or experience beyond that of a high school diploma or GED.

If you wish to carry a concealed weapon as a licensed private detective in the District of Columbia, no permit is required. However, all firearms must be registered with the Metropolitan Police Department.

She then decided that Mark might have found a means for her to live out a fantasy she'd always had but would never have pursued if he hadn't offered to help. She took a two-month online course, passed an FBI background check, took out a bond that Mark fronted the cash for and, before she knew it, she was a licensed private investigator. In a way, she found becoming one disappointingly easy, given the high esteem in which she held the fictional characters she so admired.

Ironically, since all of her cases involved documenting insurance fraud, photographing cheating spouses or finding lost pets, in the end she found small-time private investigation not to be anything like the novels. In fact, it was mostly petty and boring work.

But the business broke even. Besides, it nearly sent her mother and ex-husband into seizures every time they thought about it.

Mark reappeared with her dinner on a white plastic plate. The utensils were also plastic, but the food was tasty and cheap. Zooey leaned over the counter and bit into the hamburger as Mark stood close by polishing a glass with a dirty bar rag. This was his idea of what bartenders did with their free time. In a way, Zooey reflected, they were birds of a feather, in that they both enjoyed playing roles very different from the kind of people they had been growing up.

"What happened to my hot drink?" she asked.

"Irish coffee?"

"Sounds perfect."

Mark poured a shot of whisky and a shot of Bailey's Irish Cream into a tall white ceramic cup, filled the cup with coffee and then squirted a topping of whipped cream from a can under the bar. He slid it to her. "Did I ever tell you about Squanto the pig?"

Zooey shook her head, her mouth full. Mark's farm stories were famous.

"He was the only pig my father let me keep as a pet. I could do anything—push him over, order him around—and he'd put up with it. He was smart. But my mother wouldn't let him in the house."

"What happened to him?" she asked.

"At five hundred pounds, he got too big to feed. We ate him."

Zooey threw a French fry at his chest. "That's terrible!"

"Yeah. I wouldn't touch dinner until they gave me a dog. Then I forgot all about it."

"A typical example of what happens to faithful and enduring love. But here's a toast to the memory of old Squanto the pig." She raised her cup.

Mark raised a can of Diet Coke from behind the bar. "You don't really believe in love, do you, Zooey?"

"Love is a topic I know nothing about." Zooey licked a mouthful of whipped cream from the top of her coffee and changed the subject. "At least I didn't spend the day tracking down someone's lost dog."

"What about this Joe Quigley case? Any news on that?"

She nodded, and he leaned across the bar.

"Anything big?"

"Not really. He hired me to find a reporter for the *Spirit* named Virgil Fitts, whose friends think he's off on a binge. Interestingly, the police and some Russian thug are looking for him too."

Zooey pulled a photograph from her shoulder bag and handed it to Mark. "I visited the *Spirit* this afternoon and picked up this picture of Fitts."

She filled Mark in on the details of the case.

"What about the article that Fitts wrote about the suspected suicide of Mary Gentry?"

"I found that in the *Spirit*'s online archives and made a copy. Do you want to read it?"

"Sure." Mark leaned over the counter.

Zooey pulled the article from her bag, handing it to Mark. "It's a page four story."

WOMAN DIES IN SINGLE CAR ACCIDENT

Until her death last week, Mary Gentry was a system maintenance worker at the experimental Blackstone Nuclear Plant outside of Washington. She left the Blackstone facility midmorning last Tuesday and as she approached Washington at a high speed on County Road 5, her car broke through a guardrail and rolled down a hill. Gentry died immediately.

The accident received an unusual amount of publicity, since Gentry had, several weeks before, contacted a reporter from this paper with allegations that irregularities in the handling of the Union pension fund and of a number of safety regulations at the nuclear facility where she worked were being ignored. She claimed that the leadership of the Union of Nuclear Power Workers, an organization to which she belonged, was being paid by the plant's management to ignore safety practices as an economy measure. Gentry's co-workers stated that when she left the plant midmorning on the day of her accident, she explained her sudden departure with the excuse that she had an appointment with a reporter from the Washington Spirit.

Suspicions of foul play centered on Gentry's allegations against the plant and the Union, and on the fact that she died in such an unusual accident. However, after a week of thorough investigation, police concluded that Mary Gentry's death was not the result of foul play.

First, contrary to her statement, Gentry did not have an appointment with anyone working for the Spirit on the day of her death. Second, while it is true that Gentry had contacted this newspaper concerning certain fears for her safety at the Blackstone Plant, no evidence was uncovered to substantiate pension fund fraud or safety irregularities. Finally, it was reported by colleagues that Gentry had become increasingly unstable over the last several months and was prone to hysterical outbursts and paranoia concerning her job. Her condition worsened when the relationship with her fiancé, Joe Quigley, a design engineer at the

35

Blackstone Plant, deteriorated. Police have ruled her death a suicide given these circumstances.

"That sounds conclusive," Mark said. "Another chance at a big case washed down the drain, I'm afraid."

"Yes, if you believe what you read in the papers. Joe Quigley swears that Mary wasn't suicidal."

She poured another blob of ketchup on her plate and finished the last of her French fries.

"This story sure sounds familiar. Wasn't there a similar case like this about forty years ago?"

She nodded. "Joe Quigley mentioned something about that. I hadn't heard the story."

"It was something about a woman being killed after she'd made some accusations about a nuclear plant up north somewhere."

"Could be. We'll hear what Fitts has to say about it. Unfortunately, he's disappeared into a bottle, but I did get a tip on where we can find him. A high-class spa called the Orchid."

"I've never heard of it."

"Of course, getting us to stake out a bathhouse may be Durnam's idea of a bad voyeuristic joke."

The more she thought about Durnam, the more plausible that seemed.

"I've got an idea," said Mark. "I'll pose as a customer and case the joint."

"Sure, and I'll front you $4,000 of Joe Quigley's money to make sure you have a good time. No, we need someone to hang around outside the place for a few days. Is Gillie sober? Or sober enough?"

Gillie Webbs had once been a top-notch detective on the industrial spy circuit, but now he did occasional watchdog service for Zooey. She'd offered him a permanent job with the office, but booze always tripped up his good intentions. He seemed to prefer the low life.

"I'll see that he's on the job tomorrow morning," Mark said.

"Show him Fitts's picture and plant him outside the Orchid."

She passed Mark the address.

"Tell him to play the part of a street bum, but try to make sure that there's Kool-Aid in his bottle instead of wine. We'll give it a couple of days and see what turns up."

Zooey tossed down the last of the Irish coffee. It was Saturday night, and she craved nothing more than a quiet evening alone.

4

Zooey drove to her office early Monday morning, hoping to catch up on some paperwork before she resumed the search for Virgil Fitts. Although it was only six-thirty, the air already felt hot and damp. The black leather vest she wore over a thin blue cotton shirt stuck to her back. A shrill radio voice ranting about "traitorous black nationalists kneeling at football games during the national anthem" was giving her a headache, so she turned it off. It seemed to Zooey that the nation had lost its mind, and she was sick of it.

Her office was on the fourth floor of an old office building across the Anacostia River in southeast Washington. A seedier neighborhood, the rent was cheap, but its elevators were so slow it was usually faster to climb the four flights of stairs. But this morning the building was still empty, and the old elevator doors clanked obediently open as soon as she pressed the button. Up on the fourth floor, she unlocked her office.

The heavy oak door pleased Zooey, with its frosted glass window, and a small brass nameplate below: "Krause Private Investigation."

Jason, her secretary, who lived in the back room of her office, shouted "Hello!" as she sat down at her desk.

The first letter off the top of a small stack in her inbox was from a former client, Mrs. Iris Pumpernell. Iris had wanted to hire Zooey to investigate the marijuana that her next-door neighbors grew in their garden, complaining that the police ignored her daily phone calls about it. She was also upset about a cord of firewood stacked in the same neighbor's front yard, insisting that it was an eyesore ruining her view of the street. When Zooey explained that growing your own marijuana was now legal in Washington, Mrs. Pumpernell hauled out her real purpose in wanting to hire Zooey: to investigate Hillary Clinton's funding of child trafficking operations in Washington pizza parlors. Zooey had tried to bow gracefully out of the job, until Mrs. Pumpernell demanded that Zooey return the consultation fee she'd paid. Zooey refused, which was the reason Iris Pumpernell still sent abusive letters to the office.

As she threw the Pumpernell catalog of antique obscenities into the wastebasket, Jason set a large mug of coffee and a plate of whole-wheat toast spread with peanut butter on her desk. He wore a black satin smoking jacket and jeans.

"Thanks," she said. Jason considered it part of his job to make sure that she ate breakfast.

"How are you this morning?" He pulled a brush from his pocket and, leaning against a corner of Zooey's desk, began untangling his shoulder-length blond hair.

"Fine, great. On Saturday I made some progress on a new case I'm working on, and I spent all day Sunday forgetting about it. I went to a double feature of Cary Grant rom-com movies, and then sat through it again. An all-day movie orgy."

"What's the new case?"

"Oh, it has to do with that guy who called late Friday afternoon. His name is Joe Quigley, and he met me at Mark's Bar on Friday night; an hour late, I might add. He wants me to find a reporter for the *Spirit* named Virgil Fitts."

"Disappeared?"

"So it seems."

"Sounds exciting. A real case for a change."

"Sure, big change," she said sardonically. "Mr. Fitts is on a drunk's holiday, and I've set up another drunk, our friend

Gil, as watchdog at a bathhouse where Fitts supposedly has friends."

"It's better than hunting down another lost poodle."

"Don't remind me." She picked up a piece of toast.

Jason wandered back to his living quarters while Zooey paid bills and balanced her checking account. A couple of hours later, as she chewed on a pencil and stared idly out the window, her cellphone rang, a cheap flip phone that could take photos and send and receive text messages. It could, that is, when she remembered to recharge the damn thing.

It was Mark, one of the few people who had her cell number.

"Hello, farmer. Any news?" said Zooey.

"Gillie just grabbed our reporter, Fitts, at the Orchid."

Zooey looked at her watch. "Terrific, Mark. Has he left, or is he still there?"

"Seems they're getting smashed together out front."

She hung up, ran down the four flights of stairs and jumped into her car.

Twenty-five minutes later, she spotted Gillie, the Deacon and Fitts from across the street, apparently in the last stages of an alcoholic stupor. They sat slumped together against a maple tree on a triangular traffic island as cars whizzed by them on all sides.

Gillie resembled a bald-headed orangutan in a flabby grey raincoat. The "Deacon" was a young apprentice drunk Gillie was instructing in the ways of the street and who, it was rumored, had been a third-year seminary student before his spiritual commitment turned to the spirit found in a bottle. He was passed out.

Zooey sighed and crossed the street.

"Dos libin' ish doc bloss sum sterin' dah," mumbled Gillie to Fitts, doddering on his shoulder. Sounded like German, Zooey thought. Gillie had once worked for a Munich electronics firm during his earlier sober days.

"Sewer," said Fitts, and he pulled an unopened pint of bourbon from his coat pocket. Pushing hard at the upper limits of middle-age, his dark brown-skinned face had the puffy cheeks typical of a drunk with money. He wore a grey tweed jacket with tan suede patches at the elbows despite the punishing heat, but he'd taken his shoes off to expose his toes, which were poking through holes in his grey nylon socks. His shoes, sporty moccasins of tan leather, lay neatly together beside his feet.

The bourbon accidentally slipped from his hand back into his coat pocket as Fitts rolled his head up and squinted, trying to focus on Zooey's face. His expression was bleary and stupefied, his big forehead shaded by curly black hair shot with silver streaks in random tufts. The textbook example, she thought, of an educated man taking a fast ride downhill and greasing the wheels.

Zooey leaned down to look closely at Fitts. "Hey lady, canna spare a dime, a quarter, a sanwich?" he said.

Zooey found herself staring down the barrel of a .38 caliber semiautomatic that Fitts pointed at her nose. His forehead was damp and his hands trembled. She spoke fast, hoping Fitts was steady enough not to shoot her by accident.

"Look, Fitts, you'd be ten minutes dead if that was on my mind."

Gillie, rallying what remained of his detective training, fell across Fitts's arm, covering the gun. Zooey immediately pulled her own small firearm from under her leather vest and pushed it against Fitts's nose. "Drop it," she ordered.

Fitts obeyed. Gillie grabbed the gun and then rolled unsteadily off of Fitts's lap.

Now Zooey's hands shook; it was the first time she'd ever drawn her weapon except to practice. She felt a sudden gratitude to Mark for convincing her to buy it. "You can't," Mark had said, "be a real detective if you don't have a gun."

Fitts froze in place, his eyes focused on Zooey's gun. "Hey," he said, "you th' lady p-eye on that Mary thing?"

She tried to say "yes" but couldn't find her voice.

"How'sh about hidin' the gun? I din' know if I cou' trush you."

She hesitated. Joe Quigley would pay extra for the years this gunplay scare had taken off her life. Slipping her gun back into its shoulder holster, she straightened up and cleared her throat. "I just want to ask you a couple of questions, okay?"

"I don' know."

"I suppose Durnam told you I'd be coming."

Fitts reached up to wipe sweat from his cheeks. "Yeah," he mumbled.

"Can we go somewhere and talk?"

He waved unsteadily at a building across the street, a nondescript storefront with brown smoked-glass windows. No sign identified it as the Orchid.

"Okay," Zooey said, "let's go."

Gillie realized they were leaving and tugged on Fitts's coat. "Say, gibba buddy da udder ha pie?"

Fitts reached for the pint again, paused, and then fell on his face, passed out.

"Hell," Zooey said, nudging him with her foot.

She sighed. "Come on, Gillie, help me drag him to the bathhouse."

Gillie ignored her and searched frantically through Fitts's coat for the pint. Finding it, he sucked down half and offered the bottle to her.

She turned away, considering the situation with Fitts. He was obviously afraid of someone, though he was doing a careless job of hiding out.

Struggling with the limp weight of his upper body, Zooey managed to prop Fitts back up against the maple tree next to him.

Nothing to do now, she thought, but cross the street to the bathhouse and ask for help, if he really did have friends there.

She pulled open the brown smoked-glass door and walked into a small entryway with a second, mirrored door and a buzzer to the right. Zooey pushed the buzzer, the mirrored door opened and a girl stepped out, costumed in what Zooey assumed was a fiancée-of-Count-Dracula outfit, her face powdered white, her eyes bruised with purple and rose eye shadow, her lips slick with carmine and her pallor exaggerated by angry tints of red and purple dye streaked through her blonde short-cut hair. She was draped neck to toe in a loose, transparent purple dress with batwing sleeves, and her black-painted fingernails curled like a lizard's claws around the doorframe.

Zooey forced back a nervous laugh. "I'm here to see Francesca."

"Is Francesca expecting you?" The voice was bright and smooth.

"No, she's not, but I would like to talk to her if she's around. Tell her that I'm a friend of Virgil Fitts."

"Your name?"

"Zooey Krause."

"Please come in, Ms. Krause, and wait in the lobby. My name is Esmeralda. I'll see if Francesca is available."

Esmeralda stepped aside to allow Zooey to walk into the lobby. It was large and impressively elegant. The girl disappeared down a hallway to the left.

Zooey looked up at the high ceiling to where a tinted skylight scattered blue light over the white marble walls, reflecting off of a star-shaped fountain full of fat goldfish. On the walls of two hallways to the left and right, she dimly made out thick maroon tapestries of an Asian design with depictions of exotic sexual positions. Zooey reflected that this was a far cry from the $100-a-nudge massage dumps she so often invaded for photos of someone's wandering spouse.

But the arrival of Francesca outshone the effect of her surroundings. She was over six feet tall, broad-shouldered, and strode toward Zooey like an athlete, her feet hidden beneath an exquisite kimono embroidered with cherry blossoms. Strangest of all was the Japanese Noh mask she wore: stark white with facial features delicately brushed in black. She looked so elegantly bizarre that Zooey thought her eccentricity might have even surpassed the repulsive Mr. Ernst Cordion, the "Washington Bug Boy" she'd met on an insurance fraud case.

Francesca thrust her hand forward. "Zooey Krause? I'm Francesca." She spoke in a cultured tone slightly muffled by the mask, though with a slight accent Zooey couldn't quite place. Perhaps French.

Zooey's first impulse was to ask whether this was a rehearsal for Halloween. But the mask, she concluded, like Esmeralda's ghoulish outfit, must have been a marketing gimmick. "Hi. I came to talk about Virgil Fitts, and it just so happens that he's passed-out drunk on the traffic island outside. Maybe you could help me get him inside?"

"Of course." She seemed unsurprised, and turned to the hefty man, presumably a bodyguard, who silently stood behind her. "Take care of our dear Virgil," she said, and then turned back to Zooey. "Thank you for coming. I very much wanted to talk with you. Please come this way."

Francesca abruptly turned, motioning for Zooey to follow her down the left hallway. She took a silver key chain from a pocket in her robe and unlocked the first door to the right.

The dimly lit room was small, hexagonal and windowless, the walls painted rose with gold accents. A rose-colored carpet and rose-colored chairs with brass fittings brought to Zooey's mind the dodgy elegance of a World War II spy novel, in which the disillusioned American sells out her country to an Oriental mastermind.

Zooey seated herself, and the Madam circled to the chair opposite.

"I realize that it's early, but please take a small glass of sherry. It's very fine."

"Why not?" Zooey said.

Francesca pushed a buzzer under the arm of her chair, and someone knocked softly at the door, paused and then entered. "The sherry, Max."

He nodded and left silently.

Francesca turned her masked face to Zooey. "Someone hired you to find Virgil Fitts."

"Who told you that?" Zooey's voice reflected surprise at her directness, and Francesca chuckled.

"I suppose I've been too abrupt."

"I know who told you, anyway," sighed Zooey. "Wallace Durnam."

"Yes, we are both friends of dear Virgil, so naturally we are interested in someone who announces that she's been employed to track him down."

The butler knocked again, and then entered with a crystal decanter and one glass. He put them on the table between Francesca and Zooey and then exited, closing the door behind him. Francesca delicately poured a small amount of sherry into the glass and handed it to Zooey.

"You're not having any?" Zooey asked.

"Ah… no." Francesca crossed her legs and folded her arms. "Zooey… may I call you Zooey? I won't waste your time since you know that I've spoken to Wallace Durnam. He told me that you want to speak to Virgil about Mary Gentry. Let me explain first that I am not Virgil's guardian, but you might say that I am looking after his interests at a time when he is incompetent to do so himself. I encourage you to speak frankly, and perhaps we can clear this matter up between ourselves."

"It would be nice if we could, but my client wants to speak to Virgil Fitts in person."

"And who is your 'client'?"

Zooey sipped the sherry. "I have to respect my client's confidentiality."

"It doesn't matter. I don't think you were hired by the managers of the nuclear plant to investigate Ms. Gentry. No, I think you've been hired by a grieving fiancé to see what Virgil knows about her death."

Zooey realized it hadn't been hard for Francesca to work out who'd hired her. Mary, Zooey was sure, must have mentioned her fiancé to Virgil during their conversations about the nuclear plant.

"So tell me," said Francesca, "what does this fiancé hope to gain by talking to Virgil? He's a conscientious reporter who has troubles of his own. And to be frank, Zooey, my information indicates that you are less than experienced as a detective. And even if you were more experienced, I wouldn't recommend that you help Mary Gentry's fiancé assume the distasteful role of avenger for her death."

It sounded to Zooey like the beginning of a lecture. "Listen, I…"

"Just one minute." Francesca raised her hand. "The most important fact here is that, as a friend, I'm very concerned about Virgil."

Zooey set down her glass of sherry. "I admit that I have nothing to lose if I decide to forget about talking to Mr. Fitts. Nothing except my client's money, but that probably means more to me than it does to you. But why don't you let me talk to your friend, Virgil, and maybe I can get enough information to satisfy my client."

"And what, besides money, do you have to gain by interviewing him? Maybe you imagine yourself an agent of good in some grand battle against corruption. In truth, I detest such attitudes. Life is too complex for such simple morality."

Zooey couldn't help smiling at her pedantic tone. "Forget morality. I'm simply wondering why he needs protection so much if he's nothing but a conscientious reporter. Not to mention, why was he carrying a gun?"

Francesca rearranged the folds of her kimono. "Then you intend to go ahead with this investigation?"

"I've already spent my client's deposit."

Francesca sighed again. "Zooey, let me explain myself. You've glimpsed the opulent trappings of my business. Regard it as bait for the men who are lured like moths to the flame of forbidden erotic indulgences. It is, you see, is a potent aphrodisiac. But all of this rests on the power of fantasy. Rumors of what happens here endow me with all manner of unlikely powers, but my 'power' is really only a surface effect."

"Like your mask?"

Francesca leaned back in her chair.

"I'm sorry if I didn't speak clearly. I meant to say that I am a symbol of protection for Virgil, but the symbol is an illusion. Illusions have power only to the extent that people believe in them. I use this and other illusions to attract customers to the Orchid.

"However, in reality, Virgil will not be safe here with me because he's terribly self-destructive, as you have observed. Dear Virgil has endured a long list of catastrophes in the last few years, the death of Mary Gentry being only the latest, and one for which he feels particularly responsible."

"Listen, I don't know anything about Virgil Fitts's problems and I really don't care. I was only hired to find him, and then Durnam informed me that I'm not alone."

"Wallace Durnam shares my concern for Virgil's safety. We were considering alternatives when you became involved. He sent you after Virgil as a trial, and to give us time to investigate you. We did conclude that you are trustworthy, if inexperienced. I only appeal to you to leave this case because I believe there is no small risk involved. It is a matter of conscience."

"Risk? Why?" Zooey had a bad feeling that she was being drawn into an invisible web. The mask showed no reaction to her questions, of course, and that irritated Zooey. "Besides, I find being run through a maze by Durnam and you an affront to my professional pride."

"Have I upset you?" The painted face stared at her.

"I don't enjoy being treated like an idiot. I don't know why you're wearing that silly mask, but I can see that the opulence here is supported by a lot more than symbolism. You know a little about politics too, or the vice squad would have buried this place years ago."

Francesca laughed. Then she reached over to take Zooey's hand. It was a warm touch; she'd half-expected cold steel. "Dear Zooey, Mr. Durnam warned me about your temper. I, too, find these tests distasteful.

"But take my word that Virgil will not be safe with me once his whereabouts are discovered. He refuses to be discreet, and for personal reasons I am unsuited to help. We could send him away, but if he continues to misbehave it will do no good."

Zooey dropped Francesca's hand and leaned forward. "But why does Virgil have to hide, if he's done nothing wrong?"

"To explain that, Virgil must be your guide. You may see him and satisfy your client."

"I would like that."

"But let me suggest a wiser course of action. Drop your client, and let me engage your services to protect Virgil."

Another surprise; but this, Zooey thought, could have been part of a strategy decided beforehand with Durnam.

"I want to talk to Virgil before I make up my mind about that."

"That is fair. Everything you need to know, he will tell you."

The "everything you need to know" grated. Still, Fitts was the focus of her investigation, no matter who had hired her. She could talk to Fitts and take it from there.

Francesca rose gracefully, and Zooey was surprised again at her height. "Unfortunately, Virgil is in no condition to speak clearly now. You will return later in the day?"

"Later this afternoon."

Francesca reached to press a button, and the butler reappeared. "Escort Miss Krause to the door," she said, her mask still facing Zooey.

Zooey almost smiled, then nodded briskly and followed the butler through the door without a word.

Francesca Darmini is a cracked china doll in an extravagant cathouse, she thought. Or a diamond set in tin. But Zooey found the whole scene too ridiculously outlandish to take seriously.

5

Zooey stepped into the heat of the midday sun and looked for Gillie on the traffic island. He and the Deacon were gone; she hoped that if Gillie had taken Fitts's gun he would give it to Mark instead of hocking it, as she expected he would do.

Virgil, of course, was gone too. She searched the grass where they'd been sitting, on the chance that something interesting had been left behind. Her efforts were rewarded; Virgil's gun lay near the maple under two empty pints of whisky and some crumpled paper bags.

Zooey picked it up and headed back to her car. She'd give it to Mark for safekeeping.

She climbed into her Mustang, shoved Virgil's gun under the seat and decided to stop by Mark's for lunch. She wanted to tell him about Francesca, Esmeralda and the oddball atmosphere at the Orchid.

The car made a clinking sound under the hood, but started. Despite being twenty years old, it was dependable, though nothing to look at. An aging black paint job was peeling off to reveal the original navy-blue color, and rust spots grew along the joints. The vinyl seats were torn, and empty cups of take-out coffee littered the floor.

As she entered Mark's Bar, the surrealist poet pushed past her going out the door, carrying a black leather portfolio. "How ya doin', Zooey?"

"Hi, Dave. What have you got there?"

"A collection of my cartoons. I'm hoping to sell a few to a magazine this afternoon. See you later." He ambled off down the street.

Mark was talking to an old man in a corner booth, and he waved at her as she walked in. The guy in the booth was retired and spent most of his time fishing in the Potomac River when he wasn't searching the trash behind the neighborhood grocery stores for day-old bread and stale chocolate doughnuts.

"Hello, Zooey," Mark called. "Jason left a message that Joe Quigley is trying to get hold of you. He tried reaching you on that antique cellphone of yours, but your reception is so lousy his call didn't go through. Who's your carrier, Grandma Moses Old Time Telephone and Telegraph?"

"I do have news for him. Put a hamburger on the grill and I'll tell you about it."

Mark tucked his shirttails into his pants. "I'd like to, but you'll have to save it for later. I've got an appointment right now to talk to my bank." He yelled back to the kitchen, "Rich!"

Rich Parker's slight, small figure stepped out from the kitchen. "Yeah?"

"Throw a burger on for Zooey, would you? And then get your ass out here and mix her a drink."

"Just hold on a minute," he said, annoyed. "I can't figure out what's what since you rearranged that mess of a refrigerator."

Mark left and Zooey took a seat at the bar, thinking about her meeting with Francesca. If she had influence around this town, it was undoubtably due to horny politicians who didn't go straight home after a hard day of collecting bribes from lobbyists. And the Orchid had the air of indulging many perverse tastes, a fact that might have explained the insistent anonymity of Francesca's mask.

But the most striking result of her visit to the Orchid concerned the seeming importance of Virgil Fitts. She wondered if Durnam had told the truth about the Russian thug who was supposedly also looking for Fitts.

Rich walked over and knocked on the bar to get Zooey's attention. "Wake up, Krause. How do you want that burger cooked?"

"Rare, and a Coke. But first tell me, have you ever heard of the Orchid?"

"The flower?"

"No, the spa. High-class place."

"Do I look like I have the money to frequent a high-class cathouse?"

He walked back to the kitchen and returned ten minutes later with a charcoal-burnt piece of meat lying on a single slice of buttered white bread.

"Don't say anything," he said. "I couldn't find the hamburger buns. Or the pickles. Anyway, I never claimed to be a cook."

"Where is the cook?"

"Out sick."

Zooey looked at the grizzled bit of leather on the plate in front of her. "Take this hamburger home as a gift to your cat. No offense, Rich, but I just lost my appetite. Just get me a couple of those little bags of potato chips from the back room."

"What back room?"

Zooey jumped down from her stool and walked to the back of the bar. "I'll get them. You find some good music on the radio. And would you get me another Coke?"

Rich glared at the black box in front of him and wiped his hands on his pants. "How do you turn it on?"

"Try the dial that says 'on.'" Zooey grabbed a bag of potato chips and a bag of peanuts, remembering that Virgil's gun still lay underneath the front seat of her car. She decided to stop off at her office and leave it with Jason. If she put it under the counter of the bar, Rich might pick it up and accidentally shoot himself.

6

When Zooey returned to the Orchid at four o'clock that afternoon, a woman dressed as a French maid answered the buzzer, wearing a frilly white apron over a short black skirt and sheer black stockings stretched over her skinny legs. A pair of black leather stilettos completed the look. Her makeup, as Esmeralda's had been, was unusual; her face was artificially pale, her lips pale pink, her eyes heavily shaded with black and green. The long spikes sticking out from either side of her head were tufts of teased blonde hair.

"Can I help you?" The French maid had a sweet smile that didn't suit her hairstyle.

"I'm Zooey Krause, and I'm here to talk to Virgil Fitts. Francesca knows I'm coming."

"Yes, she told me. Please come in and wait for a moment while I find her."

A few minutes later, the butler led her down the hallway to the left of the star-shaped fountain room. Francesca, still wearing the Japanese Noh mask, stood outside the door of a room she laughingly called "La Chambre Obscure." It was used, she explained, to accommodate the aftermath of indulgence. Her tone confirmed Zooey's impression that there was little in here one couldn't indulge.

Francesca opened the door and waved her in. "If you need anything, press the button beside the bed."

The door closed. Zooey crossed the room and opened the shutters on the only window, revealing a delicate garden court planted with roses and boxwood.

Turning away from the window, she found that the walls and ceiling of this room were ebony, and a pale blue Tibetan carpet covered the floor. Next to the door hung the framed portrait of a harlequin with a wicked grin, a touch of Francesca's humor that Zooey was beginning to appreciate.

Her reporter lay on a small bed with a black lacquer frame inlaid with mother-of-pearl. He was fully clothed in the same rumpled outfit he'd been wearing earlier in the day and he stared at the ceiling with a blank expression.

"As everyone seems to know, I'm Zooey Krause," she said to break the silence. "I'm aprivate investigator working for a friend of Mary Gentry's."

No answer from Fitts.

She approached the bed and leaned over, forcing him to look at her. "My client wants to know why you think that Mary Gentry committed suicide. Of course, your masked friend Francesca says you don't know anything, and she's willing to pay me to protect you."

Fitts gave no sign that he heard.

Zooey threw up her arms in exasperation. "Well, *are* you Virgil Fitts? Or is everyone here in disguise?"

He slowly turned his face away from her and closed his eyes. "I have a terrible headache. Why don't you come back tomorrow?"

"No. Who knows where you'll be tomorrow, and I don't want to spend any more of my time or my client's money tracking you down."

"Well, that's great, because I don't want to spend any more time talking about Mary Gentry. Why not be a good girl and get lost?"

He obviously didn't take her seriously. She decided it was time to change that. "Mr. Fitts, you're in trouble. You're a drunk, you've been carrying a gun and, not counting me, you've got the police and a Russian hood looking for you. And I have a feeling you're lucky I found you first. Maybe I can help."

"That's why you came here? To help me? Save that story for the *National Enquirer*." A weak smirk changed his expression for a moment, and Zooey impulsively grabbed the lapels of his jacket and shook him hard.

"Fitts, you're going to cooperate if I have to pull out your fingernails one by one! I'm not going home until you talk to me."

"Stop goddam rattling my headache." He massaged his forehead with a pained expression.

Zooey let go. Fitts lurched up and stared directly into her face. His eyes were sharp, a penetrating dark brown.

Zooey stepped back and leaned against the wall, arms folded and waiting. If Francesca said he needed discipline, she'd give it a shot. She tried looking unyielding.

"Francesca," he waved his hand, "thinks you're all right? And Durnam?"

"Would I be here?"

He nodded and rubbed his eyes. "What do you want?"

"Do you really think that Mary Gentry committed suicide? And if she didn't, why did you print a story saying she did?"

Fitts sighed, and began patting his jacket until he located a crushed packet of Camels in his left shirt pocket. He pulled one cigarette from the pack, examined it from tip to tip and then tapped it against his left thumbnail. He lit up and inhaled a few times before he focused again on Zooey.

"You saw the article I wrote a couple of weeks ago?"

Zooey nodded.

"Well, the story I wrote about Mary Gentry is what the Human Resources Director at the Blackstone Plant told me. It's his story."

"But you talked to Mary. Do you think his story is the truth?"

"The truth? He knew her better than I did."

"And you print everything people tell you."

Fitts looked offended. "No, as a matter of fact, I don't. Look, just drop it. Drop it! Start asking a lot of questions about the cause of Mary's death and you'll get yourself into the same kind of trouble I'm in. Then the same people who are after me will be chasing you, and believe me, they won't care when you tell them you don't know anything. Like you said, I'm in trouble. But it's nothing I can't handle."

Zooey laughed. "Getting drunk on a traffic island in front of the Orchid is your way of handling it? And pulling a gun on me?"

"Forget about it. Just take my advice and get out while you can."

"I didn't get involved in this case to look for trouble. Mary Gentry's fiancé, Joe Quigley, doesn't believe Mary was suicidal, and he said that you knew she wasn't. He's upset about the article you wrote because it implies that he's to blame for his fiancée's death. He wants to talk to you about it. So why not be a professional and give him some answers?"

"What do you know about professionalism?" Fitts sighed, pushed himself off the bed and walked unsteadily to the window. He stood with his back to her, staring at the courtyard, smoking his cigarette.

"Look," he finally said, "Mary Gentry was a mixed-up kid, and I'm really not sure why her car went off the road. I'm sorry about the accident, but we weren't close; in fact, I didn't know her very well at all. But there's one thing I do know—that the relationship between her and her fiancé was strained. He didn't like her talking to me. As you probably know, he has an important job at the Blackstone Plant, and he didn't want a scandal in the papers, whether Mary's story was true or not."

"Have you ever talked to Joe Quigley about how he feels?"

"I didn't need to. Mary was very upset, and she told me all about it."

"What else did she tell you?"

"You read about it. She thought her Union brass were messing with the pension fund and being paid off to ignore safety regulations, and she was afraid that workers might be accidentally contaminated at the plant."

"And you don't think her fears or her discussions with you had anything to do with her accident?"

Virgil hit the shutters; they banged against the wall with a loud crack as he turned around again. "All right, maybe they did. Is that what Joe Quigley wants to know?"

"Yes."

"Don't you think that's a little odd, considering that Joe Quigley's in a better position than anyone to know what's true? So where does that leave me? Mary came to me with a hysterical story about the danger at a nuclear plant, so I took it to Durnam and he picked it up even though he thought she was probably a crackpot. She didn't have many facts, so I urged her to investigate it further and get back to me. At first it seemed that a few plant supervisors and Union leaders might be involved. And then some other names surfaced, some small-time gangster types. So I figured that Mary was right, that something illegal was happening at the plant, although it probably wasn't anything big. Maybe the mob actually was running some pension fund scam.

"But then more important names started turning up, and I got excited. There appeared to be more going on than I'd thought. Mary's idealism was egging me on, I guess, and in the end I figured maybe I might have a Pulitzer Prize in the works, putting the screws to both organized crime and some high-powered executives at a nuclear plant.

"Christ, I was an idiot. A dumb bastard to think that all I was dealing with were some lowlifes. But this I can tell you: they've got cops on the payroll, and they want a cover on this bad."

"I don't understand what made you think it was a small story to begin with," Zooey said. "Pension fund corruption and tampering with safety regulations at a nuclear plant? That's big stuff, isn't it?"

"Sure, if the workers are in danger, and if you can prove it. But we didn't have anything but Mary's opinion that something was wrong. But I did have a suspicion that the real story was that someone in the Blackstone Plant management was involved with the mob."

"Okay. But what happened on the day of Mary's accident?"

"Her car smashed through a guardrail, rolled down a hill, and she broke her neck. We'll never know what she had that she wanted to tell me. I have no proof of Mary's suspicions. If I did, I'd be waving it in the headlines. Instead, I've been keeping my ass low. If they figure I don't know anything, maybe they'll leave me alone."

He leaned back against the shutters and closed his eyes. "But don't think I feel good about running away from those thugs. Twenty years ago, they would have been running away from me. I'm just not the plucky young journalist I used to be. Right now I'd rather be drunk and safe."

Zooey chewed on a finger, thinking, "Would you talk to Joe Quigley?"

"Why? What do I have to gain?"

"You'll get him off your back, for one thing. Just tell him who's spreading the rumors that Mary Gentry committed suicide. Tell him who talked to you at the plant—that should satisfy him."

"Well, I can tell him who gave me the story. That's no big secret."

"So you'll do it?"

Virgil stepped across the room to where Zooey leaned against the wall and looked hard into her eyes. "It's all a matter of trust, you understand that? For all I know, Joe Quigley is part of the crowd who's been following me, maybe figuring that I know too much about the Blackstone Plant. Right now, they're just tailing me. If they think I know something, one of those clowns might figure that I'd be better off dead."

Zooey walked away from Virgil to cover a moment of hesitation. "No," she said, "I don't believe that Joe cares about a scandal at the plant. When we met, he spent the whole time talking about how much he loved Mary; how they met, what she looked like, her idealism... He's upset that people think he betrayed her, or that something he did caused her to kill herself."

Zooey tried to sound more confident than she felt about Joe Quigley's interest in Virgil Fitts.

"Sure, I'll talk to Joe Quigley." Fitts sounded unconvinced. He was too smart not to have caught her hesitation, but Zooey suspected he might have his own reasons for finally agreeing to meet Joe.

"If I'm right about Joe, then maybe he can find out who's after you," she said.

"We'll see about that."

"There must be a phone in this place where I can call Joe. This area is a dead zone for my cell. If it's all right with you, I'd suggest that we meet him at a bar I know." Zooey headed to the door.

"Wait!" said Virgil. "On one condition. We take Francesca's car."

Zooey frowned. "Why? What's the point? I've got mine outside."

"She's got a chauffeur I trust." He smiled wolfishly. "You're cute, but for now I'd like a professional driver."

Zooey didn't like it, but she agreed and walked to the lobby to look for a phone while Fitts made the arrangements for a car. Joe agreed to meet them at Mark's Bar.

She drifted to the Orchid's doorway and peered through the two-way glass. It had begun to rain. Searching through her bag for a stick of gum, she wondered whether she had finally stumbled onto an important case, or, more probably, into just a circus of small-time criminals.

A heavy, cream-colored Mercedes limousine pulled up and Fitts, already inside, motioned to her from the back seat.

The chauffeur was a trim, young African American, with short, dark, wavy hair and a thin nervous face cratered with acne scars. He wore a navy-blue jacket, a white shirt and a navy-blue knit tie. Zooey said, "Take us to Mark's Soft Shoulder Bar in Adams Morgan."

He nodded and they sped away.

Zooey turned to Fitts, who sat slumped staring out the window. "I've been wanting to ask you about the story on Francesca Darmini. Durnam said that you two are friends. When does she take off that mask? What is it, a treat for the customers? Or does she keep her real identity a secret?"

"Look," Virgil snapped, "I've known Francesca for years, and this isn't the first time she's helped me out, and took a risk doing it. But as to her background..."

He dragged out his Camels. "Well, that's another story. Anyway, it's none of your business or concern."

Fitts's vehemence made it clear he wasn't about to say anything more, so Zooey decided to push the issue later.

Her thoughts were interrupted by the driver.

"Mr. Fitts, there's a black SUV what's been on our ass two blocks, and the twin faces up front are bad news. If you and the lady grab hold, we'll see what they've got in mind."

Zooey just had time to brace her hand against the front seat when the limo shot abruptly down a narrow one-way side street, and then charged down a large alley. The display of street-wise driving reassured her. No wonder Virgil had insisted on Francesca's car.

"Shit," the chauffeur shouted, "they're still on our asses and it looks like one of 'em's got a big piece. Get down!"

Fitts hit the floor with Zooey beside him. She didn't take their situation seriously until she rose again and turned to look back; a bullet crashed against the reinforced back window, spreading a cobweb of cracks across the glass.

Zooey found herself nose to nose again with Fitts as she shakily attempted to disentangle her gun from her vest.

"My gun! Where is it?" Fitts yelled at Zooey, and she shook her head.

She was thrown away from Virgil and up toward the window as the limo veered through an office parking lot. As attendants jumped clear of them, the driver gracefully avoided relocating any parked cars, although from the sound of smashing metal and glass behind them Zooey guessed their pursuers weren't as skillful.

"Shit!" the driver screamed. "How about some cover back there? Those sons of bitches are driving right up our exhaust!"

Zooey popped back up with Fitts as a bullet punched the damaged window, peppering them with glass. Zooey shoved Virgil to the floor and jerked up, trying to fire through a fist-sized hole in the window. It took a few seconds of panic to discover her gun wasn't jammed; the safety was on. This gave time for another shot to smash against the window with a thud that sent her to the floor again.

"Can't you move this crate faster, for Christ's sake?" she screamed.

Fitts grabbed Zooey's gun. With Zooey beside him, he crouched forward and propped the gun's snout against a broken edge of window glass and fired two shots. Immediately, another bullet hit the glass near Zooey's face and they ducked, Zooey wondering where in hell the police were. Virgil jumped up again and fired the remaining five shots. Zooey, moving slowly up beside him, saw that two holes had pierced the window of the car behind them, and the gunman held his shoulder as his car swerved and hit a building.

The clatter of screaming glass and metal behind them mixed with the hammering inside her chest. Then the gap between the two cars widened until the pursuers disappeared. In the distance, Zooey heard police sirens.

"Hey!" Zooey leaned forward. "Make sure they can't tail us, Mr., uh…"

"Sharps, lady. Rashid Sharps. I think Mr. Fitts got a lucky shot at one of them."

"Lucky is right," Fitts said, "so make sure no one gets a fix on us. Including the cops."

A line seared his right cheek where a flying piece of glass had grazed it. A thin trickle of blood slid toward his chin, but otherwise he looked unhurt.

"Who the hell was shooting at us?" Zooey said, her voice shrill.

"I don't know," Virgil said, handing the gun back to her. He wiped his face and noticed the blood. "But this is the first time anyone has fired a gun at me. Until now, folks I've pissed off have been content to follow me around town and throw a punch."

"You must have some idea who it was."

"If I knew, I'd tell you."

Zooey pushed wet strands of red hair from her face and felt mildly hysterical. "Then do you think it would be all right to explain to me why Francesca Darmini owns an armored car? I'm not complaining, understand, but it obviously came as a surprise to those nice men who were chasing us."

Fitts gingerly touched his face wound. "Some of her wealthy foreign clients are very security-conscious."

"Nothing I need to know about, I'm sure."

Virgil shrugged.

She trembled. Only now did she get the chance to be scared. "Well, I see that Francesca was right about one thing: you're not going to be safe at the Orchid. They must have tailed us from there, although I don't know why they didn't shoot when you were drunk outside this morning. But we're going to have to think of a way to protect you tonight. How about the HighRoad Hostel on Belmont Road in Adams Morgan? It's cheap, and Rashid could keep an eye on you."

"Why the sudden concern for my wellbeing?"

"I told you, didn't I? Francesca offered to pay me to protect you."

"Great protection. A pint-sized junior P.I. who can't shoot."

"That's quite a complaint from Mr. Sobriety. Now, how about the HighRoad?"

"Are you kidding? These guys aren't playing around. If you're really going to help protect me, then we'd better stick together."

Zooey didn't care for that suggestion. "What's your idea?"

"Why don't you rent me a room for the night?"

Fitts did have a point, she decided. Partly to keep her ex-husband off her back, she'd rented her apartment under a phony name. No one, except for Mark, knew where it was. Even Jason only knew her cellphone number, and he never gave it to anyone without her say-so. It made her apartment a safe hiding place, and she didn't want to surrender her privacy, especially to this drunken reporter with his string of deadly fans.

The car rolled slowly down Wisconsin Avenue. Obviously Sharps was circling, waiting for instructions. She decided to stall. "Let's concentrate on talking to Joe Quigley right now, since he's probably waiting for us at Mark's Bar. Later we'll come up with something."

"And another thing," Virgil said. "Where's my gun?"

"You left it on the traffic island when you passed out," Zooey said, "but I picked it up, and I'll see that you get it back. Rashid, please drive us to Mark's Bar."

63

7

Rashid Sharps parked, hopped out and limped back to open Zooey's door.

"Thanks," she said, looking down at Rashid's lame left leg. He acknowledged her glance without embarrassment.

"Rashid, I'm Zooey Krause."

"S'all right, Miz Krause. Just one thing. What kind a gun you got?"

Zooey pulled out her Llama IIIA. It was small, light and about as feminine as a gun can be.

Rashid examined it skeptically. "Not bad if you wanna shoot squirrels on Rock Creek Parkway."

"What's wrong with it? It's light and it never jams." She took it back and holstered it. Her gun was a mark of her style.

Rashid shrugged. "Sure, it's light, but so is a handkerchief." He ducked into the front seat and pulled out a .44 Magnum. "It's one of these babies what punched the holes in our reinforced back window. I'd have thrown mine back to you if I'd known what you had." He dropped it into Zooey's hands.

The gun sank like a weightlifter's barbell. "Forget it, Rashid! I'm just a short kraut with underfed biceps. You keep it."

Rashid shrugged. "Thought I'd tell you."

Virgil leaned across the car. "Rashid, we'll be staying at this bar for a while. Are you waiting?"

Rashid nodded. "Francesca told me to stick by you." He glanced up and down the street. "Just in case."

Zooey steered Virgil across the sidewalk and asked him, "Don't you really know who was chasing us?"

"Your guess is as good as mine."

"That's hard to believe."

She looked at her hands, disappointed to find that they were still shaking. She hoped Virgil didn't notice.

She pulled open the door to Mark's Bar.

"This the kind of bar you like?" Virgil glanced around the room, taking in the afternoon crowd: Eleanor at a table by the window with her shopping bags stuffed into the booth beside her, muttering while she shoved crackers into her mouth and sipped a can of soda; Dave the fat surrealist at the center table wearing a ripped tunic, with comic books and drawing paper spread before him; a local watch-repair shop-owner and small-time arsonist who was always available for hire—he was playing a hand of gin rummy at the bar with a local bookie. Mark whistled as he swept the floor behind the bar.

Virgil waved at the tall, narrow windows of stained glass that rimmed the twenty-foot ceiling. "What is it with this place? Looks like a church."

"It was a church. Now known as Mark's Soft Shoulder Bar and my favorite place in town. The owner is my partner in the detective business; that's him behind the bar."

Virgil looked scandalized. "How could your partner change it into a bar?"

"He didn't. That honor belongs to the original minister's son. But that's all history, nothing you need to know."

Virgil gave her an exaggerated sigh. "Touché."

"Joe Quigley hasn't arrived yet." She pointed out a booth in the back corner. "Go ahead and sit down. I'll get us something from the bar."

Zooey walked up to the counter where Mark twirled the dials of his radio. "Hello, sharecropper. You haven't seen Joe Quigley, by any chance?"

"Not today. Why, are you expecting him?"

"Any minute now. I thought he might have arrived before us."

Mark looked at her closely. "You okay? You're pale as a ghost."

Zooey shook her head dismissively. "I'm fine."

Mark furrowed his brows. "I think not. Out with it."

Zooey shrugged. "I guess I'm okay, except that a couple of creeps with big guns followed us part of the way over here, and I think we shot one of them. Damn, I was scared."

"A couple of creeps with guns? Who were they? Where are the cops?"

"Look, we got away before the police arrived, I'm not hurt and I don't have time to fill you in just now. By the way, see that guy over there? That's our lost reporter."

"Virgil Fitts?"

"In person. Why don't you send him a cup of coffee?"

Mark poured a cup from the pot of thick day-old brew and walked it over to Virgil. When he stood back behind the counter, he gave Zooey's appearance another careful examination.

"You're shaking."

She still was.

"Look, would you mix me a gin and tonic? I want to talk with Fitts for a few minutes before Joe gets here."

"Sure." He pulled down a glass from a rack and polished it before pouring the gin. "With big guns?" he asked again, concern in his voice.

"And would you keep an eye on the door?" Zooey squeezed an extra lime into her drink. "I don't think anyone followed us here, and a chauffeur from the Orchid is watching the street outside, but let's make sure because I've had enough surprises for one day. And why don't you keep that gun of yours under the register handy?"

"I will," he said—a bit too eagerly, Zooey thought.

She walked over to the booth where Fitts sat studying his coffee. When he saw the drink in Zooey's hand, he brightened.

"Is that for me?" he asked.

"Don't you think you've had enough for today? Besides, I need you sober."

"Thanks, Mom." Virgil grabbed her glass and took a sip.

"Gin." He frowned. "Awful stuff." He gave it back to her.

"Right. Now, I wanted to ask you about... oh, there's Joe Quigley."

Joe's thin figure hesitated at the door. He was dressed more casually than he had been during his first appearance at Mark's, wearing a blue polo shirt, a pair of snug-fitting brown corduroy pants and brown suede running shoes; the upper-crust version of slumming it. When Zooey raised her hand, he ambled over to join her.

He looked pale; not sleeping much, she guessed. She doubted she would sleep much herself that night.

He sat across from Virgil, next to Zooey, the corners of his small mouth tightening as he stared at Fitts.

"So you're Virgil Fitts?"

"That's right." Virgil stretched out his hand.

Joe looked surprised but he shook Virgil's hand. "I'm Joe Quigley."

Zooey hadn't known what to expect from Joe, but his calm manner pleasantly surprised her.

"It's been quite an afternoon, Joe," she said, waving at Mark.

Mark walked over to the table, staring first at Fitts and then at Joe Quigley. "A Black Label, please," Joe said. "On the rocks."

"Now here's a man who knows how to drink," Virgil said. "The same for me."

"It's your funeral," Zooey said, though she suspected that both would talk more freely if the scotch loosened their tongues. The drinks were quickly delivered.

"Getting straight to the point," Joe addressed Fitts politely when the drinks arrived, "what makes you think that my fiancée, Mary Gentry, committed suicide?"

Virgil took a quick gulp of scotch and shuddered. "First, let me tell you that I'm sorry about Mary's death," he said. "It was a real kick in the teeth to find out about it, and I want you to know that it wasn't easy to write that story. There are many lousy aspects of newspaper reporting, and having to discredit the reputation of a woman like Mary didn't make me feel good. But I wrote the story as I saw it, and that's what the business is all about."

"Look, I know that. I'm not planning a vendetta against you. My only interest is the source for your story—maybe I didn't make that clear enough to Zooey when I hired her."

"It was clear," Zooey said.

Virgil pulled out his Camels. "Look, I'll give it to you straight: A few days after Mary died, I got an appointment with the Director of Personnel at the Blackstone Plant."

"Herb Calcut."

"That's right, and he made me aware of some facts that had escaped my notice. Such as, that Mary had been seeing some kind of psychiatric therapist for years, but she didn't put that fact on her application form for employment at the Blackstone Plant. It was only after she died that this information came to light. And then there was the testimony of her co-workers, saying that Mary had thrown more than one hysterical fit at the plant in the last few months, apparently unprovoked, screaming and crying and frightening everyone. The first time Herb Calcut just sent her home with a tranquilizer from a stash he had, figuring that she must be having some problems at home to make her act that crazy.

"But when Mary starting acting more and more paranoid, saying that people were following her in cars…"

Virgil took a second gulp that emptied his glass. "The problem was that she made all kinds of crazy accusations and not many made any sense. I mean, I have to admit that sometimes when she came to my office, I got the feeling that she was living on the edge of something. I didn't know what, but she expressed feelings that had nothing to do with the story we were supposedly investigating. Some of those other feelings concerned you, Joe. You were the most important part of her life, and you hadn't supported her suspicions. Am I right?" Virgil swirled the ice in his glass with a swizzle stick. "Suicide does seem like a possibility to me."

Zooey watched the expression on Joe's face grow into one of satisfaction.

"You're wrong about Mary," Joe said, "but I couldn't prove it to you now. Still, seeing a psychiatrist is no proof that you're crazy or suicidal."

"You're right about that," Virgil said. "And I may be wrong. If I am, I apologize."

"I thought it was someone at the plant who had spread that rumor," Joe mused, "but I wouldn't have guessed it was the Director of Personnel. That's very interesting. The plant found itself in trouble when additional articles came out after Mary's accident, stories that raised questions about Mary's allegations and the suddenness and nature of her death. From what you're telling me, I now believe Herb Calcut decided to release false information about Mary's psychiatrist and to drop a few hints about the trouble between us. It certainly made a very convenient diversion for those who might have wanted to probe further."

"I see it, all right," said Virgil. "But nobody lied. Mary *did* see a psychiatrist, she *was* upset with you and she *did* throw one or two hysterical fits at work."

"Sure, that's great," Joe said. "Paint half the picture and you get less than half the truth. Come on, Mr. Fitts, admit that you know she had more sense than that."

"I thought she made sense in the beginning concerning her observation of certain questionable practices at the Blackstone Plant and with the Union. It was you who thought she imagined things."

"Hey," said Zooey, "you got the information you wanted, Joe. Now why don't we drop the subject?"

Joe shook his head. "No. I want to know if this man has evidence to support any of Mary's allegations. Mr. Fitts stated publicly that he found no evidence to support an investigation into the Union at the Blackstone Plant, a conclusion that was exactly what I thought. If he feels differently now, I'd like to know."

"You're right, I found no evidence," Virgil said.

"What about the car that chased us this afternoon?" Zooey said.

"What car?" said Joe.

"I haven't told you everything, Zooey," said Virgil. "So drop it."

"Drop what? Who was chasing you?" said Joe.

"I'll bet that the men who chased us were hired, expensive guns," Zooey said. "And I'll bet they're probably hard-to-trace out-of-towners. We have almost no hope of turning up anything on them."

"I've made plenty of enemies along the way, and I'm working on some other hot stories concerning the mob and Union tampering," Virgil said. "That's what today was about, I'm sure."

Turning back to Joe, Virgil said, "Look, Mary was worried about the safety of the system maintenance workers, which is understandable, and about their pension fund."

"But that's silly." Joe's voice was indignant. "I work at that plant too. Do you think I'd put myself in that kind of danger?"

"No, I don't think anyone would. But I don't think that's what this is about at all. The Union leaders at your plant are being paid off by somebody, for what I think is a pension fund scam."

"What makes you so sure?"

"You mess with the Union and the mob, and you've got trouble." Virgil shifted uneasily in his seat and glared at Zooey. She glared back.

"Look, Zooey," said Joe, "you've done what I asked you to do. I finally know who started those rumors about Mary and me, and why, and who's trying to lay the blame on me for something that wasn't my fault. So maybe now I can do something about it. I'll pay your fee and let's just leave it at that."

"I'll type up a brief tomorrow and send you the bill."

"Thanks." Joe began to push out of the booth. "Nice to meet you." He shook hands again with Virgil.

"Sure," Virgil said. "Good luck. And I really am sorry about Mary."

"So am I," Joe said. He turned, walked to the counter and paid Mark, and then strode quickly through the door and out of sight.

Virgil stared straight ahead like a toy doll behind a shop window as he absently crushed a half-smoked Camel against the Formica tabletop.

"You're not telling the truth, are you, Fitts?" said Zooey.

Virgil frowned. "Some of it."

"Why not all of it? People tried to kill you today, and me along with you. This is about a pension fund?"

Virgil shrugged. "Could be. I'm not sure."

"So why not tell Joe?"

Virgil shook his head. "You're some detective."

"What's that supposed to mean?" Zooey snapped, irritated.

"You don't know Joe. I don't know Joe. I have no reason to trust him. Why do you? I told him what he wanted to hear, or at least I told him what I wanted him to hear. He's satisfied. Leave it at that."

A silence fell, and the bar radio, that had been playing filler music, switched to a news bulletin.

"This just in. A video was posted today on Facebook and YouTube by Louis Farrakhan announcing his organization's declaration of war on white America and the police. On the video, Farrakhan called on all communities of color to join him in jihad against the corrupt, racist white government that oppresses all people of color."

Vigil jumped up, pointing to the television. "For God's sake, turn that damn thing on!" he shouted. Mark did, and CNN immediately lit the screen, "BREAKING NEWS" scrolling across the top.

Wolf Blitzer announced: "…and the video our reporters discovered earlier uncovered a disturbing proclamation by Louis Farrakhan announcing a race war on white America. We can show you this much of it."

The picture changed to a grainy black-and-white image of Louis Farrakhan. "We have suffered long enough. We have been the targets of brutal white police officer murders of unarmed men, women and children of color long enough. The founding racism of this nation, which built a decadent prosperity on the backs of chattel slavery, and which has refused to recompense the victims of that injustice, has driven us to the breaking point. We are the *Black Lives Matter Armed Brigade,* and we have captured the three police officers involved in the murder of an unarmed black teenager in Milwaukee, Wisconsin. They were exonerated of any wrongdoing in a white man's court, because no white man's court will ever give us justice. But we demand justice. White America, stand ready to suffer the wrath of God Almighty. Leave this country now, while you can, before the heavy hand of Allah exterminates your wicked race for taking this land that was never yours, but was stolen from people of color and built on the backs of the people of color."

The video changed to a scene of three police officers bound and gagged and on their knees. Behind them stood three masked men with swords. The voice of Farrakhan proclaimed, "Execute justice upon these, our oppressors."

The scene turned back to Blitzer. "We will not show you the execution. It is too horrendous and shocking to show. This outrageous, brutal and cowardly act is deserving of the condemnation of us all, no matter what race, religion or ethnicity. Police in Milwaukee confirm the recovery of the bodies of three of its officers, found dumped on the side of a highway, beheaded.

"We take you now to Washington, D.C., for comment by the Justice Department."

"Mark," said Zooey, "for God's sake shut if off. I don't want to see anymore."

The screen went dark.

"It's hard to believe," Zooey said. "What's next?"

Virgil rubbed his chin, looking tired. "God help us."

8

Zooey strolled down 19th Street past Kalorama Park at six o'clock on Tuesday morning; her problems felt abstract but clearer than the night before. A light fog slowly melted in the soon-to-be numbing heat as the sunshine crept up the sides of the buildings. It was the beginning of the kind of day that would set off tempers all over the city, and she was glad she'd taken advantage of the early morning for her walk.

Because she'd been over-tired and still anxious from the shooting and the national news, sleep had been slow in coming. She'd awakened early with the desire for a walk to clear the cobwebs from her head, relieved that Virgil had been so easily persuaded to stay at a hotel. It gave her time to think.

Her dampened red hair clung to her forehead and didn't stir as the first breeze of the day pushed a newspaper away from the curb. She glanced at the headlines: "Farrakhan Still at Large" and "African American Neighborhoods Attacked by Mobs in Milwaukee."

Feeling discouraged, Zooey headed back home.

Back at her apartment, she unlocked the front door and wandered into the kitchen to fill a lead crystal snifter with an inch of cognac. She carried this to an antique roll-top desk sitting under the windows next to the door to a balcony that overlooked the brick wall of the townhouse next door.

She set the snifter next to the computer on the roll-top desk and began making notes for the brief she needed to draft for Joe Quigley. Reduced to facts, there wasn't much to tell, and ten minutes later she finished it off with: "The terms of my engagement have been satisfied (i.e. determining the location of Mr. Fitts). One thousand dollars covers all charges to date; no additional charges are anticipated unless you wish to resume an active investigation."

Then she turned on her radio, curled up on her nearby couch and drifted off to sleep.

Two hours later, she awakened slowly to a syrupy version of "Smoke Gets in Your Eyes." She switched it off and called her office.

"Krause Detective Agency," answered Jason.

"Hi Jay, it's me."

"Hi boss. What happened to you yesterday? You said you'd call at five o'clock. Did you hear the news about Milwaukee?"

"Yeah, I heard. Thank God it's halfway across the country from here.

"Look," she went on, "the Quigley case developed complications. Bad stuff that I don't want to go into just now. I won't be coming into the office for a few days. How much money do we have in petty cash?"

"I'm not sure. About five hundred dollars."

"Take all of that and get lost for a week. Take an advance on your regular check as well. Consider it a paid vacation."

"Paid vacation? Why?"

"To tell you the truth, there may be someone watching the office and I'd rather there wasn't anyone there to watch. Don't panic about it, just take a short trip to Fire Island or something. Before you go, though, did the secretary for the wallpapering firm who wanted dirt on her husband call about the photos?"

"Yes, she did. Twice."

"Okay, call and tell her they're in the mail. Then go down to the post office and mail them on your way out of town. On my desk there's a list of lost dogs that I haven't been able to find. I think there's just Buddy and Lily Lolita left. Call and tell their owners that I'm hot on the case and should have some news by next Tuesday or Wednesday."

"I think they ran away because they didn't like their names."

"No doubt. When you finish, straighten up and take off."

"When should I come back?"

"Next Monday should be fine."

"Okay, I'll see you then. Thanks for the vacation."

"You're welcome. Bye, Jason."

"Bye, boss. Take care."

She hung up, thinking what a blessing Jason McPherson was after her previous secretary, a jerk who'd robbed her blind. She'd blackmailed one of Zooey's customers under Zooey's name and then skipped town with the cash, leaving Zooey with an irate client and a police investigation into her business, slim as it had been two years ago. The woman had finally resurfaced on a robbery charge in Illinois, and Zooey had been cleared.

Jason was a second-rate abstract painter, a master of organization and the best-looking secretary she'd interviewed. Gay, of course. The office redecoration scheme he'd invented and then carried out, with Zooey's instructions to "make it look like an important private investigator works here instead of some young hack," turned her office into a something that looked like a chic art gallery—all glass, chrome and bright primary colors. It wasn't the setting for Sherlock Holmes and Watson, but she supposed that it improved her first impression with clients.

She could afford him because, besides Jason's small weekly salary, he lived in the back room of her office.

Zooey called the HighRoad Hostel to check with Virgil.

Sharps answered. "He's flown, Miz Krause. He took off while I grabbed some sleep this morning. Left a note:

'Checking out leads.' Wants you and Francesca to meet him at a bar called The Tombs near Georgetown University at seven tonight."

"That crazy drunk."

She hung up, annoyed, and walked to the kitchen to make a sandwich. How was she supposed to protect a man who was wandering the streets unescorted? She should have contacted him earlier. And what was this "checking out leads" all about?

Maybe he'd decided that the Mary Gentry case was worth a little more investigation. She wondered if Fitts was up to it. Her next phone call was to Francesca, who was unimpressed by Virgil's flight.

"How can one protect such a man?" she said in a silky, indulgent tone.

But when Zooey asked if she knew about Virgil's "leads," Francesca had an idea. It seemed that Virgil had asked her about a man by the name of Vlad Sakorski, and though she said she wasn't sure who this might be, she suggested that he could have been the Russian who'd asked about Virgil at the Westerner's Bar. Zooey felt sure, once again, that Francesca knew more than she was telling, but decided to use her own channels to investigate the man's identity.

She called another investigator, Max Rohand, a kind of bounty hunter who knew the names of most of the hoods on the East Coast, and most of their covers. For a two-hundred-dollar fee, you could buy five minutes of access to his extensive mental library.

"Max, what have you got on a character named Vlad Sakorski? Russian, maybe."

"Yeah," came his answer, "Vlad Sakorski." He coughed a few times in mock concentration. He liked to give the impression of strain when earning his fee. "Yeah, right. A mob hitman originally from New York. Heavy on the muscle. He did a number on a Miami cop two years ago in a bar, something personal, like Vlad figured this cop was making eyes at his Miami girlfriend and blew him away. Hot temper. Yeah, he killed the sucker. But I ain't heard nothing on him since then.

"Now it could be the mob is hiding him, or it could be they blew him away. He wasn't paid to be creating headlines—not those kinds of headlines, anyway. The Miami cops would pay anything to get their hands on him. You know where he is?"

"No, but I heard a rumor that he's here."

"Could be, but I ain't heard nothing about it. Vlad was one of the best hitmen in New York, though."

"Thanks, Max. I'll have your fee in the mail."

Zooey stewed around her apartment for an hour, thinking. If this hitman was after him, Virgil was lucky to be alive. It made her feel even more nervous about having left him at the HighRoad Hostel for the night, even with Sharps on guard.

Remembering that she'd have to stop at the office to pick up Virgil's gun, she pulled out her own Llama IIIA and studied it, deciding Rashid might be right. She couldn't intimidate New York hitmen with a swank but inadequate gun. She changed from shorts into a pair of jeans and walked down to her Mustang, which Francesca had been kind enough to have dropped off at a nearby location. Zooey hadn't given the exact address.

Half an hour later, she pulled into the parking lot of Burpee's Armory and Pawn Shop across the Potomac River in Arlington, Virginia. It was its usual tacky brightly-lit self, with large window signs shouting: "DEALS!!! WOW!!! WORLD WAR II RIFLES $99.35!!!!" Burpee's had good values, and she didn't want to spend a lot of money for a replacement gun.

Burt Burpee himself, a bald eagle of an old man sweating profusely in his poorly air-conditioned store, greeted her gleefully from behind the wired, bullet-proof cage.

"Hiya, Missus Krause! Haven't seen you since you last bought ammunition for that bee-you-tee-ful Llama IIIA. Nice day, ain't it? A little warm, yes, but God forbid it could be worse. Snow, maybe! Say, what can I do for you? You want more bullets, maybe, for your bee-you-tee-ful Llama? Lovely... nice weather, right?"

Burt always spouted lines like that. Stuck in his grey metal box all day, dealing with fanatics shopping for a "little extra" security and nuts erotically fondling the steel-blue sheen you only get off a gun, it was no wonder he made such crazy chatter.

"Hello, Burt. Yeah, the weather's great and so's my mother. But I'm not here for bullets."

"Hey, Missus Krause, you're not buying from the competition? None better 'n mine, no ma'am. Never a misfire. Guaranteed."

"No, no, your bullets are great. But I want to trade in the Llama on a larger gun."

Burt shook his fringe of hair and giggled.

"What's a good deal on my Llama?" She handed the weapon to him.

As she expected, Burt assumed the wary face appropriate for talk about money, not weather.

"Oh, that Llama IIIA is such a small weapon, basically ineffective, and yours looks particularly worn. A bad scratch here ruins that nice finish, lowers the value for buyers who go for image. I'll give you, well..."

He shuffled through an endless pile of yellowed papers behind the glass. "I'll be fair. As a down payment on this Luger, I'll pay $50."

"Don't hand me that crap, Burt. I paid $230 for this gun during one of your 'special sale' weekends, and I only used it once except for target practice. So I want $100 at the least. And forget that Luger; I'm not joining the Third Reich."

He gently laid the Luger back in its case, unsuccessfully covering a chip on the barrel with his finger.

"I'll give $80 towards this $350 Glock 19. It has fifteen rounds to the clip and weighs only thirty ounces fully loaded. Very impressive-looking. Used to belong..."

"To an old lady who plugged sewer rats with it from her porch on Sundays. I know, I know."

He slid the gun out to her. It did seem perfect. Bigger, but in her shoulder holster not heavy enough to give her a permanent slouch. And fifteen rounds to the clip was good.

"Okay, I'll take it if you throw in a box of cartridges."

Burt cradled the Llama in his hands. "A bee-you-tee-ful gun."

She also bought a new black leather shoulder holster.

9

The Tombs turned out to be a Georgetown University haunt in a converted nineteenth-century townhouse serving beer, spirits and bar food. A random line of tables swarmed the bar, and Zooey squeezed her way to an area still empty of customers.

At a few minutes before seven, Virgil breezed in, saw her and sat down. He looked brighter than before, more purposeful. He'd also taken a bath, shaved and put on a fresh pinstriped shirt. This revised version of Virgil Fitts differed so radically from the booze-soaked and soggily reluctant reporter she'd discovered in front of the Orchid the day before, that Zooey began to reassess her negative first impression. Today he carried an air of sober concentration that put Zooey on guard. She watched as he ordered a scotch and turned smilingly back to her.

"Have a good day?" she asked, sliding him his gun under the table wrapped in a brown paper bag.

"Excellent." He pushed the bag into his inside suit pocket and took a long pull on his drink. "My first," he announced with a self-mocking nod.

"Meet any nice people?"

"One or two."

Zooey strained for an offhanded tone. "Did anyone else try to put a bullet through your face today?"

Virgil sat back and scanned her expression thoughtfully. "Take it easy."

"What I'm trying to say is that I wish you'd waited for my call this morning. Francesca hired me to look after your welfare and that's just what I'll never be able to do if you go flying around Washington alone with a two-foot-wide bull's-eye painted on your back. Now I know what Francesca meant when she described you as self-destructive."

She cursed herself silently for sounding so melodramatic.

Virgil coughed a few times by way of lodging a humored protest. "Zooey, please cool off and let's start over: are you sure that your car wasn't followed while you were driving to the bar?"

"I took a cab. And it wasn't followed."

"Great. Now let's pretend that we're working together. Okay, so why did you stick me in a hotel without your address? And no phony excuses, please. I know your neck's on the line, but so is mine."

"Maybe I didn't feel like any unexpected company."

"And maybe I didn't feel like sitting around all morning waiting for your permission to leave the room."

Zooey grudgingly smiled. "Have you made it your personal mission to point out my inadequacies as a private investigator?"

"Okay. Truce. I don't find fault with you, and you don't with me."

Zooey signaled for another beer. The young waitress, wearing her long pumpkin-colored hair in a braid, carried a red plastic bowl of popcorn to their table.

She probably thinks I'm here with my father, Zooey thought.

Lively conversations erupted from the tables filling up around them; most of the customers were young kids very different from herself. She'd never gone to college, and had never even held a full-time job until the year before her divorce.

She focused again on Virgil, who was watching two men at the next table set up a pocket-sized plastic chess set. "How did you find out about Vlad Sakorski?" she asked.

"Ah, now that's an interesting question," he answered, turning back to her. "But first, we've got to set a few things straight. The first thing is, why should I trust you?"

Zooey grinned. "Do you even trust your mother?"

He pulled at his silver-black curls so that they stuck out even further around his head, making him look a little mad.

"What's the matter? Don't tell me your mother is a sneak thief," she said. "The kind who looked through your drawers when you were away at high school football practice."

"I put a combination lock on my bedroom door."

Zooey groaned skeptically. "Really?"

"Yes, but come on, Zooey, what's your stake in this thing? Now suppose I do have evidence to indicate that Mary Gentry's death was not accidental. Nobody's paying you anymore to investigate her death and nobody will, including me. What good will it do you to know what I have? I have…"

"Look," she interrupted. "If you've got this evidence, and I'm sure you do, this could be a big break for both of us. A chance for me to gain a reputation as a seasoned investigator and, of course, a big story for your paper. Why don't we work together? Francesca's paying me to watch you anyway, so if we work together, we're killing two birds with one stone. If we get something hot, maybe Joe Quigley will join in. Otherwise, I can look at it as an investment in the future. My future, that is."

Virgil frowned. "It's more dangerous than you think. You make this sound like a Nancy Drew mystery."

"What makes you so sure it's dangerous?"

"Do you know who Karl Neibor is?"

Zooey shook her head.

"Let me fill you in. Karl isn't the biggest, most powerful hood in Washington, but he's dangerous. And it's his name that surfaced in connection with the Union tampering. Now, if you'd like to go and ask him a few questions, he'd be happy to send you floating home face-down in the Potomac River. I think Mary discovered something important on the day of her accident, and obviously she never got to tell me about it. My belief is that someone ran her off the road."

"That's your evidence? The name of Karl Neibor?"

"And the fact that the police are sitting on her accident." Virgil sipped his scotch and then leaned forward and grabbed Zooey's wrists. "And I mean sitting hard. I visualize the accident report as a clean white page, with a blurry photo of a bloody front seat."

"That means collaboration between the police, the Union, the mob and someone at the power plant? Sounds damn unlikely."

Virgil released her wrists and leaned back again, taking another sip of scotch. "Sometimes I think we should force the police department's hand. Make them reopen the case."

"Sure," Zooey said. "Somebody shot at us, or so says an alcoholic reporter and a two-bit detective looking to make a name for herself. That should make page five in the *TV Guide*. You know, one of those human-interest blurbs next to the hair growth ads. Just enough to let Karl Neibor know that we're still interested."

He nodded. "Maybe. They're still not sure if I have any evidence."

"You *don't* have any, do you?"

A sudden lull of conversation in the bar led Zooey to see that Francesca had arrived. She and Rashid Sharps strode quickly toward their table, Francesca still wearing her kimono and mask.

Now there's an extreme obsession with privacy, Zooey thought. No doubt the students assumed she was with the theater program on campus since, after a few stares, the noise picked up again. Virgil had chosen this location wisely.

Francesca sat down, sweeping her kimono around her legs, while Rashid limped through the scattered tables to the bar.

"My dear Virgil," she laughed, "I see that you are playing the game you like best: keeping secrets and leading your friends on a wild goose chase. But I can also see you're in good spirits once again."

"Hello, Francesca. You arrived just in time. Zooey was pumping me for information about Mary Gentry and the Blackstone power plant." He winked at Zooey and she frowned.

"Francesca's the one who put me on to Sakorski," Virgil said. "When Durnam told her that a Russian had been looking for me, she started asking around."

"Did you know he's wanted by the Miami police for killing a cop in a bar fight two years ago?"

Virgil nodded. "How did you know?"

"Sources of my own. He's been out of sight ever since, probably hiding here in Washington. It's unlikely that he'd be hired just to watch you, Virgil. According to my information, he's one of the best hitmen around."

Francesca's mask nodded agreement. "He is also highly placed with the Russian mob in this country. Very dangerous, indeed."

Virgil ordered another scotch, and the pumpkin-haired waitress asked Francesca if she'd like something.

"Nothing, thank you," she answered.

"Rashid thinks that it was Vlad that I winged yesterday," Virgil said. "Following us in the car, I mean."

"But who hired Vlad Sakorski?"

"Karl Neibor," Francesca said.

"I should have known you'd know about Karl Neibor too," said Zooey.

"She knows," Virgil said.

"Are you planning to pursue Vlad Sakorski?" Francesca asked Virgil.

"I'm going after Sakorski, I'm going after Neibor and I'm going after anyone who's illegally mixed up with the Blackstone Plant." Virgil tossed a handful of popcorn into his mouth and looked cheerful.

"I don't like it," Francesca said.

"Well, what would you have me do?" said Virgil.

"Let this blow over. Leave town for a while."

He shook his head and laughed. "The answer is no. I've tried hiding out, and I didn't like it."

"Forget about Karl Neibor," Francesca said. "You think you are helping me, but you're not. I am a practical woman, not given to foolish acts of vengeance. You should learn from my example. If you had, none of us might be in this situation."

Zooey had no idea what Francesca was talking about. "What do you mean about foolish vengeance? Vengeance for what?"

"I've known Karl Neibor for a long time, Zooey," Francesca said, "but let it stand as a private matter between Virgil and me. I can assure you, this particular story has no bearing on what happened to Mary Gentry. You should know, however, that Karl Neibor is a dangerous man."

"That's what Virgil said." Zooey shifted uneasily at another mention of things she "didn't need to know," and wondered if she should get involved with a potentially dangerous investigation about which no one would give her complete information. Whatever secret game Francesca and Virgil were playing, they weren't sharing the rules.

Virgil put his hand on Francesca's shoulder. "You know that I need help to find Sakorski." He looked steadily into the slits in her mask as some private understanding worked between them again.

Zooey sighed loudly but no one noticed.

Francesca said, "I hadn't intended to mention this, but Vlad Sakorski called me today from New York."

"He called you?" Zooey mused again about all of Francesca's apparent underworld connections.

"He knows that Virgil and I are friends, and he's in trouble. Killing the policeman two years ago was a mistake that angered his bosses. He is now trying to make amends for it by silencing Virgil. By failing, he has put Virgil on guard. Now he claims he possesses the documents for which Virgil is searching, and he will exchange them for $20,000."

"Documents?" Zooey asked.

Virgil nodded slowly. "It's possible that Mary was carrying important evidence in her car when she died. For example, she could have had proof of a money transfer between Neibor and a Union leader. And maybe, though this is stretching it, Sakorski was at the wheel of the car that ran Mary off the road. If he *was* the first person on the scene after the 'accident,' he would have found what she carried in her car."

"No," Francesca said. "I would never trust this man Sakorski. He has presented you with what I see as a strikingly simple-minded ruse, intended to help him finish his job of silencing you. I think he has returned to New York, where he still has friends, in the hopes that after two years the heat from Miami to find him has died down. He hopes to lure you there so he can finish his assignment and regain the trust of his employers. Don't be stupid enough to take his bait."

Francesca spoke with conviction, and Zooey was inclined to share her opinion of Sakorski's offer.

"He claims that he…" A round of laughter interrupted Francesca's comment, and Zooey looked up to see a student with an acne-scarred complexion and long blue-black curly hair approaching their table. His pale blue eyes stared hypnotically straight at Francesca while his friends from the next table collapsed in giggling fits.

"Uh, excuse me, but my friends were wondering whether you're singing as Madam Butterfly at the Kennedy Center this week."

Francesca turned slowly toward him, and he took a step back.

"I'm sorry, but you are mistaken." Although she spoke calmly, the answer evoked howls from the table behind them. Zooey turned to inspect the three young men who leaned back in their chairs, laughing and pointing in Francesca's direction.

"Get lost," Virgil said.

Another student shot up from the table and stood behind the first. "Bert's just shy," he said. He shoved "Bert" in Francesca's direction, causing him to stumble and nearly fall into her lap.

"If you don't want anyone to know who you are, you shouldn't wear your opera costume into this bar. Lots of theater majors hang out here," the second student said as Bert slumped away. "And Bert wants to know if you'll come to a party at his house tomorrow night. Just the two of you, right, Bert?"

Bert hid his face with his hands and groaned.

"How about taking off that mask so Bert can see what he's missing? We'd all like to see the famous…" The student made a mock grab for Francesca's mask, and Virgil, to Zooey's surprise, leaped forward to grab the kid's shirt at the collar.

"You idiot, get your ass out of here before I beat you senseless."

He knocked the kid sideways, ripping his shirt. The kid was clearly astonished at Virgil's fit of temper.

"Hey, be cool, we're just kidding around. Bert is a fool about opera; he's got standing room for the Kennedy performances on all seven nights. We just thought we'd give him a hard time…"

The kid backed away and Virgil sat down.

What a temper, Zooey thought. The kids hadn't meant any harm, and it was curious to see Virgil's temper spark at their drunken antics. It was Francesca's fault, anyway, for assuming such a grandiose disguise in public.

"I'm sorry," Virgil said to Francesca.

"It doesn't matter." Francesca's dignity was unfazed. "What I was beginning to say was that Vlad Sakorski insisted that he would only deal directly with you, Virgil, and that you must come to New York to meet him. He claims, of course, that he is now afraid to stay in Washington. I don't think you should go."

"Suppose it *was* Sakorski who ran Mary off the road," Zooey mused.

"If he found any documents," said Virgil, "he might have kept them as insurance, so he'd have something to bargain with. Maybe he always intended to sell them."

Virgil looked at Francesca. "Will you make me a loan?"

"Dear Virgil, do you mean that your misplaced sense of duty will cost me money?"

"Damn right it will. Temporarily, I hope."

"Of course," she said, and to Zooey's shock, she pulled a flat brown envelope from the leather bag she carried and slid it across the table. "I would not dream of coming unprepared."

Zooey wondered how much cash it would take to make such a large bulge in the envelope. Enough to satisfy Virgil, apparently, since he didn't bother to look.

Virgil turned to Zooey. "I leave for New York on the next train. Want to come?"

"I sincerely hope," said Francesca, "you will not allow Virgil's misguided sense of duty to draw you into danger as well."

"I thought you offered to pay me for protecting him."

"It would be a mistake to go with him to New York. I will continue your payments only if you stay in Washington. You may resume your job when he returns."

Zooey considered for a moment. Not only was Virgil's scheme half-baked, but it was clear that something other than the desire to clear Mary Gentry's name was behind his change from drunken evasion to an all-out hunt for evidence. "I had other plans for investigating Mary's death. Maybe I should stay here and continue with that," she said cautiously. All this talk with Virgil about trust had disturbed her; she wasn't sure she did trust *him*. He had more information that he was concealing from her, she was sure of it. What she couldn't figure out was whether he was crazy or just dangerous. Probably both, considering the involvement of Vlad Sakorski and the Russian mob. Anyway, it was surprising how quickly her attraction to the danger of the case faded when she was forced to decide whether to accompany Virgil to New York.

"Virgil, is there anything else you know that could affect me here in Washington?" she asked.

He avoided her eyes for a moment, and she knew the answer. "No, Zooey, nothing that could affect you. Just make sure that you're not being followed. Why don't you come to New York with me?"

But Zooey was fixed now. "The answer is 'no.'"

Francesca reached across the table and took her hand. "Excellent for you, dear Zooey. I had hoped you could act as a bodyguard to Virgil, preferably in some safe location far away from here. But what can one do with this man?"

Zooey sighed with relief and frustration.

"I have my chauffeur here. We'll drive Virgil to Union Station to catch his train," Francesca said. "May we give you a lift somewhere?"

Virgil rose and took Francesca's arm, a silly picture to Zooey's mind, since the masked woman towered at least three inches above his head. As Rashid limped toward them from the bar, Zooey decided that she wasn't ready to let either of them know where she lived.

"No, thanks. I think I'll just hang around here for a while and soak up some student innocence."

Virgil studied her face. "Be careful, Zooey."

"I will."

The three of them left the bar: a lame chauffeur, a rumpled reporter and a giant in Japanese disguise. What a sideshow. As soon as they disappeared, a voice called out from the neighboring table: "Hey, can I buy you a beer?" It was Bert and his friends.

"No, but thanks anyway." Zooey sat for a long time, looking to any stranger's eyes like a cute graduate student, lost in thought about nothing more serious than finding a date to the homecoming football game.

10

Late the next morning, Zooey walked to Mark's Bar. Mark stood talking with Dave, the only customer. Both were intently watching the big-screen television above the bar, which was, surprisingly, tuned in to a news channel. Mark seldom watched the TV and mostly listened to his antique radio.

"What's up?" asked Zooey.

"Shhh," hushed Dave.

Zooey recognized Wolf Blitzer on the screen. "Breaking news. The terrorist organization calling itself the *White Power Second Amendment Nationalists Front* fulfilled its threat to attack an African American urban center. Their leader, David Duke, issued a video thirty minutes ago warning the people of Baltimore, Maryland, to leave before drones exploded above the city dispersing toxic material onto the city center. In the video, Duke warned that this attack is in retaliation for the murder of the three white policemen in Milwaukee. The clip is edited for language."

The picture changed to a clip of David Duke dressed in Klan robes. "Three white policemen were brutally slaughtered like cattle. We, the white race, must finally stand against this debasement of our society by an inferior race, a blight on our nation. We, the sons of the *White Power Second Amendment Nationalists Front*, have tolerated enough of the inaction by our corrupt government, a government aiding and abetting the destruction of our white nation. This country, founded by white men, built by white men and made great by the white men, will not be displaced by ni(bleep) and Jews. We stand armed and ready to take back our country and purge our land of the urban hellholes that are eating like a cancer at the very fabric of white society. The blow against this urban rat-infested nightmare called Baltimore is just the first of many to come. I call on white America to join us in our crusade to rid our shores of this black and brown scourge."

"Oh, sweet Jesus," said Zooey.

The picture changed to a reporter standing on a street corner holding a microphone. Behind him, crowds of panicked people sprinted in every direction, one colliding headlong into the reporter.

Recovering, the reporter announced, "Just minutes ago, Wolf, the domestic terrorist group calling itself the *White Power Second Amendment Nationalists Front* released a warning of an attack on Baltimore from the air. Three drones were, in fact, spotted high over the city. All three simultaneously exploded. We have obtained exclusive cellphone video of the event."

The picture changed to a jerky video of a spidery drone high above the city exploding in a fireball.

The picture returned to the reporter on the street just as another panicked man ran into him, knocking him to the ground. "Out of the way, moron!" he screamed, pushing the camera aside.

Getting back on his feet, the reporter continued, "The group's statement warned that the drones dispersed enough poison over the city to fatally kill anyone who comes in contact with it, especially if it is inhaled. The manifesto goes on to state that the goal of the group is the annihilation of the Black and Brown races in America.

"The explosions have set off mass panic, Wolf, as you can see around me. A massive gridlock caused by fleeing motorists has brought the city streets to a standstill."

The reporter hunched down as shots were heard in the background.

"Fights are breaking out in the gridlock, and I hear gunshots, Wolf. I am getting reports of break-ins and looting. Police, unable to move through the crowds, are helpless to stop it."

Suddenly, the picture went blank except for the audio. "Screw this crap. I'm not breathing poison."

"Wolf, my cameraman just threw down his camera and has fled. I'm on my own here."

The picture changed to Wolf Blitzer. "Ron, are you safe? Are you all right?"

Cursing, and the sound of a fight, were followed by silence.

Wolf Blitzer glanced anxiously off camera, and then resumed: "We have lost the feed to our reporter in Baltimore."

Zooey turned to look at Mark, who stared back with a grim expression of dismay.

"If any of this is true, the cleanup alone could cost billions," said Dave.

"It's a war," said Mark.

11

Zooey awoke at eight o'clock on Wednesday morning. It was a cloudy day and cooler than it had been in a month, the streets and sidewalks slick with early-morning rain. She carried her first cup of coffee to her balcony and stood watching kids playing basketball in the alley below. A book she'd left lying out on her porch chair was drenched from several nights of rain, and she reached to pick it up.

"Hey, lady," a kid called, looking up at her. "Want to come down and play?" He smirked at her.

Zooey smiled as she turned back to her apartment, shaking her head. She sat down at her laptop and located the number for the Blackstone Nuclear Plant. She stared at it a moment. No one was paying her to continue her investigation into Mary Gentry's death, but an urge to see justice done for this woman she had never met, yet somehow felt she knew, pushed her on.

She dialed the number and an operator answered the phone. Zooey asked to speak to Mary Gentry.

"Mary Gentry?" The voice sounded surprised. "Let me connect you with the Human Resources Department. Hold on and I'll transfer the call."

"Mim Dresser," chirped a young voice twenty seconds later. "Who's calling, please?"

"My name is Carol Pelicort. I'm a friend of Mary Gentry."

There was a moment of silence Zooey had anticipated. "How long has it been since you've seen her?"

"About three months. I've been out of town. Why, isn't she there?"

"I'm afraid I have some bad news. Mary's had a car accident about a month ago on County Road 5. I'm afraid she didn't survive." The voice sounded genuinely grieved.

"Mary? Dead? I can't believe it. How horrible! My God, it's so sudden... were you a friend of hers too? I think Mary might have mentioned your name to me. Mim, isn't it?"

"That's right, but I don't think Mary would have mentioned me. I didn't know her very well."

"Is there anyone there at the plant I could talk to about her?"

"Well, there's Herb Calcut, the Director of Human Resources. Just a minute."

After a pause, a new voice said, "This is Herb Calcut." The tone of his voice was deep and authoritative.

"I'm a friend of Mary's," Zooey said. "But I've been out of town for three months, so I didn't know what happened to her."

"I'm sorry you had to find out about it like this."

"Listen, I don't want to keep you away from work, but could I come by and see you? It feels so strange to suddenly come back and find she's gone, without knowing how it happened."

"You want to come to Blackstone and talk to me?" He sounded interested.

"If you wouldn't mind. I mean... you're the only person who can tell me about it. I didn't know any of her friends at work."

"Are you as attractive as your voice sounds? How about we meet for dinner tonight?"

Oh boy, thought Zooey, a player. Well, she decided, he buys and I get the information I want.

"I'd like that."

"How about a place called Pizzeria Da Marco on Woodmount Avenue in Bethesda."

"Say, at six-thirty?"

Calcut agreed.

Pizzeria Da Marco turned out to be a modern pizzeria/ bar, the dinner crowd young and dressed casually expensive. Zooey lingered at the door, wondering if this was type of bar Mary had enjoyed. A waitress wearing a long, full black skirt with a white blouse swished between the tables, taking orders and serving drinks. A poodle with rhinestone eyes was embroidered above the pocket of her blouse.

At the counter to her right, Zooey saw a middle-aged man. He was classically handsome, with a Clark-Gable-style mustache, sitting by himself and sipping what appeared to be bourbon on ice. He glanced sideways to the door and saw Zooey. She nodded, and he nodded back.

More than one pair of eyes studied Zooey as she crossed the room. She'd decided on a flashy dress as the right sort of look for questioning Mr. Calcut. It was a backless black satin dress with thick brass bangles on each wrist. Her red hair swung loose behind her.

"Herb?" said Zooey.

"And you must be my dinner date?" he answered, surveying her. His smile showed his appreciation for what he saw.

"Hi. Yes, I'm Carol Pelicort." Zooey sucked in her breath; she'd almost said "Zooey Krause."

"I'm Herb Calcut." He wore a black shirt with pleats down the front and black stovepipe pants along with a black suede blazer.

"Nice to meet you," he said. "You were a friend of Mary's? Sit down."

"Yes." Zooey sat on the stool next to him. "You're the Director of Human Resources at the Blackstone Plant?"

"That's right," he said. "I'm sorry about Mary."

The bartender approached. "Gin and tonic, please," Zooey said, "with an extra slice of lime." She turned back to Herb. "I don't understand. What exactly happened to Mary on the day she died?"

"Mary was troubled. I did all I could to try and help her, and she was often in my office. In fact, as I explained to the police, I saw her for a few minutes at work the day she died.

"I know she came to work that morning as usual at eight o'clock. Wendy Corcoran is a good friend of hers, and I interviewed her after the incident to see what she knew. She said that they had coffee together, as they always did, during their ten o'clock break. Wendy did say, however, that she didn't look good. Rather sweaty and flushed, as if she was sick with the flu. Wendy said she asked if she felt okay, and Mary just shrugged it off. She thought Mary looked worried but didn't want to pry.

"According to Wendy, they sat down in the cafeteria at lunch and talked about nothing in particular for ten minutes, and then Mary said that she had to make a phone call. A little later, when Wendy saw her back at work, she said Mary told her she was going to have to leave work early because she had an appointment with a newspaper reporter. Wendy said she seemed upset, but when she asked her about it, Mary wouldn't say why."

"How upset was she?"

"Oh, I don't know, just a little shaky or something. She'd been like that a lot lately."

"Did she say what she was upset about?"

"As I told the police, she didn't say anything to me. Wendy said Mary just told her she had to leave right away, and she asked Wendy to cover for her if anyone noticed she was missing."

"And then she had an accident on the way to see this newspaper reporter?"

"Yes. There's a sharp curve on County Road 5 where she slid off the road and then down a hill; the police said she died instantly. I'm told Joe Quigley, her fiancé, arranged the funeral. She's buried at the Prospect Hill Cemetery in Northeast Washington."

"Thank you for telling me all of this," Zooey said.

"Maybe you know this, but it's a truism of human resources work that five percent of your workforce causes you ninety percent of your problems. I'm sorry, since Mary was your friend, but Mary was that five percent. She was always going on about some ridiculous claims that the Union at the plant was corrupt and working with senior management to cut corners on safety."

Herb sighed. He then smiled and absently squeezed Zooey's thigh. "I did what I could for her."

Instead of batting his hand away as she wanted to, Zooey patted it and smiled.

"Before I left in May, Mary shared with me that she was having some problems," said Zooey. "Problems with Joe, I mean. She also confided in me that she'd lost her temper a couple of times at the plant."

Zooey watched Herb's face as he slid his hand a bit further up her leg.

"I don't know Joe well, but I can tell you half the single women at the plant would do anything Joe asked of them, and the other half would at least consider it. I did sometimes wonder whether he fooled around. There were rumors.

"As to her outbursts, well, there were a few incidents at the plant I had to deal with. I can say Mary was seeing a psychiatrist. But I suppose you knew that, being her friend."

"And then there was that thing," said Zooey, "about the newspaper reporter she talked to. What was his name?"

"Virgil Fitts, a real scumbag from what I hear. I did have to talk to him once."

Herb pulled a comb from his coat pocket and ran it through his hair, temporarily relieving Zooey of his hand on her thigh.

"But," he continued, "he told me that he hadn't talked to Mary on the day she had the accident.

"Look, if you ask me, Mary was unstable and unhappy. The police concluded this was a suicide, and I believe they're right. I'm sure that's upsetting to hear, but maybe Joe Quigley was seeing someone else and she found out that morning."

Zooey smoothed her dress and asked off-handedly, "What did you think about the things she said about the plant? About the Union, I mean?"

"She was wrong. I mean, I'm in management. The Union reps are not high on the list of people I like to talk to, and they are a bunch of jerks, everyone knows that, but they're not doing anything illegal. Mary got carried away trying to get dirt on them.

"Say, where did you get to know Mary?"

Herb placed his hand on her thigh again, smiling seductively.

"It's funny, but I met her one day in a department store. She looked like someone I'd gone to high school with."

"How about we take this conversation back to my place?" His hand slid further up her thigh as he leaned in closer to her. "I'd love to get to know you better, beautiful. I'm sure we'd have a lot to talk about."

"Listen, I'm holding you up," Zooey said, jumping off her stool. "It's been kind of you to talk to me. And here's ten dollars to pay for my drink." She slipped the money from her tiny gold bag on to the bar.

"I thought we were having dinner," Herb protested, reaching out and squeezing her shoulder.

"Some other time."

Yeah, she thought as she turned on her heel and walked out of the restaurant. Sometime around the end of never.

12

Zooey returned home on Wednesday evening after her talk with Herb Calcut. She'd now heard differing stories about Mary's mental health, and maybe Mary's death really had been suicide or simply an unfortunate accident.

Or maybe not.

But would a plant executive hire a mob hitman like Vlad Sakorski to reassure himself of Virgil's intentions or information? Of course, she only had Virgil and Francesca's word that Sakorski had been in Washington; her informant hadn't heard of it.

But who were the men with magnums who'd chased Francesca's car? But then again, what if the attack had nothing to do with Mary Gentry? Maybe it involved some other investigation of Virgil's she knew nothing about.

Zooey found the night to be as surprisingly cool for this time of year as the day had been, and she felt chilly in her backless dress.

What a dress. She'd bought it with her ex-husband's hard-earned money to wear to a cocktail party thrown for his New York manager. Alec had loved the dress to the point of obsession—he'd actually followed her around the room all evening—and there had been a familiar but frightening scene in their bedroom after the party. Alec became cruel and abusive when he drank too much. In the early years of their marriage, before her pregnancy, she'd accepted his occasional lapses. But after getting pregnant she'd decided that her days of silent suffering were over. She became angry and defensive on the many occasions when Alec expressed his disappointment with her. But it was also true, she had to admit, that she hadn't really been much of a wife. At least, not the kind he wanted.

On the night after the cocktail party they'd screamed at each other. In the end, Alec hit her. He never hurt her badly; he always battered her confidence and self-respect much more than he inflicted any physical injuries on Zooey. But this night was the worst.

She slumped in a dining room chair, absorbed in her own angry history until she shook herself and sat up, disgusted. She walked into the bedroom, pulled off her dress and hung it carefully in the closet, wondering why she'd even worn it to begin with, and pulled on a loose white dress of Indian muslin with butterfly embroidery that didn't remind her of anything but the import shop where she'd bought it. To chase the flashbacks away with finality, she sat down at her desk and made notes on her conversation with Calcut until she felt tired enough to attempt sleep, which came more quickly than she would have guessed.

The first thing she did the next morning was call Joe Quigley at the Blackstone Plant. She wondered whether he would be willing to rehire her, now that he'd had time to think about the fact that his personnel manager had possibly lied about Mary to the press to save the plant's reputation. The operator switched her call from line to line, but finally she heard Joe's voice.

"Quigley here."

"Hi Joe, it's Zooey Krause."

"Zooey! I've been thinking about you."

"Good thoughts, I hope."

"Listen, I really can't talk here at work. But I'd like to see you, if you have time this week."

"Sure. What do you have in mind?"

"How about dinner? There's a restaurant I know that serves great German food and beer, and I had, actually, thought of stopping there tonight. Care to join me?"

Zooey thought for a moment. "That's fine. Where is it?"

"I could pick you up."

"Well, I'm going out and I don't know what time I'll get back home. It would be better if I met you there."

"Anything you say. It's the Old Europe Restaurant, on Wisconsin Avenue near the Naval Observatory."

"That'll be easy to find. What time?"

"How about if we make it early? Say, six-thirty?"

That evening she arrived before Joe and she settled back comfortably with a German beer at a table near the bar. The bar television was on with more distressing news about Baltimore and violent demonstrations around the country. Zooey was thankful that the sound was off, as she was more interested in listening to a hefty blonde wearing a gold sleeveless blouse describe her new lover to a dark-skinned woman companion.

"We've worked at the same bookstore for three years, but he lived with a girlfriend who was going to law school. Then one day, about two months ago, she packed her suitcase and ran away with a man who works as a clown for the Ringling Brothers Circus. She…"

The companion laughed.

"No, really! She…"

Joe came up behind Zooey and put his hands on her shoulders. "Hi."

She jumped. "Joe! Don't you know better than to take a private investigator by surprise? You could get shot."

He smiled. "I don't suppose you are often surprised."

"No, that's not true. People surprise me all the time." She watched while he ordered a beer. He'd obviously changed clothes after work and now wore a pair of pleated, white cotton pants and a thin, collarless white gauze shirt. Speaking of surprises, his slim frame in these casual clothes had a grace and proportion she found unexpectedly attractive.

After a bit of small talk, they both ordered bratwurst and hot German potato salad, along with rye bread and a pitcher of beer. Joe asked about Virgil Fitts and then said, "Are the two of you still investigating the Blackstone Plant?"

"Why, are you still interested?" This was her opening, but she'd decided to hold back asking him if he wanted to pursue it further for a while.

"If you think there's something of substance in what he says, I can't help but feel curious—out of respect for you, not him. After I left the two of you at the bar the other night, I found myself getting more and more angry. I think he knows Mary didn't kill herself, but he printed that story anyway because he was afraid of someone at the plant. I hate journalists who print lies, and I don't think someone with his lack of ethics has any business on the staff of a newspaper."

"It sounds like your friend Mary wasn't the only one with ideals," Zooey said. "But Virgil's no criminal. A sloppy journalist, maybe, but he's not a criminal."

"Then why did he print those lies? Have you wondered about that?"

This was exactly what Zooey had been wondering. "Maybe he believed them at the time."

"I doubt it. And it pisses me off. I mean, maybe I resented Mary's contact with Virgil too much, and maybe I should have paid more attention to what she said. But it seems so much clearer now that I know that my Human Resources Director lied to shift attention away from any more questions about her accident and the plant.

"But I never lied to Mary, Zooey. She always knew exactly where I stood. Virgil, on the other hand, betrayed her trust when there was nothing she could say to defend herself, and I wonder now whether the duty to correct that doesn't belong to me. I *know* that Virgil never thought Mary killed herself. She *couldn't* have. Nobody who knew her would say that."

"He said that he didn't know her very well."

Zooey wondered why she was suddenly in the position of defending Virgil, a loyalty she wasn't convinced he deserved.

"But what do *you* think?" said Joe. "Do you think she killed herself?"

Zooey picked up her glass of beer and looked at Joe. His question had been serious, but his eyes, as before, showed a bit of detachment from his words. It made her wary, but also curious.

"Why do you look at me that way?" Joe said. Some of the detachment in his eyes turned to curiosity. When she didn't answer, he asked again. "Why do you look at me that way?"

Zooey smiled. "It's nothing, I was just thinking about the bratwurst. Where is it?"

"Food!" Joe laughed. "That's all women ever think about."

"That's not true. I think about other things, like about good German beer, buying a new car and especially about movies."

"You see a lot of movies?"

"When I have time."

When the food finally arrived, it was delicious, and both of them ate in silence until their plates were empty. Joe finished first and poured them each a fresh glass of beer after wiping his mouth with a corner of his napkin.

"So what is Virgil doing now?" he said.

"Following leads."

"What leads? I thought he was trying to convince me the other night that he didn't have any leads."

"I'm not sure he does, but he obviously thinks he might."

"That's interesting."

"Is it? Why do you think so?"

Joe lifted his chin. "What do you mean?"

She reached for her beer and took a sip, feeling that she'd rushed it a bit. "Well, I'm just wondering if you wanted to hire me to resume the investigation into Mary's suspicions about the plant."

He shook his head. "Not now. I want to do something to clear Mary's reputation, but I'm not sure what it is." He reached over and lightly tapped her wrist. "I'll think about it, though."

Zooey left the restaurant at ten o'clock, later than she'd intended. Joe walked with her to her Mustang, then stood relaxed in the street, both hands in his pockets, beside her car door as she pulled out her keys.

"Let's do this again sometime," he said.

"What, more food?"

"More food, more beer, more conversation. I'll call you."

Zooey paused in the act of starting the car and looked up at him, scanning his eyes for their intent. What she saw stifled the dismissive remark that had been on the tip of her tongue. Instead, she said, "You do that." She started the car and drove off.

13

On Friday morning, Zooey called Francesca, wondering if she'd heard anything from Virgil.

"Very little," said Francesca.

"But he did call you?"

"Yes, he called on Wednesday night. He seemed to be in good spirits, but he was silent as always about his activities. However, I do know that he has not yet contacted Sakorski."

"What the hell is he doing there, picking his nose?"

She heard Francesca's muffled laugh. "I don't know, Zooey, and I doubt that he would tell me unless it was absolutely necessary. But I suspect he has adopted an admirable caution and will try to obtain more information before he agrees to the meeting with Sakorski. As for your part, I hope that you are not continuing the investigation?"

"I've found out a few things, but I haven't got much information to continue with. I'd hoped that Virgil could have helped me out by this time."

As she wandered into the bathroom to comb her hair, she realized that she was restless, and that the day had become depressing. She supposed she should pick up on the lost dog cases she'd accepted before she'd met Joe Quigley, but the prospect of searching out a lost mutt was a letdown after her involvement with Mary Gentry's death. Yet she felt at a dead end until Virgil turned up something in New York. As much as she disliked depending on him for information, she was afraid to advance further alone. She still wasn't sure of the real motivation for Virgil's interest in the case, and whether he'd told her the complete truth about Mary.

She felt stalled.

The day was hot and sticky, and pulling the hair off her neck didn't cool her. The walk to Mark's Bar for lunch was a struggle, with the thought of its air-conditioning her only spur to move.

When she arrived, even the seldom-glum Mark looked unhappy, with his chin sunk in his palm, leaning over the bar.

"You look cheerful," she said to him.

"So do you, sweetheart," he said. "Why don't we both throw ourselves under a truck?"

"Good idea. That'll give old Virgil Fitts something to think about." She settled herself on a stool and covered one of Mark's big, brown hands with her own. "What's bothering you?"

"Nobody bothers about me, that's the problem."

"Argh." Zooey covered her face and moaned. "We can't both be low at the same time. It's my turn. Now cheer up or I'll punch you in the face."

"And what about you? You look like Dracula's widow," said Mark.

"You mean it?"

"No, I'm lying. You look worse than that."

"That's the spirit." Zooey pounded her fist on the bar. "Bartender! Get me a drink!"

"Sure, babe. Gin and tonic?"

Zooey nodded and he pulled down a glass from the rack above the bar.

"And would you ask the cook to grill me a cheese sandwich?"

"Sure." Mark sauntered back to the kitchen while Zooey surveyed the other customers and saw no one familiar.

Dave's table was empty but littered with balled-up paper, and there was an empty Coke can on the floor beside his seat. She went and picked up the litter, then tossed it into the waste can behind the bar. Lingering for a while by a window, she watched a sweaty noontime crowd tramp by across the street.

She still had Joe Quigley on her mind. She realized she wanted to see him again, but also thought the last thing she needed was to have the hots for a guy like Joe; sweet-tempered and nice to look at, but conventional, safe and settled-down. Like Alec. Too much like Alec. Except for the sweet-tempered part.

Now why couldn't she have a quiet little affair with Mark?

Because she just couldn't feel it. Though she had an idea he could.

He called to Zooey, "Here's your drink."

"Thanks." She sat down again and sighed, noticing that Mark's face, too, was sinking into its previous sour mood. She watched as he washed and rinsed the bar sinks, then pulled out three limes for slicing.

"Anything new on the Gentry case?" he said.

"No," said Zooey, "and if you get a call on it, tell them I'm vacationing in Afghanistan."

Mark held a lime to the light, examining it wistfully. Zooey knew his whole repertoire of bartender stances, along with the moods they were meant to convey. The Gentry case intrigued him, but he was afraid that it, like a few of her other cases that had promised real adventure, would fade into something dull and predictable. The car chase and her introduction to the masked Francesca were her first encounters with what felt like real detective work.

"Do you sometimes want to get out of being my partner in the P.I. business?" Zooey asked.

He looked startled. "No, never. It's just that with those insurance and divorce cases you sometimes handle, it's hard to tell whose side we're on. Now with Virgil Fitts, you have a shot at something real."

"If I get killed, that would be something real."

Zooey saw that her off-handedness offended him. "Look, those divorce cases discourage me too. What about that lowlife husband Roger Morris whose wife got screwed in the divorce by the dirt I dug up on her? The only way I justify it is by saying I just provide information. If my investigation puts someone in a bad light, well, they got caught in the act. It's not my fault they did something they're ashamed of."

Mark nodded and resumed slicing limes. "I know. But usually you deal with such petty and personal misdeeds. Half the time we're not even sure who's at fault."

"That's the truth."

A neighborhood patrolman strolled into the bar, and Mark sold him a can of Coke. After he'd left, Mark asked Zooey, "What about Mary Gentry? What happens about her?"

"My gut tells me if we touch that case, we're likely to get burned."

"That makes it sound more interesting."

"We're hardly Sherlock Holmes and Watson." Zooey drained her gin and tonic, and Mark set up another. "But I don't mean to be so negative. I do hope to continue with Mary Gentry, after I get some news from Virgil Fitts in New York."

A group of construction workers filed into the bar, and Mark took their orders for sandwiches and booze. Afterwards, he leaned against the bar and rubbed his thick farmer hand through his hair, then waited on some new customers. Zooey knew that part of him wanted to sell the bar and go into a full-time active partnership with her. He wouldn't suggest it, though. First, because he'd always dreamed of owning a bar like this; and second, because he knew she wouldn't like it. That wasn't the agreement they'd made.

She finished her drink, paid the tab, waved goodbye to Mark and went home.

Later that weekend she spent much of her time at the movies, her favorite escape. With no word from Virgil, she felt further and further away from the Mary Gentry case. She'd half-expected to hear from Joe Quigley and even found, to her discouragement, that she'd jumped a few times when the phone rang. On Monday morning, her secretary Jason returned to the office sporting a dark gold tan that glistened through a thin white peasant shirt laced up the front. His glow of health and good spirits was depressing, but she summoned up the energy to be cheerful.

"Jay, you look terrific! What did you do, go down to Acapulco for the week?"

"I wish I had." He had a dust rag in his hand and was busy polishing her phone and desk. "Actually, I stayed with a friend at a beach house at Cape Cod. Wonderful place with a sauna and a front porch overlooking the sea, and we went sailing and swimming every day. You should take a vacation like that."

"Maybe in my next life."

He finished dusting and replaced her papers in neat stacks.

"But my time wasn't wasted; I brought back a dozen soft-shelled crabs for our salads at lunch. Want to see?"

"Of course."

She followed him into his office apartment, bright with abstract art and bowls of flowers. The tiny freezer compartment inside his refrigerator was stuffed with frozen transparent crustaceans.

"They're lovely," Zooey said doubtfully.

"And I brought back three bottles of French wine, compliments of my hosts. You see, I always take care of you. Now sit down and I'll make a pot of fresh coffee. Have you had breakfast?"

Later that morning, Zooey took on an insurance job, a whiplash case the insurance company thought fishy. She agreed to follow the claimant to see if he kept his neck brace on, and after a day's watch, Gillie spotted the man without his brace.

He called Zooey, and she rushed over to take photographs. By three o'clock Wednesday, she'd developed the film, Jason had typed up the paperwork and she was without work again.

She'd gone home early that day to brood over her finances when Jason called to say that Joe Quigley had phoned the office asking for her. She called the plant and the operator put her on hold for ten minutes, but then was told that Joe had left work.

Shrugging it off, she walked downstairs to her mailbox and found a check for a lost pet case. She'd located a brown-and-white spotted beagle puppy named Junior by answering an ad in the Lost and Found column of the *Spirit*. Not much effort expended, but the owners had been effusively grateful, and the check included a generous bonus in addition to her regular fee. The wife had written "Thanks!" with round loopy letters in red pen, followed by a couple of happy, fat red hearts at the bottom left-hand corner of the check. Zooey decided to cash it right away and spend another night at the movies.

Her neighborhood theater was showing a film about a young New York cop—a Hispanic who'd uncovered a narcotics rings in the Bronx. Unfortunately this hero cop, who aspired to the job of police detective, was shot dead in his front yard at the end of the picture. His killer was a long-haired punk who'd been annoyed by a speeding ticket. The theme was dark and pointless, as if bravery, discipline and moral strength have failure as their only reward. Zooey left the theater with a stomach uncomfortably full of popcorn and an equally uneasy headful of Mary Gentry. There was still nothing definite from Virgil Fitts, though Francesca had claimed that he was all right and relatively sober, still investigating the background of Vlad Sakorski in New York. Zooey felt half-offended that Virgil hadn't called her himself, though maybe she'd stay safer if he didn't.

On Thursday she had little to do and no cases to work on, so she spent the morning at target practice with her new gun. She drove downtown afterwards with the idea of wasting time, and she ended up shopping. She bought two pairs of jeans on sale and was wandering the sidewalks aimlessly when the smell of hot cheese and spices attracted her to a pizza stand. She ate lunch standing at an outdoor counter, braving the heat. Only two other people ate at the usually packed pizza stand, while the sidewalks filled with lunch-hour office workers sweating their way to restaurants with air-conditioning. She finished, and while wiping grease from her mouth and fingers with a waxed paper napkin, a sullen voice asked for a dollar. She turned to confront a drunk with a ruddy and swollen face. He was wearing rags of scratchy army surplus wool, and his feet were crusted black where they stuck through his shoes. She dropped a couple of quarters into his grubby outstretched hand, and then he mumbled while following her, "God bless you," followed by sarcastic compliments on her unusual generosity. It was just that kind of a day.

She walked into Mark's during the after-dinnertime lull. The only customers were a tattered old man listening to the bar radio and Eleanor, a broad potato-shaped woman draped in a butter-yellow tent dress, sitting alone in a booth by the front door.

Mark hovered over the radio and listened to the end of a newscast. More news about Baltimore and the race riots. It seemed a few cities had declared curfews and called out the National Guard. The President's caustic Tweets weren't helping much.

"Hi, Zooey," he called. "Goddam, I knew we hadn't heard the end of this mess."

"What's that?" She hopped up on the stool next to him.

"The same ones who attacked Baltimore are issuing videos of David Duke threatening more to come. And Farrakhan is also airing more videos threatening more police attacks. The FBI can't find either of them.

"What are you drinking, the usual?"

"Right."

He reached for a glass. "It's just come out. Duke threatened to nuke another major American city, but won't say which one or when. He demands the release of all incarcerated White Supremacists and fifty million dollars' worth of diamonds and gold by the end of next week."

Eleanor had been mumbling to herself at the front booth since Zooey had walked in, but suddenly she started to shout. Most of the time she was a sweet-tempered old bird who pushed a two-wheeled shopping cart around the neighborhood, a cart permanently loaded with brown paper bags containing second-hand clothes and broken toys, but her eccentricity sometimes tipped into manic raving.

"Bastards! Sons of bitches! Shit-eating whores! Jews!"

Mark walked to her booth and spoke soothingly, "It's okay, Eleanor, relax. Keep it quiet, now. You want another Dr Pepper?"

"Goddam Dr Pepper, he's a goddam Jew," she growled, but then nodded without catching his eye, so Mark brought a can with a straw to her table. She sipped and temporarily lowered her one-way conversation to a whisper.

"Would you throw me a bag of potato chips?" Zooey said when Mark strolled back behind the counter. "It sounds like Eleanor's having a bad day."

"Yeah, she sure is." He ripped open the bag and emptied it on a paper plate. "She's been sitting at that booth since ten o'clock this morning. Say, did I ever tell you about the old single-piston tractor a neighbor of ours had in Iowa?"

Zooey shook her head as she crunched chips. Mark's tractor imitations were as famous locally as his pig stories. "You talk about tractors so much there isn't a single regular customer who can't tell the difference between a John Deere Diesel and an International Harvester Gas Six Cylinder, down to the engine vibration."

"Well, this thing," he said with a grin, "was a four-stroke, and it vibrated like hell because you didn't have two pistons swinging in opposite directions to counteract each other. Used to hop like a rabbit across a field. Went CRACK, plop, plop, fum, CRACK, plop, plop, fum, like that."

At the explosion of Zooey's laughter, Eleanor dropped her can of soda, spraying Dr Pepper on her yellow dress and plastic sandals. She wailed. Mark rushed over with a bar rag as Eleanor grabbed her red vinyl shopping bag, clasping it to her lumpy bosom.

"Thieves! Whoring, goddam thieves! They stole my cat!"

Mark spoke softly. "Eleanor, your cat just took a vacation and wandered away for a couple of days. He's probably hanging out with some young females in the neighborhood. He'll come back when he's tired."

"No," she insisted. "You don't know what happened. Three big, heavy men broke into my apartment while I was sleeping last night, about three o'clock in the morning. They broke the lock on my door, pulled me out of bed and tied me up, the whoring bastards. And then they picked up Rex, poor Rex, poor pussycat, and stuffed him into a burlap sack, and then threw the sack into the trunk of their car. Just like they did last time, only worse. He'll suffocate in that sack, or starve to death with nothing to eat."

"It's okay, Eleanor. Hey, calm down and I'll clean this mess up; I'll even bring you another Dr Pepper. No charge. No more talking now, just sit quiet and I'll wipe your dress." He brushed at her yellow tent with his bar rag.

"My feet too."

"Right, right." He dabbed at her feet.

"But what about my cat?"

Mark walked back to the sink. "He'll come home, I promise you."

"No more soda pop. I'm going home." She stood up, putting a crumpled dollar bill from the side pocket of her dress on her table, and tugged at her shopping cart. "Rex

115

might get away from them like he did before. He escaped, and then I heard him crying at the door in the middle of the night. So I better get home in case he comes back."

Mark and Zooey watched Eleanor slowly push her cart out to the dark street.

"I hope her cat comes back," Zooey said to a stranger who had just returned from the bathroom in the back of the bar.

He nodded vaguely and then he, too, paid for his drink and left.

Zooey twitched her nose. "Do you smell gasoline?" she asked Mark.

Mark shook his head and said, "No, but I have a terrible sense of smell. I wouldn't know it if a dead skunk lay on the bar next to you."

News about race riots still droned on the radio, and as Zooey reached to change the station, she noticed a large black leather briefcase next to the barstool where the old guy had been sitting. She spit out the ice cube she was sucking and said, "Hey, Mark, that old guy who just left forgot his briefcase. Maybe I can catch him."

Mark nodded. "I'll put it in the back so no one grabs it if you don't catch him. He can pick it up later when he realizes he forgot it."

Zooey ran from the bar and down the street, searching for the ragged figure of the man who'd left. After several seconds, she gave up and turned back.

A loud explosion rocked the sidewalk, and a ball of flame shot from the bar, slamming Zooey backwards to the pavement. In a panic, she crawled across the street, feeling blood drip from her face.

When she'd crossed the street, she looked back.

The bar was a smoking ruin, doors and windows blown out and the building on fire.

"Mark! Oh Christ, Mark!"

She ran back screaming.

14

It wasn't until several hours later, as she sat on a hospital bed in the Emergency Room of George Washington University Hospital, that Zooey began to fully comprehend what had happened. She winced, and the doctor who was stitching up a gash on her chin thought that he'd hurt her and pulled aside the curtain that secluded her bed to signal a nurse from the desk. Nurse Casa, a thin, tired-looking Hispanic woman of about twenty-four, put a gentle arm around Zooey's shoulders and tried to calm her. Zooey was having trouble understanding what the doctor was doing to her chin, and she wondered why her head felt so fuzzy. She remembered that she'd been crying and guessed that Nurse Casa had given her an injection of a sedative.

"Okay," the doctor said, "it's all finished. Now, that wasn't so bad, was it?"

Zooey stared blankly at his reassuring smile.

"Can she be discharged?" said the nurse.

The doctor nodded as he consulted her chart. "You can put your shoes on, Zooey. Check with Nurse Casa at the desk before you leave."

Both doctor and nurse exited, and as soon as the nurse pulled the curtain closed around her bed Zooey reached down and crushed her face into a pillow. She hadn't been able to find a trace of Mark's body before the police pulled her from the rubble and forced her into an ambulance. But there was no doubt about what had happened.

Mark's dead, she thought. Her mouth felt full of blood.

She cried weakly for a few minutes, and then wiped her face with the pillow. Easing herself slowly from the Emergency Room bed, she slipped on her shoes, planning to tiptoe past the nurse's desk. But after a nurse called out her name, it took ten minutes to complete the insurance forms and a medical release. When she was finally free, she searched the waiting room for the policeman who'd accompanied the ambulance to the hospital.

He was young and lean, a black cop named Clarence. He observed her charred and torn clothing and her bruised and stitched face with sleepy eyes.

"Miss Krause. I'd like to take you down to the station for some routine questioning."

"I'll give you all the help I can."

"Follow me." He took her arm and steered her carefully through the crowded waiting room, past a woman holding a bloody handkerchief to her forehead, a crying child who looked pale and scared, a group of drunken high school students who laughed and attracted stares and a few scattered old men who looked relaxed and right at home.

Zooey climbed into the back seat of the patrol car and tried unsuccessfully to make conversation with Clarence up front. The driver, also black, seemed more sympathetic, winking at her in the rear-view mirror as they pulled up to the precinct station. She smiled back, feeling dizzy again and unclear about what she should tell the police about the bombing. In the ambulance, she'd wanted to scream the whole truth about Virgil Fitts and Mary Gentry to anyone who'd listen. Now she felt tired and disgusted with herself, reluctant to let anyone know how stupid she'd been by getting involved in the case.

Walking between the two policemen, she climbed the worn stone steps into the old precinct office building, beginning to seriously wonder who'd planted the bomb. Was it the mobster named Karl Neibor that Virgil had mentioned?

When she was seated in a back room of the station across from Clarence, who had paper, forms and a full ashtray of stale cigarette butts spread in front of him, she decided to tell him everything she knew. Her small detective agency meant very little without Mark, anyway.

Clarence leaned back with his eyes half-closed. "All right, Miss Krause, what time did you arrive at the Mark's Soft Shoulder Bar tonight? That's what it's called, correct?" He consulted a report.

"That's right. About six o'clock."

"Now tell me every detail of what happened after that."

She described everything she could remember, searching for details about the tattered old man with the briefcase.

"It's the old man who was sitting at the bar that you should be looking for," she said.

"Yeah, why's that?" Clarence pulled a thin cigar from its cellophane package and stuck it in his mouth.

"Because the bomb must have been in the briefcase he left next to his barstool. The old man walked out of the bar only a minute before it exploded."

"That's not the way it looked to the arson squad. The fire looks as if it was deliberately set, according to their preliminary report." He pointed to another paper in his stack.

"While the explosion didn't start the fire," he continued, "there was an explosion. Listen to this." He read from the report in front of him. "On-site evidence of a gasoline spill in the storage room next to the kitchen gives the immediate and most likely explanation for the ignition of the blaze. The explosion that followed was probably caused by the detonation of two propane tanks stored in the back room, and a third one connected to the cooking grill. It appears the grill had been left on, but extensive damage makes that impossible to determine with certainty."

He turned to another paper and lit his cigar. "This is a preliminary report, of course. We'll have to check into his insurance records."

"But I'm telling you that that's not what happened! I'd been sitting in the bar until just sixty seconds before the explosion. I've been working on a case and..." Zooey, without realizing it, was shouting.

"Pipe down!" Clarence shook his head and looked weary.

"I'm sorry, but Mark Ramos was my closest friend, my partner in the detective agency I run, and I can tell you he didn't burn down that bar for an insurance claim. He loved running his own bar, and he put his whole life savings and inheritance into it when he came here from Iowa seven years ago. As for finances, he wasn't doing so badly, which I'm sure you'll find out if you look at his books."

"Records that were probably destroyed along with the bar. I've seen this type of fire too many times in that neighborhood." He made some notes on the back of another form.

Zooey stared at him. "Check with his bank! Why would he burn down his bar while he was inside? Fat chance of using that insurance money!"

"Maybe we'll answer that question when we see who his beneficiary is. You were his partner; maybe you set the fire."

"You're crazy! There was a bomb in the suitcase that old man left in the bar! I'm sure your arson squad will uncover the evidence tomorrow, when it's light outside. I'm working on a case concerning the Blackstone Nuclear Plant, and there's already been some violence connected with my investigation. It's possible that organized crime is involved. You see, an employee at the plant contacted me at first..."

She sketched out some of the details concerning her investigation.

"Virgil Fitts?" Clarence said after she'd finished. "I've heard about him." He emptied the ashtray, slamming it against the steel wastebasket beside him. "What you say is all very interesting, but we'll have to rely on the arson squad for a final conclusion. They report that this is a type of fire that they investigate once a week in this city. Several this year in this precinct alone."

"I don't understand." Zooey shook her head. She couldn't seem to muster much resistance; her brain still wasn't functioning clearly. "Maybe whoever is after me did set a fire. I thought I smelled gasoline just when the old guy left. Maybe that is what happened, and it wasn't a bomb. I don't know. I can't think straight right now."

An idea clicked. "But the old man still could have done it. He went to the bathroom at the back of the bar and could easily have sabotaged the kitchen without us seeing it. He left as soon as he got back."

"Anything is possible, I suppose, however unlikely. Well, you can go home now. We'll call if we need you."

"I guarantee you're taking the wrong line with this. If you'll give me time, I'll prove it to you."

"Sure. When you've got the proof, send it over special delivery."

"I will!"

"And I suppose you've had ten years' experience with the arson squad? Look, some of my colleagues there were investigating fires while you were still learning your ABCs in grade school."

Clarence rubbed his eyes. "Let me give you a tip. Keep your ass away from that crime scene, especially if your name appears on the insurance policy, because the city's very hot right now about prosecuting suspects in these kinds of arson cases. There's a lot of public pressure, and don't forget that this is an election year."

"Is that a warning?" Stunned confusion crossed Zooey's face.

"Just file it under the category of friendly advice. Now go home. It's five o'clock in the morning, and I got three hours' worth of reports to finish. We'll call you in again if we've got any more questions."

Zooey rose, alarmed at how her knees trembled. Bright spots swirled in front of her eyes for a moment, fading as she found herself stumbling away from the desk toward the next room. When she paused for a moment at the precinct's front door and swayed unevenly, the man at the front desk rushed forward to steady her.

"Easy now," he said. "Where are you going?"

"Home. I need a cab." She found it hard to focus on the man's face.

"There's usually a cab or two around the corner to your left, just a block or two down. Think you can make it?"

"I'm all right. Just tired." She moved slowly to the stone steps and down to the sidewalk, keeping a firm grip on the wrought-iron bannister as she descended the small stairway. The street was empty and silent, except for the early-morning delivery trucks that had started their rounds. About halfway down the block, she smelled fresh bread, bagels probably, and stopped for a minute.

Maybe food will make me feel better, she thought, and stepped into an alley that ran beside a delicatessen bakery. The narrow passageway was dark and wet, but through an open door at the end she saw five white-aproned bakers mixing dough at a long table. It was a cheerful sight, the figures illuminated and framed by the doorway. The warm bread smells made her stomach rumble. But when she reached the door, a stifling wave of heat blew out from the ovens, and she saw how the workers, drenched with sweat and ruddy-faced, looked dour and exhausted.

Pulling a five-dollar bill from her purse, she entered the open door and approached a heavy woman who'd just pulled a tray full of bagels from a tall oven. "I'll give you this for a fresh bagel." She tried to smile, waving the money.

The woman, unnaturally red-cheeked from the heat, tried to smile too as she took Zooey's money. She folded it carefully and pushed it into a pocket of her red stretch pants under her baker's apron, and then handed Zooey a hot bagel.

"Thanks," Zooey said.

She immediately gobbled down half the bagel and had finished the other half by the time she was halfway down the alley. A wave of nausea bent her over when she'd almost reached the street; again, she relived the moment of the explosion—the deafening blast, the shattering windows, the slap of hot air punching her to the ground.

She tried to imagine a different scene, one where she had discovered the briefcase and then instantly realized what it contained.

She saw herself fling it, in a panic, out into the empty street. And then it exploded, maybe breaking windows, but harmless to Mark and herself, who both watched it from inside the bar. She heard Mark congratulate her quick thinking.

That's what she should have done; or rather, that's what any experienced detective would have done. But then, no experienced detective would have put her partner's life in danger by taking on such a half-baked case. Or, if she had taken the case, she never should have hung around Mark's Bar.

She turned back into the alley and leaned up against a brick wall, panting for air. She would've done anything to change the last few hours so that the explosion had never happened and Mark was waiting for her back at the bar. Always, throughout difficult times during the past three years, she'd turned to him for common-sense advice and humorous companionship. Feeling guilty and afraid of facing what she'd done to her friend, her stomach knotted up again. She stepped further back into the darkness of the alley and, doubling over, she threw up.

15

Zooey realized, when she awoke the next morning, how stupid it had been to return to her apartment after what had happened. Yet it appeared that, still, no one knew where she lived.

She called Jason to fill him in about the small *Washington Post* article in the Metro section entitled "Fire at Mark's Soft Shoulder Bar." Her name wasn't mentioned, luckily, though Jason said that Joe Quigley had already called her office three times that morning. She told Jason to relay the message that she was all right if he called again.

The police had called Mark's relatives in Iowa the night before while the doctor stitched her up in the Emergency Room, so she left Jason in charge of seeing that flowers were sent and any questions from Mark's relatives answered. She couldn't face the idea of talking to them herself. Almost certainly she had been the intended target of the bombing, if it was a bombing, and her intention was to avoid feelings of guilt by finding Mark's killer.

After lying to Jason for the third time by reassuring him that she really was all right, she walked into the bathroom to brush her teeth, catching sight of her face again in the mirror. She looked awful. Her face was peppered with small cuts, and she had five stitches in her chin. Besides that, her eyes looked red and swollen, evidence that the thought of Mark had kept her wide awake and restless long after she'd finally turned out the lights and crawled into bed.

She decided that her first move was to get some real answers from Francesca. She quickly dressed, grabbed her car keys and headed for the Orchid. She wasn't in the mood to appreciate the man who opened the smoke-glass door. He was dressed as a demon, in a red cape over black tights, with war paint streaking his face scarlet and blue. He did, however, recognize her name, and answered her request for Francesca by leading her into a part of the Orchid Zooey hadn't seen before. He left her waiting in a bizarre room full of giant toys, including a five-foot-high jack-in-the-box, a towering stuffed elephant, a pony-sized purple giraffe lying on its side, a white rat as large as a Great Dane and some adult-sized baby dolls. It could have been cute but it wasn't. The elephant, instead of having soft grey fur, was covered in silver foil with red button eyes. The purple giraffe had a lime-green mouth and black teeth.

There were no chairs, only bright velvet cushions on the floor. Zooey wandered to the far wall where a glass cage of real macaw parrots stood under a skylight. They had a clever and well-furnished house inside the cage, including a small pool with a cluster of pink and gold lilies, parrot swings festooned with tiny vines and perches clustered near the skylight roof. She didn't like the way the parrot in front stared at her. He sat on a swing and picked at his leg, twisting his head to glower at her, and then he screeched. She winced at the shrill noise.

The grief of the night before was turning to anger at the way she'd been tricked and fed half-truths by Francesca and Virgil. She wasn't going to leave the Orchid this time without answers.

It was half an hour before Francesca opened a door into the toy room.

"I'm sorry that I kept you waiting, but something upsetting occurred this morning." Her voice was tired behind the mask.

"A man asked to sleep here last night because he had ingested a large quantity of both amphetamines and alcohol. He was an important man with an excellent national reputation, and we've only just discovered that he died of a heart attack during the night. The matter must be handled with great delicacy. His body cannot be discovered here; it would mean a disaster for his family. We are preparing to move him to where he will be discovered in a more appropriate setting."

Zooey stared at Francesca and felt sick. "Does death always follow you this way?"

Francesca looked straight at Zooey. "What on earth happened to your face?"

"You don't know? Very funny. Either your gossip network isn't working as well as it should, or you're very good at faking surprise."

"Zooey, believe me, I don't know anything! Please explain it to me."

"You don't know about the explosion at Mark's Bar last night? Someone planted a bomb that was intended for me. Instead, it blew up the bar while Mark was inside. He's dead."

"Oh, no." Francesca came closer and tried to lay a hand on Zooey's shoulder.

Zooey hit Francesca, knocking her backward, her strained control giving way to rage. She shouted, "I didn't want this! You know I didn't want this! Now you're going to tell me just what the hell's going on! No more mysterious answers! And take off that fucking mask! You're going to tell me everything you know and I want to see your face when you say it!"

Zooey stood rigid, her heart pounding. She felt like something inside had broken. The anger she'd used as a shield overwhelmed her and she couldn't speak.

Francesca stood straight with her hands at her sides. "Perhaps you don't believe this, but I'm so sorry, Zooey. He was your lover?"

Zooey shook her head.

Yes, he'd loved her. She'd ignored it, but it was true. Her tears spilled and she involuntarily released a pathetic sob. Francesca moved forward and hugged her close.

"Shit, Francesca, some friend, some goddam friend I was to Mark. It wasn't him they were after, it was me. And like a goddam amateur I ignored it. I should never have gone back into his bar until this whole thing was over. Shit." She cried into Francesca's sleeve.

Francesca nodded, patting her shoulders. "Come, let's go into a room down the hall. It's more private and I'll make you tea."

Zooey gratefully allowed herself to be led from the nightmarish nursery down the hall into a calm white-furnished room nearby. A large wooden Buddha sat on a stand in front of a window facing the courtyard of roses and boxwood she'd seen before. She settled into a low couch while Francesca plugged in an electric teakettle on a counter in the corner.

"Take this," Francesca said, handing her a large white handkerchief. Zooey wiped her eyes.

"Have you heard from Virgil?" Zooey said finally.

"I've heard nothing."

"I don't understand it. What is he doing in New York?"

Francesca didn't answer, but continued with her tea preparations. Zooey watched her, saying nothing until a brass tray with a teapot and cups were set on the table in front of her. Francesca poured pale green tea into a delicate china cup and handed it to Zooey.

"Francesca," Zooey finally said, "you've got to understand that I need answers. I've never been sure how much of what Virgil told me was the truth. He said Mary was capable of suicide, but Joe says that's impossible. Virgil says he has no evidence to support Mary's allegations about Union tampering, but then he gives all kinds of mysterious hints and disappears to New York. And then a bomb explodes in Mark's Bar. For all I know, he's joined the other side."

"I can understand why you'd think it, Zooey. Virgil has not told you everything he knows; some of his information actually has little to do with Mary's death, and more to do with his desire to protect me. Yet now you deserve the entire truth, and so you shall have it."

Francesca stood and walked calmly to the only window and closed its shutters, then flipped a switch to turn on the lights. When their privacy was assured, she turned back to Zooey. Slowly she raised her hands and lifted the Noh mask away from her face and down, holding it at her waist.

"Oh God," was all Zooey managed.

It was as if someone had carelessly sculpted Francesca's face out of slippery red clay, then smudged it without eyebrows or lips. One eye glared white. Zooey had had no idea that Francesca's disguise and careful movements were more than a stylish affectation.

Francesca turned away. "Karl Neibor is responsible for the ugly thing you see. Hydrochloric acid. He did this to me seven years ago, and he is the man Virgil wants to destroy."

Zooey shakily set down her teacup and leaned forward on her chair. "Why didn't you kill the son of a bitch?"

"Avenge myself on him?" Francesca shook her head, still facing the shuttered window. "I don't believe in it. Revenge is a luxury for those who can afford it."

"Don't talk that nonsense to me! You can't stand still and let a man do a thing like that to you!"

Francesca turned to Zooey again, her face as unreadable as when she'd worn the mask. "You don't understand. Nothing I do now will change what happened."

"Of course, I don't understand. Nobody tells me anything." Zooey sighed and picked up her cup again. "Here, sit down and have tea with me."

"Yes." Francesca sat and laid her mask on the table.

"Was it Karl Neibor who blew up Mark's Bar?" said Zooey.

"I don't know."

"But how did you get involved with him?"

"It's a long story, and you must know something about my background in order to understand it." Francesca poured herself a cup of tea and leaned back in her chair, stretching her long legs under the kimono.

"I grew up in a luxurious apartment in New York, in a family never lacking for money. My father worked for the 'underworld,' as it is so quaintly termed, and it was his idea that I manage a business like the Orchid. In fact, most of the financing was a loan from him and his friends.

"I hated my father and his 'friends.' I was afraid of everyone, except for my self-pitying mother, who was equally hard to love since she allowed my father to abuse her. Nothing she did was right in his eyes. Once, I saw him throw a pot of boiling water at the sink where she was washing dishes because she'd forgotten to make his coffee. At the dining table, he'd throw a plate of food on the floor if he didn't like the way it was prepared. Even though we had money to hire a cook, he insisted that she prepare all the meals for him and any friends he chose to bring home, even when he hated the food she prepared and ridiculed her in front of guests. When he was drunk, he beat her. It sounds impossible, but honestly it was the only way they knew how to live, as well as the only way they knew how to be married.

"To gain support for her martyrdom, mother encouraged me to hate my father, although it was she who disappointed me the most. I swore that I would never passively accept such abuse from a man, although you will quickly discover that I failed. Perhaps it is not so surprising that I failed; so many of us relive our parents' quarrels. Mother loved me and tried to pamper me, but the only time she opposed my father was when she learned of the plan for me to manage the Orchid, and then he beat her the worst he ever had. After three weeks in the hospital, she swore to the police that she'd only been injured by a fall down the stairs when she'd had too much to drink. Nobody believed her, of course."

The story sounded like a depressingly familiar scene from Zooey's own marriage and her experience with divorce cases. She nodded sympathetically. "Where are your parents now?"

"My father died nine years ago. Murdered, of course. So silly."

"And your mother?"

"I purchased a home for her in California. She lives there now on a small trust I established in her name. The ridiculous woman; her needs are so modest that she saves most of her income."

"And then there was Karl Neibor."

"Yes. I'm sure you'll understand now why I first explained about my family. It's so difficult to simply tell you what happened, without trying to vindicate it by all those years with my father. Of course, there is always a dark side to passion, which has little to do with the experiences of childhood. Most people avoid the passionate fantasies that disturb them and choose something safer—more conventional. That was never the case for me. I hadn't intended to imitate my parent's example of abuse, yet sometimes our demons emerge, no matter how much we intend otherwise.

"You have seen only the outer rooms of this house, the elegant rooms and retreats. But I cater to many sordid tastes for pleasure in this business. Actually, these outer rooms are seldom used. You must know by now that few men desire real beauty, and men most often come here because they are willing to pay enormous sums of money for something quite different."

Zooey closed her eyes and tried not to imagine what kind of perverse activities Francesca sponsored in the dark halls behind the star-shaped fountain.

"Do you find me repulsive?" Francesca's voice was calm but slightly tentative, which surprised Zooey.

"No," she answered, and was fairly sure she meant it. She sensed that she and Francesca understood one another better than she would have guessed.

"Ten years ago, Karl Neibor and I were lovers, although I don't mean that I loved him. He held a powerful and inexplicable attraction for me, driven as he was by sadistic pleasures. Like my father, as I'm sure you've concluded. Maybe I despised my passion for him when we were apart, but still I indulged it for a few years. I actually began with the idea that he might murder my father as a favor, but fortunately someone else arranged it before we put our plans into action.

"Eventually, I grew weary of Karl's abuse, as I began to understand my own motivations and grew tired of hating myself. Of course, I understand it better now than I did then, but leaving him was not so simple." Francesca gently touched her face. "On our last night together, he did this."

"Why?"

"He marked me, like a dog marks a tree. It gave him a permanent hold over me. It also gave him pleasure to disfigure me after I turned away from him. I made the mistake of telling him how much he disgusted me, and a man as brutally insecure as he is does not bear such an insult with grace.

"I could hardly go to the authorities; Karl knows far too much about my business, and revenge would cost everything. If anything happens to Karl through my instigation, certain evidence will be forwarded to the police. Much of it is false, but I would be destroyed in proving it so, and there is certainly enough of it that is true to send me to prison. I would lose everything. So you can understand now why Karl and I have reached a stalemate."

It seemed to Zooey that there were other alternatives, but this wasn't the time to go into that.

Francesca stood, replaced her mask, walked to the window and pushed open the shutters again.

"Let's have a whisky," Francesca said.

"Best idea I've heard all day."

Francesca opened a cabinet and pulled out a bottle of Blanton's, pouring them each a stiff shot without ice. Francesca drank hers in one neat gulp after she pulled up her mask and stood behind the shutters out of sight. Then she handed a glass to Zooey, who drained it and shuddered. She had never developed a taste for bourbon.

"I haven't enjoyed telling you these stories," Francesca said, "but you should be warned about the danger involved in investigating Karl Neibor. I must plead with you not to involve yourself further in this affair. Leave it with Virgil."

"I tried that, Francesca. I haven't done anything involved with Mary Gentry for days and look what happened."

"Then you must contact the police. I know this is a strange request from me, but it certainly makes the most sense now."

Zooey's head tingled. "I tried to talk to the police last night after the explosion, but they're insisting it was arson for the insurance money. They even suggested that I might be Mark's beneficiary, which, if it's true, means that I'll be a suspect in the fire. The guy who questioned me didn't have the slightest interest in what I had to say and, besides, we already know that the police ignored Mary Gentry's accident. Maybe Karl Neibor paid them off. Only three of us might know the truth, but we don't really know what's happening and we have no proof."

"But Zooey..."

"All I know is, I won't hang around the police station downtown for the next two weeks while the cops play games and insult me. I'm going to New York to see Virgil. I've got no other choice."

"There are other options, as I've always tried to explain to both you and Virgil. The best is a trip away from here and far away from New York. You have no experience with these people, and Virgil does. You've seen what Karl Neibor did to me. Don't be a foolish would-be hero and let him do the same or worse to you."

"I know you're right, Francesca. I'm way out of my league. But Mark's gone and I can't turn away now."

The mask nodded and Francesca sighed. "I understand. Perhaps there is no safety now. To be truthful, I don't understand why there is so much violence surrounding the death of Mary Gentry. These men are ruthless, but they always act for a reason. The stakes are high, you can be certain. But I'll arrange for a flight to New York that leaves this afternoon, and Rashid will pick you up and take you to Reagan National Airport. Meanwhile, I will call Virgil and tell him what has happened. I know he will be glad to see you, dear Zooey."

She paused.

"Still, it is most odd the risks which Karl has taken to silence both you and Virgil. I fear that Virgil is indeed close to a discovery in New York."

Zooey shook her head. "I'm scared," she muttered. "But I don't know what else to do."

On her way home, Zooey couldn't resist the impulse to drive by the ruin of Mark's Bar. She parked down the street and stared. She wasn't alone; Dave, the artist, was slouched twenty feet further down the street, sloppily dressed and stony-eyed, with paper bags under each arm and completely oblivious to the presence of her car. Finally, as he turned to walk in the opposite direction, she called to him.

"Dave! Over here!"

He squinted mournfully for several moments until he recognized her face, substantiating Zooey's theory that he didn't see well. Slowly, he walked over to her open car window.

"Two survivors surveying the scene of disaster," she said. "How did you find out about it?"

"I was just down the street when the bar exploded." Dave gently touched the stitches on her chin. "You got your face cut up. How did it happen? The papers said it was arson."

"That's what the police decided, but don't you believe it. I'll find the bastard who did it, though, and rip both his arms off."

133

"I'd help you if I could, but I'm afraid I'm pretty useless." Dave shook his head, then shifted both packages to his left arm so he could straighten his glasses. "I feel really bad about Mark."

"Me too."

"An understatement, huh—I don't guess there'll be a funeral or anything here in Washington?"

"His relatives will probably take what's left of his body back to Iowa."

"Yeah, I guess so. Well, I'll see you, Zooey. That is, if we end up drinking at the same bar one of these days."

"I'll be around."

"Yeah, sure." Dave wandered off.

At home Zooey packed her bags, folding a dress, a pair of jeans and several blouses into a small green valise that was a relic of the third anniversary of her marriage. It was a perfect example of the practical gifts her husband had bought her for special occasions, like the vacuum cleaner he'd decorated with green ribbons and dragged through the front door for their first anniversary. "But it was expensive!" he'd complained in reaction to her sulking.

She remembered Jason and called to tell him about her four o'clock flight to New York, and that she didn't want anyone else to know where she'd gone. Jason asked if he should give Joe Quigley her cell number if he called. She considered it, and then told him no, to just take a message.

An hour later she stood on her balcony dressed in a purple blouse and slim black skirt, sipping coffee and watching kids chase each other through the alley below.

Zooey wondered why Virgil was so loyal to Francesca. It had to be more than simple friendship, considering the wad of money she'd given him for his trip to New York. He must have been amazed when Mary Gentry walked into his office with a perfect frame-up for the man who'd destroyed Francesca's face. Of course, he'd never explained that to Zooey, and he had probably never explained it to Mary Gentry either.

All this evasion made her furious, considering how Mark and she had paid the price of his silence. And yet Virgil was the key to making sense of what had happened.

A half-read book lay open on the balcony chair and reminded her of how long it had been since she'd had the peace of mind for reading. The book was titled *The Perfect Murder*, and she remembered something about a detective in India. As she reached for it, the downstairs buzzer rang and she jumped. Until now, nobody had known where she lived, and she hadn't even known what the buzzer sounded like. She'd been too tired to resist when Francesca insisted that Rashid Sharps drive her to the airport.

She walked into the kitchen and poured the rest of her coffee down the sink, then picked up her suitcase and sighed. After one more look around the apartment, which had once felt like a safe escape but did no longer, she fixed her mind on New York.

16

Zooey walked into the La Guardia airport terminal at six o'clock on Friday evening and retrieved her small green valise at baggage claim. Virgil, looking tanned and healthier, stepped immediately from the crowd and hugged her. She was too tired to resist.

"Okay, okay," she said.

She knew she resembled Frankenstein's monster with her stitches, and he stepped back and frowned.

"Francesca called and told me everything," he said. Then he hesitated. "I don't know what to say about Mark, Zooey. I'm sorry. But I'm sure saying that doesn't help at all."

"It's all right," said Zooey.

"No, it's not."

Zooey turned and headed for the exit. Virgil walked beside her. "No, it's not all right," she said. "Now tell me about the weather."

"I found Vlad."

"I figured you had."

"Why do you say that?"

"It's probably the reason someone tried to waste me in Washington."

Virgil slowed. "Are you blaming me?"

Zooey stopped walking. "I've been thinking about this ever since the bar blew up, Virgil, and everything is beginning to make sense. You were chasing Karl Neibor from the beginning because you knew he was behind the corruption at the Blackstone Plant. You never thought he was a 'comedian gangster' like you told me at first. Mary Gentry came to you with an angle on a man you'd hated for years, and you thought you'd finally found a way to take him down."

"What's wrong with sticking it to Neibor? I told you who he was."

"That's not what I'm saying," Zooey said. She couldn't eliminate the hard tone of bitterness from her voice. "You wanted revenge for Francesca, so you put Mary's head on the chopping block. Joe Quigley was right: you used Mary for reasons of your own and then, when somebody killed her, you pretended to believe she'd committed suicide. I think she really did have an appointment with you on the day she died; in fact, she was rushing to your office when someone ran her car off the road. Then, instead of helping to find her killer, you lied about it by printing a story that Mary Gentry was suicidal in order to save your ass. Did you ever warn Mary about what she was up against?"

"Of course."

"Or did you let her walk blindly to her death, like Mark? And almost like me? Did you tell Mary what Karl Neibor did to Francesca?"

Virgil faced her squarely. His face was red, his expression grim. "She knew," he said firmly.

"She knew what? About Francesca?"

"Damn you, I told her Neibor was a dangerous man. She knew he was behind the corruption at her plant. The difference was, she didn't walk away from it."

Virgil's face went stony. They were nose to nose and Zooey didn't care that they were drawing attention.

"Then either her information was bad, or she was a damn fool!"

"Nobody asked you to fly to New York, Zooey!"

"Wrong! You asked me that night at the restaurant and I refused! Only, it turned out to be too late! Next time you withhold information you don't think I need to know, I swear I'll save Neibor the bullet!"

"You didn't need to know what Neibor did to Francesca. I told you who he was. Why I hate his guts is my business, and it hasn't a damned thing to do with why Mark was killed."

Zooey slapped him hard and he flinched. Then he turned and walked stiffly down the corridor and out of sight in the press of people. As Zooey stood trembling, someone asked if she was all right. Without answering, she shoved her suitcase into a corner and sat on it.

She forced herself not to cry. Like Joe Quigley, her quiet life had crumbled, and now she was in New York without a reason. Yet it didn't seem safe to go back to Washington.

After ten minutes, she picked up her bag and walked outside, when someone came up from behind and took her suitcase.

"That was a lousy start," said Virgil.

They stopped. Zooey glared across the exit filled with people and honking cars.

"I'm tired and my stitches hurt. I feel guilty about Mark but I don't know who to blame. No matter what happens now, if we nail Neibor and the whole goddam police force, it's still a loss. Mark should have had thirty more years to tell farmer stories at the bar. Nothing that happens now will change that."

She grabbed his arm. "Virgil, if you hide things from me again, I don't know what I'll do. Don't lie to me. I mean it."

Virgil briefly stroked the cuts around her left eye and nodded.

"When you first turned up, I wasn't admitting to anyone, least of all myself, that I let Mary get in over her head."

"Okay, let it ride for now. Let's get out of here."

Driving away from the airport in Virgil's rented car, Zooey sank back and closed her eyes. With a headache like breaking glass, she wondered if the world of two weeks ago had ever existed. It was exactly two weeks since she'd met Joe Quigley.

"Tell me what really happened on the day Mary died," she said. "Everything you can remember."

Virgil shrugged. "I'd pretty much dropped her story as a dead end. I was working with a friend taping interviews at a nursing home that was being investigated for wasting federal funds, when Mary called me there about mid-morning. She was calling from the office and sounded hysterical about something that had happened at work, but I couldn't get her to tell me what it was. She kept saying there was only 'one,' and I asked her, 'One of what?' But she wouldn't say. She also said that she had evidence, but I couldn't get her to tell me what. She didn't say anything about the papers that Sakorski claims he found at the scene of the crash.

"She sounded irrational to me, Zooey, like she'd cracked under the strain. I told her that I'd leave the nursing home and drive to her office, but she said no. She said she had to get away from there and that she wanted to meet me at my office. I tried to talk her out of it. I told her that she was too upset to drive all the way into town, and then she said something strange, like 'It's too late for me, anyway,' and hung up. I was waiting for her to arrive at my office when her car ran off the road.

"The police supposedly searched the car, but if she was carrying something it was already gone. Her trunk had popped open in the accident, and all they found there was a smashed radiation detector. Her lunch bag was on the floor in the front seat.

"I got an interview with the Personnel Manager at the Blackstone Plant, like I told Joe Quigley. I could see that the police weren't pushing her case, so I just printed a misleading story and disappeared. I was worried Neibor thought I knew too much about this scams, and I was concerned he'd come after me. And then you found me. That's all there is, Zooey."

"And the Personnel Manager said she'd been seeing a shrink?"

"Right. He told me confidentially that she'd been a first-class loony, but they'd been afraid to fire her because of her accusations. It might have looked bad."

"Right. I saw him and he told me the same thing." She scratched her chin carefully around the stitches. "But why was she carrying a radiation detector?"

"Mary used it to test for contamination around the plant. It was part of her job."

"What about her lunch?"

"Just a sandwich and a Snickers bar. They weren't radioactive, if that's what you're thinking."

"So we're back to Vlad."

"Tomorrow night, ten-thirty at the Alsatian Nightclub, we've got an appointment to meet him. I didn't call him until two days ago. I wanted to put my ear to the ground first and see what I heard."

"Two days" rang in Zooey's ears, but she said nothing.

"I didn't hear much," Virgil said, "except that he's still wanted by the Miami police for the time he shot a Miami policeman. It seems odd that he'd come here, unless this is the only place where he still has friends.

"But I'll tell you this. He says he'll give us something to think about."

Zooey believed it.

17

Highball glasses rose and fell, chairs shuffled on thin, black iron legs, and in the dark corners of the Alsatian Nightclub, large table candles cast dim circles of light on a cold wall of expressionless faces waiting for the show. Hands flashed, lifting drinks off small, round-topped tables draped with pink linen.

A band tuned up behind the stage curtain, but Zooey couldn't see well in the semi-darkness. She and Virgil sat at a circular bar. An eerie wail drifted from the stage and Virgil, chin in hand, watched as the curtain parted on a New Wave rock band.

Am I bashful?
No, I'm not.
Am I honest?
Not a lot.
I twist a knife of snow
and see I'm striking oil.
My favorite occupation
is the cold.

The four-member group, dressed in grey plastic jumpsuits, mirrored sunglasses and army boots, droned the lyrics while a bare-chested G-string clad woman pranced in a shallow tray of dark mud.

Vlad was due and the hair on Zooey's neck stood higher with the passing minutes. The atmosphere didn't help. On top of everything, Virgil had already soaked up his third whisky. They'd done practically nothing but argue since she'd arrived.

"Look, Virg, what say you hold the boozing down?"

"The little lady's feeling jumpy?"

"Damn scared, if you want to know."

He shook the ice in his glass off-handedly. "And here I thought you were such a tough ass. Don't tell me you might need my help?"

"I goddam hope not," she muttered. His crack had hurt. Now that her initial gung-ho anger had worn off, this scene felt like more than she could handle. She was afraid that if a safe way out appeared, she might take it.

Virgil watched these thoughts cross her face and set his glass down with a clunk, nudging her elbow. "Hey kid, you look like hell," he laughed.

She shrugged. "Thanks."

"The truth is," he sighed, "we step on each other's raw spots one hell of a lot. At the airport, and ever since…"

Zooey waved her hands. "Don't remind me."

"Come on, partner." He raised his glass. "Here's to vengeance and a Pulitzer Prize." He drained his fourth whisky and started to signal for another when he caught Zooey's dark look, grinned and dropped his arm.

"All right, Zo, but I didn't know I'd be working with the Women's Prohibition League."

She let the crack pass.

"I have a sudden urge," she said, "to leave for Oregon and get a job as a cocktail waitress. You know, something safe and dignified where a pinch on the ass is the biggest risk you're expected to take."

"How the hell did you start in the business anyway? The only other woman P.I. I know is Sal Mason, and she's twice the size I am. She's not the kind of gal you treat delicately; in fact, she'd punch you for it. I've seen her pick up a thug by the collar and throw him halfway across a room."

Zooey shrugged.

"I suppose it's nothing I need to know," he said.

She smiled weakly. "Not much of a story."

She grabbed the drink Virgil had just ordered despite her objections and downed it. It burned, but it helped shake off her mood of morbid nostalgia for Mark. Virgil looked forlornly at his empty glass.

"Of course," she said, "the romance of this job quickly faded. I've chased down so many poodles that I start lifting my leg when I pass a fire hydrant."

Virgil laughed. "Yeah, but it's the same with my job. But while I'm an open book, you play it close, Zooey. What the hell makes you so tight-lipped?"

"Right now, it's simple nerves."

"Sakorski?"

"Does that surprise you? Let's just look for Vlad the rest of the night."

The customers sat like corpses. Everyone's chief motivation seemed to be boredom, and Zooey decided that she'd have to drink the contents of a distillery and be hanging from a meat hook to feel like she fit in. Besides, she didn't like the careful way Virgil watched her or his close cross-questioning. He was sharp in his own eccentric way, and he obviously had the reporter's knack for drilling down on a story.

She noticed the guy who sat next to her had no arms. He was dressed in a black velour outfit and looked like a wingless Prince Hamlet. He drank through a straw and talked to a heavily rouged blonde transvestite who managed to look prim and proper in a green sequined dress.

"I seemed to have it all," he was saying, "and that, you understand, is what I found depressing. You see, despite the adoration of millions and the acquisition of every material possession I deemed worth having, life meant nothing. A great *nada*. I was financially fulfilled and yet unhappy, so I laid my arms on the hydraulic paper cutter intending to die. Fortunately, I was saved, for my nurse was a most gloriously innocent girl from International Falls, Minnesota, and I married her. Now I am completely happy."

Zooey rested her head on the bar. Virgil poked her, puzzled.

"This place is a mausoleum," she said.

Then, as if to contradict her, the band changed pace. A new beat pulsed loud and fast, and many of the ghost-like figures around her rose to dance between the tables.

Hello, I'm Modern.
I walk the Modern Way.
Hello, I'm Modern,
so you'd better keep away.

"Hey, Zo, is that our newsboy?" Virgil pointed with his swizzle stick past the dancers to a small corridor that presumably led to the toilets. A short, slim, olive-skinned man with his right arm in a sling was outlined against the hall light.

"Damn, Virgil, who knows? He looks Russian, anyway." Her heart raced, keeping time with the music. "Gesture him over, I guess, and let's see."

Virgil waved tentatively and the man nodded, then started toward them.

I realize your presence. I shut you out.
I push around your ribs until you shout.
You're deep within this stone and getting thin.
I'm into the Modern Spin.

It wasn't until the stranger was halfway across the wide room that Zooey noticed his left hand was stuffed inside his over-sized coat pocket, creating a bulge that definitely wasn't a memo pad to write her phone number on. As he pulled it out, Virgil's glass of whisky exploded in his hand and he suddenly found the floor to be the most comfortable seat in the house.

A few people screamed and overturned their tables, sending alcohol and their large candles spilling across the rug. People rushing helter-skelter bogged down Sakorski's progress, but he'd already shot through the crowd and was obviously unconcerned about innocent bystanders. Zooey jumped from the bar and desperately grabbed a table, flipping it over to shield herself and Virgil as she drew her gun. Virgil was busy tying a napkin tightly across his heavily bleeding hand.

A bullet smashed the flimsy Formica barrier and burned a streak across the rug beside Zooey. She raised her arm, firing twice into the ceiling, then raised her head to take a hurried glance around the room. There was no sign of Sakorski, and she decided he must have ducked behind a table of his own. Meanwhile, bar patrons were screaming as they made for the exits. Several small fires smoldered on the rug set by the candles knocked off their tables. Sakorski would soon be able run through the fleeing crowd and shoot them both.

"Virgil! Get up! Sakorski's going to kill us! Come on, get up!"

Virgil's eyes looked dazed and his left hand still bled steadily. She figured he was in shock and they both needed to act, so she pitched him toward the door. Another shot shattered a table next to her and Zooey shrieked.

With a strength that came from panic, Zooey pulled Virgil down behind another table. Sakorski jumped up to fire another round, but a quick ceiling shot from Zooey sent him down again. There were still too many people standing around them for her to risk returning firing. She searched for a safer place to take cover.

"Goddam, clear out!" She hollered louder than she would have thought possible, but, incredibly, the band ignored her.

Then Sakorski leapt up and ran forward, peppering her table with bullets. Without thinking, and in a moment she'd relive endlessly in nightmares, she rolled from behind her table and emptied her clip at Vlad. One shot hit him directly in the center of his chest, shoving him sideways over a table and down in front of panicked bystanders. One of them, so drunk he could hardly stand, reached over and picked up Sakorski's gun, waving it in front of his terrified friends. Laughing, he unloaded it into the ceiling.

Zooey dropped her own gun and ran to Sakorski. While most of the crowed had now exited, incredibly, the band was still performing. When she reached him, she saw he had spilled so much blood the rug around him was soaked. She held his head up and tried to staunch the flow with a pink tablecloth, but it was like trying to dam a river. Virgil crawled up next to her to help, but it was an obvious lost cause.

In her disgust with the band, Zooey forgot for a moment to be scared. As she pressed hard on Sakorski's chest with the tablecloth, she realized that she was looking at the body of the first human being she'd killed. The last footing of her life dropped away, and she wondered whether she'd ever recognize herself again. Probably the only reason she'd survived was the fact that Sakorski's right arm had been wounded, most likely in that car chase in Washington, and he'd had to shoot with his left hand.

Sakorski held up his head for a moment and struggled to talk. He gurgled, "You… what…"

"Sakorski! Where's the evidence?" Zooey shouted.

"Uh… uh…" He gasped out a choked laugh. "Only you," he gagged, "can do what we want. Only you." He coughed and fell back, his fingers twitching, his face going white.

"Who planted the bomb at Mark's Bar? Tell me, dammit!" She dropped the saturated tablecloth, grabbing Vlad's lapels, and shook his head with all her strength. "Only I can what?"

Virgil, foggy as he was, took her shoulders and forced her toward him. "Zooey, this guy is dead. Let him go and let's get the hell out of here."

Her hands were covered with blood, and there were smears across her face. She stared at Virgil for a moment, then shook free of his weak grasp, throwing herself at Sakorski again. She pounded his chest with clenched fists.

"Talk! Talk, you bastard! Goddammit, you owe me everything!" She pummeled him with all her remaining strength until, slowly, awareness returned and her arms went limp. She wrenched herself away, resting on her knees, panting. Sakorski's waxy eyes were fixed on the ceiling. She realized Virgil was right. He was dead.

Virgil yanked her away from the body, with blood dripping from her fingers, and led her to the door.

"Come on, Zooey, get clear. We've got to get out of here before the cops arrive."

Zooey didn't answer but let Virgil pull her along. He picked up her gun from the floor on the way out. Behind them, the band rocked to the rhythm of their music, apparently so stoned and focused on their ear-shattering music they still had not registered what had just transpired before their very eyes.

Hello, I'm Modern.
I speak with Modern Calm.
Hello, I'm Modern.
I sing a Modern Song.

18

Zooey almost cried again, this time because of nerves, while a doctor looked at Virgil's hand. She was sitting in the flowery living room of a suburban home, the home of a friend of Virgil's. They'd driven directly from the Alsatian Nightclub to this quiet and moneyed neighborhood, with its sweep of gently curving, tree-lined streets.

Virgil directed Zooey to turn up a semicircular driveway leading to a miniature edition of a Southern plantation house, a white pillared home with an ornate white front porch and a large wooded backyard behind the house.

Virgil rang the front doorbell under a brass plate inscribed "J.C. Norris, M.D.," while telling Zooey that it didn't matter what excuse he gave about his injury; this doctor was a longtime friend and would keep things quiet. J.C. Norris, a handsome, white-haired African American man in his fifties, warmly greeted Virgil at the door and immediately invited them inside. Virgil quickly explained that he'd been inadvertently caught up in a bar fight, and "J.C." swept Virgil off to a back room, motioning Zooey to sit down in the living room while he shouted upstairs for his wife.

The television was tuned to a news program blaring the latest details of the continuing escalation of violent clashes between White Supremacist militia groups, National Guard forces and African American communities. In addition, more

148

police had been shot by groups claiming to represent Black Nationalists. Farrakhan and Duke, still releasing videos urging their followers on, still had not been captured by the FBI. Casualties from these clashes now were reported to exceed 800.

Zooey found the TV remote and shut it off.

The doctor's wife, a white, plump, cheerful woman named Lily with a teased bouffant hairdo, brought coffee for Zooey and found her looking depressed. "There, there, now, Virgil's going to be fine, dear," the woman clucked. She gave Zooey a quick hug that smelled of scented bath powder. "Have some coffee."

"Thanks," said Zooey, warming up to Lily's mothering tone.

"Virgil never comes to visit anymore, not since he and Alice were divorced years ago. Alice and I were very good friends when J.C. had his practice in Washington, but then we moved back to New York. And then, oh my, Virgil and Alice got divorced, and now we never see either of them. Alice is living in Texas, I hear."

"Virgil doesn't talk much about it."

"No, I don't suppose he would, poor man. I really don't know what got into Alice's head, leaving him that way. Have a piece of my sour cream chocolate layer cake. No, come on, you'll love it, everyone does! It's my specialty, and my, you can certainly afford it. How on earth do you keep so slim?"

"It's in my genes, I guess." Zooey took the plate with an enormous slab of cake and dug in. It was delicious.

"I've only been skinny one time in my life, and that's when J.C. was courting me. He likes skinny women and he's been begging me for thirty years to lose weight, but I just can't do it. Some people are just that way, don't you think so?"

Zooey jumped as a cry of pain from Virgil rang out from another room.

"Poor Virgil. But don't worry, J.C. will fix him up just fine. Imagine it—getting involved in a bar fight. Isn't that awful? Now tell me, what kind of work do you do in Washington?"

"I'm a private investigator. I have my own small agency."

"Oh my! Isn't that something? How times have changed. No girl I knew would ever have thought of having a career like that. I don't suppose you're married?"

"No." Zooey squirmed uncomfortably.

"I'm too nosy, that's what J.C. says, so never mind. Young girls today don't get married like they used to. You should meet my daughter Sue Ann. She's getting her master's degree in engineering at Florida Tech, and she tells me that she's just not interested in getting married now, she's that busy with her schoolwork. Pretty as she is, with all the dates a girl could want in high school, the Snow Queen at the Christmas Prom during her senior year, and all she cares about are computers and building design."

Zooey wondered what this well-meaning but naïve woman would think if she described what had really happened at the Alsatian Nightclub. And that she'd killed a man. "I tried being married but it didn't work. I'm divorced," she said.

"Oh, I'm sorry. I've been talking too much. J.C. always tells me that I talk too much. Here, have some more coffee, please. "

"Thanks."

Zooey looked up as J.C. and Virgil walked into the room and Virgil sat down beside her. He looked pale, and he had one hand wrapped in white gauze.

"A few deep gashes from breaking glass, but that's all," he said. "No big deal."

She patted him on the back. "Good. Have some sour cream chocolate cake? It's Lily's specialty."

Lily grinned. Zooey couldn't help liking her.

When they arrived back at their hotel lobby at midnight, Virgil suggested a nightcap in Zooey's room. She agreed, and he knocked on her door ten minutes later carrying a bottle of scotch and a cannister full of ice. They sat down at a tiny table shoved into the corner of her room.

"Have a shot?" he asked, pulling two plastic glasses from their cellophane wrappers.

"I don't think so. I really don't like scotch."

"You should have said so. I could have bought something else."

"No, maybe I'll order a cup of tea from room service." Zooey paused, and then said, "Listen, Virgil, what happens now?"

"I've called Francesca and she's arranged for us to catch the first flight to Washington tomorrow morning. You'll have to get up at about five-thirty, though. We should leave by six."

"That's it? What about Sakorski?"

"Do you want to visit the police and tell them what happened?"

"Hell, no."

"Well…"

"But Virgil, he's dead. I killed him. It's going to take me a while to deal with that."

"I don't blame you for that."

"Have you ever killed anyone?"

"No." He poured a healthy punch of scotch, dropped in a handful of ice chips and sipped. Then he pulled out his Camels.

"Let me have one of those." She lit one of his filterless cigarettes and choked. "Man, these are strong.

"Look, Virgil," she continued, "this detective thing was more of a game with Mark and me; I never thought anything like this would happen. I just don't know how to deal with killing Sakorski."

"Forget it for tonight, kid. If it hadn't been him, it would have been me or you or both of us lying dead on that nightclub floor. Think about how many people Vlad has wasted and remember what happened to Mark and Mary Gentry."

"Yeah." She sat smoking and then reached for Virgil's bottle and poured herself a small shot. "Do you think Vlad really had any evidence?"

"No. Francesca was right, as usual. He just wanted to waste me to make his reputation right with his employers."

Zooey nodded and they sat in silence for a while.

"Lily said you've been divorced too," she finally said.

"That's right."

"Your wife left you?"

"Yup."

"Why?"

"Why do you want to know?"

"Oh, I don't know. Just small talk, I guess. To take my mind off Vlad."

Virgil ruffled his hair and it stood out in tangled curls around his ears. Despite everything, she couldn't help liking his battered quality, like an old car you've driven so long you can't bring yourself to junk it.

"You know, I'm a talker," he said. "I like people and normally I don't mind telling a complete stranger the story of my life. Most reporters I know are like that; it's part of the job, I guess, to gain people's confidence, but there's something about your insistence on knowing everything that bothers me. It's like, you don't really want to know about me, you just want to know."

Zooey sat up straighter. "Really?" She crushed out her cigarette. "You're a fine one to complain about my questions. You're always badgering me with the same thing."

"It's not the same thing. Part of you always stands back; you don't get involved."

She shrugged. "Maybe you're right. Keep the world at a distance, I always say."

"Now why would you say that?"

"Well, it's a good quality for an investigator, wouldn't you say?"

"Not really, kid."

"Maybe it's just my manner that's too abrupt. Anyway, I shouldn't have asked about your divorce, it's none of my business and God knows I hate to talk about mine. But there is one subject that I have a genuine interest in, and that's Francesca. I like her, but there's some connection between the two of you that makes me uncomfortable because I don't understand it."

Virgil frowned, studying his plastic cup. "I loved her once, if that's what you mean."

"I thought that might be true." She paused, and then ventured another question, without really understanding why she wanted to ask it. "Do you still love her?"

"Yes, but there's no sex, and there hasn't been for years. We're like war buddies. We've been through a lot together and we stand by each other when no one else will and no matter what happens."

He took a sip of scotch and shook his head. "Francesca knows all the reporters, not just me. You might say it's in her best interest to find out about things and give out tips. Little things, mostly, but there's an occasional big story she gets wind of and lets somebody know. In return, she gets left alone. If something happens at the Orchid, the papers ignore it or say it happened somewhere else. Keeps the heat off her, you know, like little indiscretions by the mayor or a congressman or the police that don't wind up as front-page news.

"This is a long-time arrangement. I met her about twenty years ago, before she got hooked up with Karl Neibor. She was beautiful, a knockout, and let me tell you it wasn't hard to fall in love with her or just die a lingering death of terminal lust. I slept with her as often as she'd let me, which was often enough until Neibor entered the picture. Now that was a weird situation; I could never figure out what she saw in that bastard. Shit, what a bastard."

Virgil stood up and limped across to the bathroom. "Be back in a minute. I think I must have twisted my knee, it's so damn stiff." The bathroom door banged shut.

Zooey took another Camel from Virgil's pack on the table and lit up. There was a cheap oil painting on the wall over the bed of a ship sailing into a golden sunset. She stared at it for a moment and then looked around at the quilted bedspread, the standard issue nightstand with built-in radio, the all-purpose avocado-green carpeting and the aluminum stand that supported her suitcase.

Virgil returned, limping worse than ever. "Damn this knee." He sat gingerly on the edge of the bed.

"Hand me my drink, would you?"

She gave him the plastic cup. "So that's why Francesca gave you all that money to come to New York? Because you'd once been lovers?"

"Well, that's not the whole story, but let's save some of the good parts for later. I can't tell you everything in one night; it would spoil my aura of the man with a mysterious past."

"Right." Zooey smiled. "Have you got any other masked-lady lovers hanging around Washington?"

"Plenty. But what about you, Zooey? Why are you so mysterious about your past? You're the only detective I know who lives in an apartment under an assumed name, and your secretary is the only one who knows your cellphone number. So who pulls your tail?"

Zooey took another tiny sip of scotch. "I'm a little obsessive about my privacy, I guess. I'd never lived alone until I came to Washington. I went straight from my family home into marriage after high school, and after my divorce my ex-husband and mother kept threatening to kidnap me and take me back to North Carolina. So I had a legitimate reason for lying low. Besides, I don't like people hanging on me and asking prying questions about my past. The only reason I've been pushy with you is because I need to know anything that might affect our investigation. That's why I had to know about Francesca. I'm sorry if I've pushed too hard."

"Oh no," Virgil laughed, "you've forgotten that I'm a reporter, and I know how to dig too. Knowledge is power, Krause. Now some people might say you're a voyeur looking into other people's lives, but let's call that a cheap shot and say you're afraid of something. Or someone, maybe. Am I right?"

Zooey kept silent, turning her plastic cup in her hand.

"Maybe just yourself?" Virgil said.

"Drop dead."

Virgil looked up in surprise. Zooey clutched her cup so hard that it snapped, and she cursed as scotch leaked out onto her pants. Virgil took a couple of steps toward her and stumbled.

"Damn," he said. "Forget the glass and come here."

When she rose, Virgil leaned forward and kissed her. It was the last thing she'd expected, but the most surprising thing was that she found herself kissing him back. It was a long and gentle kiss, each touching only at the lips.

She pulled away and sat down on the edge of the bed, and Virgil sank down beside her. He slipped his arm around her waist and traced the outline of a scar he felt through her shirt across her side.

"What's this?" he said.

Zooey looked at his face and the heavy rough lines around his eyes and flushed cheeks, wondering if she'd made a mistake. She'd already made so many. She lifted her blouse and showed him the scar.

"It looks terrible, doesn't it?" she said.

Virgil shook his head. "I've seen worse, believe me. What happened?"

"Appendicitis."

"I've never seen an appendicitis scar that big."

Zooey leaned away from him slightly. "My father was a strict German Catholic," she said. "He believed that pain was in the mind, something you could choose not to feel. When I was six I got a bad side ache and was afraid to tell him about it. I didn't say anything until I couldn't stand it anymore, and when I finally told him he said a stomachache shouldn't bother me, that God was just testing me and I must be brave. It was part of his personal religion to heal me with prayer. When my appendix ruptured three hours later, I went into a coma and they had to rush me to the hospital in an ambulance.

"If the hospital hadn't been close by, I'm sure I would've died. It was a week before my fever came down and they knew I'd pull through. Kids are amazingly resilient; they said an infection like that would certainly have killed an adult. The doctors had to scrape inside my entire abdomen to clean the infection out, and that's why the scar."

"Your dad sounds like a great guy."

She smiled a little. "Well, he had his beliefs. He wasn't really a monster. In his own way, he loved us and wanted us to be happy, but his extreme beliefs also set him apart. His religion twisted his feelings and exaggerated his shortcomings into something dangerous. If he'd been less of a fanatic, it might have been all right. We could have shared his religion; it might even have drawn the family closer.

"When I was ten, I was watching television with some friends in our living room on a Saturday afternoon. Dad was outside mowing the lawn, when the noise of the lawnmower suddenly stopped and he came staggering into the room. We were watching a monster movie, and he came staggering in like he was Frankenstein or something, sort of lurching around with his face all purple. I'd never seen him do anything like that before, and it freaked me out a little, but my friends were giggling. They thought he was kidding about the movie until he finally collapsed. He died on the way to the hospital. The doctors said his heart burst, or something like that. I was only ten, so they didn't tell me much.

"But I never really felt bad about it, Virgil. It scared me, and I cried at the funeral, but it almost seemed like somebody else's father had died. I spent years feeling horrible because I never missed him."

They sat silent for a while, Zooey wondering what it was about Virgil that made her confide in him that way. Maybe the deaths of Mary Gentry, Mark and then Vlad Sakorski had made her think about her father's death. In any case, it was a story she hadn't told anyone in years.

"What time is it?" she asked.

Virgil glanced at his watch. "One-thirty."

"Hey, we better get some sleep."

"Yeah. You take the bed," said Virgil. "I'll take the floor. I'm not leaving you alone tonight."

Zooey rose and kissed his forehead. "I'll take you up on that offer."

She fell asleep in less than a minute while Virgil, still sipping scotch, lay awake on the floor.

19

Zooey paced around her apartment nude on the Sunday after she'd arrived back from New York with Virgil. She'd just awakened to a grey and sultry early afternoon, the sort of weather that hardly deserves clothes. All the blinds were pulled closed and the rooms were dark, her fans slowly whirring. She briefly considered turning on her air-conditioner, a cheap unit she'd bought on sale during the last hot summer, but resisted the temptation since it made a racket like a cage full of rats playing with jackhammers.

Francesca and Rashid had met them at the airport the day before, Saturday morning, all cheer and concern. They'd wanted to take both Zooey and Virgil to the Orchid for safekeeping, but Zooey insisted on returning to her apartment. At least she'd found out the reason why Virgil never seemed to have a place to stay; Francesca had insisted that he give up the lease on his apartment and put most of his belongings in storage when Mary Gentry died. Francesca had stored the rest of his stuff somewhere in the Orchid and given him a room.

By the time she'd showered and dressed, it was already two o'clock in the afternoon. After chasing away the numbness of waking up with coffee and two frozen waffles, she became aware of how much her whole body ached. She wandered through the apartment and turned all the fans on their highest setting, creating a hot breeze that rattled the papers on her desk. She ambled to the balcony and watched some kids in the alley throwing rocks at pigeons, the flock fluttering away like a cloud of confetti. Picking up a half-read detective novel from her balcony chair, she stepped back into the living room and lay down on the couch intending to lose herself in someone else's danger for a few hours. But after skimming a few pages without comprehension, she realized that she was too restless to concentrate and strolled back to the balcony. Normally, she would have headed to Mark's Bar. Now, she felt like walking in circles.

It was depressing how little she knew about Mary Gentry. What had she really looked like? Where had she lived? Even after three violent deaths, she lacked any hard evidence to support Mary's original suspicions about Blackstone and had little idea about how to get it.

She felt sure that it was time to start investigating Mary's death from the beginning again. She hadn't seen Mary's apartment. She'd also never visited the police lab to inspect the items found in Mary's car: a lunch and a radiation detector, according to Virgil. A visit to the nuclear plant was risky, but according to Jason, Joe Quigley had called almost continually during her absence. An idea began to form in her head: Joe was the one who'd originally hired her, and he certainly had a strong interest in the case, as well as a lot of information about the plant. If she could use him to get some inside information about the Blackstone Plant... well, it was a start. At least following up on it made her feel like a detective again.

On Monday morning at the office, Jason greeted her with a now-familiar astonishment. His mouth dropped open.

"Zooey! You look terrible!"

"Don't be silly, Jay. These stitches were expensive. I spent all weekend at a punk beauty salon to get this look."

"They did a good job," Jason mumbled as he straightened some papers on her desk.

Looking down and then back up at her, he said, "Look, I'm really sorry about Mark. I know how much he meant to you."

Zooey sighed. "I'm sorry too."

"So what happened in New York?"

"Oh, I had a great time. Nightclubs, music, adventure. All that stuff you read about in the society column."

"Yeah?"

"Sure, it was great. Now what's new around here? Did anyone want to question you about the explosion at Mark's Bar?"

"Nothing about the explosion. As to business, some lady lost a diamond ring. She thinks her caterer stole it during a party, but I have a feeling you'll find it mislaid in a drawer. But that's it, except for junk mail. I guess all your fans are on vacation."

"Good." She glanced down at her desk. It was immaculate, as usual. Jason had not only dusted and arranged her papers, but he'd set a bouquet of asters in a brown pottery vase next to the canary-yellow trim line phone he'd picked out the month before.

"Shall I pour you some coffee? I just made a fresh pot."

"That sounds terrific. Put some milk and sugar in it, because I didn't have time to eat breakfast."

This was Jason's cue. "No breakfast? Sit right down and I'll bring you something to eat."

Jason disappeared into his illegal apartment while Zooey read junky advertisements. A few minutes later, he reappeared with breakfast set on a bamboo tray covered with a white linen napkin: fruit, yogurt and a blueberry muffin.

"Thanks, Jay," Zooey said with a wry smile. "My own mother never treated me so well."

"Did you pay your mother's salary?" He smiled and disappeared.

Half an hour later, her desk sprinkled with muffin crumbs, she called him back. "Why don't you sit down for a few minutes, Jay? I have a few things to talk to you about."

He sank into the chair across from her desk. "Shoot."

"First, tell the woman with the diamond ring to take her business to my competitors. From now on I'm concentrating solely on Mary Gentry, although if I don't learn something soon, you'll read about my adventures in the obituaries. If they're interested.

"If I have any savings left, which I probably don't, you can have it all. There's a will in the safe. Make sure I'm cremated."

"Come on, Zooey, what's all this morbidity supposed to mean?"

"It means that this case with Mary Gentry is dangerous, and I want you to keep a close watch on yourself and on the office. You still have that gun?"

"Yeah."

"Keep it loaded and handy. I'm not kidding about this, Jason, and I can't afford to send you away again since Mark's gone. There are some very dangerous characters following Virgil Fitts and I'm sure they know something about me, because they bombed Mark's Bar. So please watch out."

"I will. Don't worry, Zooey, because you know I grew up in a tough neighborhood and I know how to handle myself with a gun."

She nodded. "I'm counting on that. Now let me explain more about this case."

It took a while to explain about Sakorski, so she didn't have time to call the Blackstone Plant until eleven o'clock. After the usual delay, she reached Joe.

"Quigley here."

"Hello, Joe, it's Zooey Krause."

"Zooey!" Joe shouted.

"Look, Joe, not so loud."

"You're all right!" he shouted again.

"No, Joe, this is a voice from beyond the grave," Zooey chuckled. Then, for an instant, she thought Joe believed her.

"Jesus, I've called so many times and your secretary wouldn't tell me a thing. Wouldn't give me your number, wouldn't tell me where you were…"

"Those were my instructions to him and he did a good job. I'm sorry if I worried you."

"Well, after what happened to Mary… I guess I overreacted. Anyway, I'm glad you called. That was an awful thing at Mark's Bar."

"Yes, it was."

"It doesn't have anything to do with…"

"Let's not discuss this over the phone," Zooey interrupted. "I'd like to talk to you, though."

"Sure. How about dinner at my place tonight? I'll pick up a couple of steaks on my way home from work."

"That sounds nice, but I'm busy tonight. How about Tuesday evening?"

"At seven?"

Zooey got directions to his home, hung up, and then sat absently chewing a fingernail until Virgil called.

"How's life, kid?" His voice sounded bright.

"About what you'd expect. How's your hand?"

"It's healing. It's my knee that's giving me hell. Well, what's on the schedule today?"

"I've got a plan for us, if you're willing."

20

When Zooey approached the door to the police headquarters late Monday afternoon, she wore a tight leopard-skin dress, knee-length black leather boots with spiked heels and rhinestone sunglasses. She'd also teased her hair up and carried a green snakeskin bag. Virgil, limping as he held her arm, wore a colorful Hawaiian print shirt and red checked pants. Sunglasses and an enormous straw hat shaded his face.

"This is a stupid idea, Krause," he said, his voice slightly muffled by the hat. "I don't know how I let you talk me into it."

"Come on, Virgil. Nobody's going to recognize you." She turned to look at him and laughed.

"Funny, is it? What a harebrained scheme." Virgil made a face at her.

"Nothing's going to happen."

"Oh no? If somebody recognizes who I am, it'll be years before they get through with us. I'll be the laughingstock of the whole police force. Nobody will ever take me seriously again."

"Enough already." Zooey pulled open the door.

Ten minutes later, they sat across the desk from Lieutenant Jim Buckley, the man who'd overseen the Gentry case. When he'd walked into the small office where Zooey and Virgil waited, he was obviously shocked by Zooey's bruises and stitches, but said nothing about it. Instead, he offered his hand with false enthusiasm and introduced himself.

"Hello, Lieutenant," said Zooey, extending her hand limply. "My name is Mrs. Wilson and I am Mary Gentry's sister. This is my husband, Duane Wilson."

Virgil, trying to keep his face hidden under the hat, mumbled a greeting and pretended not to see the lieutenant's hand.

Zooey was unimpressed. The lieutenant was a short young man with a blond blow-combed haircut and a trim mustache. He looked like a beer drinker, with a paunch the size of a volleyball straining the bottom buttons of his uniform shirt. But the thing she disliked most about him were his eyes, eyes that crinkled into slits when he smiled. Unsympathetic as only a policeman's can be, she thought.

"We hadn't heard that Mary Gentry had any relatives," he said.

"Nobody did, I guess. You'll have to excuse our appearance but we just returned from a long stay in Mexico. We volunteered our help as Christian missionaries in poor villages on the Yucatan Peninsula, and as you can see, they were less than grateful. Not that we mind; we look for our reward in heaven. But I'm afraid that we've been out of touch with Mary, out of touch with all our friends for that matter, for two years."

"What brings you to Washington now?"

"Officer, we just returned to California yesterday, when we heard about poor Mary's accident. So, of course, we flew out right away."

The lieutenant smiled and his eyes disappeared. "What can I do for you?"

"Oh my," said Zooey with a trembling voice. She took a green handkerchief from her snakeskin purse and blew her nose loudly. "Poor Mary. It was such a blow, Lieutenant."

Virgil gave a hidden poke to her ribs.

"Of course, with all the scandal in the newspapers, we wanted to know, I mean to find out, what really happened, Lieutenant."

Lieutenant Buckley leaned way back in his chair and pressed the tips of his fingers together under his chin, looking solemn. "It's too bad about the papers, Mrs. Wilson. I'm afraid they only confused the truth in this instance. Your sister simply lost control of her car and slid off the road. She was driving much too fast, I'm sure, but other than that, there's no evidence to indicate anything out of the ordinary. She died instantly, according to our medical examiner, so you can rest assured that she didn't suffer."

Zooey nodded solemnly. "But we heard she was bringing something to a newspaperman. And you found nothing?"

The lieutenant shook his head and smiled. Zooey wanted to nail both ends of that smile to the corners of his eyes. "Mere rumors, Mrs. Wilson, fabricated by a drunk reporter whose specialty is empty gossip. Unfortunately, he disappeared before we could question him. His colleagues report that he's off on another drinking binge. It's a shame when the media is so irresponsible. Fake news is the order of the day. The police will question this reporter whenever he drags himself off the floor of whatever bar he's disappeared into, but I guarantee that his stories will be nothing but a blast of hot air."

Virgil choked and Zooey patted his back.

"Allergies," she said. "He's very sensitive."

"Can I get you a drink of water?" asked the lieutenant.

Virgil shook his head. "No, thanks, I'm all right."

"I can't tell you how this sets my mind at rest," said Zooey. "It was such a shock to think poor Mary might have committed suicide."

Lieutenant Buckley smiled graciously. "I understand, Mrs. Wilson."

Zooey lifted her right hand to her lips, "There was only one thing, Lieutenant. I mean, simply so we can know certainly about this matter. Was anything at all found in the car? I'm sorry if I'm being a bother, but any mementos?"

Lieutenant Buckley frowned and looked at his watch. "Only a bag lunch, a Geiger counter and some clothes were in the trunk."

"Oh, I see," said Zooey.

"We did a thorough analysis of those effects and found nothing at all out of the ordinary."

"I'm glad to know that you personally conducted the investigation to clear this matter up."

"The analysis of her effects and postmortem were carried out by our lab." The lieutenant's face brightened as he glanced again at his watch. This was what Zooey had hoped for.

"I could take you to the lab if you like, Mrs. Wilson, and you could speak to the man in charge."

Zooey smiled. "Would you? Oh, that would be so nice. Just to see such a place."

Lieutenant Buckley conducted them to the lab, introduced them to a Dr. Kepler and quickly excused himself.

The lab was a white, antiseptic-smelling place, and the doctor looked like he'd been born there. He was a soft, stout old man with a scrubbed-pink face and a completely bald head. At the long tables behind him, assistants poured chemicals into test tubes amid a crowd of equipment and examination slabs.

"Ah, yes," the doctor said, "I remember the Gentry exam. The result of the analysis was most routine."

The frequency with which people used the word "routine" galled Zooey. If it had been as routine for them as it had been for her, half of them would be dead.

"What were her effects?"

Glancing at a report, he said, "There was an ordinary radiation detector, but smashed very badly in the accident, I'm afraid. And a lunch, let me see... an alfalfa sprout sandwich with mayonnaise on whole wheat bread. One peeled carrot and a bag of peanut M&Ms." He beamed at them. "They all checked out as normal."

"M&Ms, her favorite candy," sighed Zooey.

"And, of course, her clothes, which she was wearing, including a smock, blouse and one pair of trousers. White. And shoes. We examined these but found nothing out of the ordinary. Nor did the postmortem turn up anything unusual. The cause of death was determined to be trauma from the crash; specifically, a broken neck."

Very routine, thought Zooey. "Do you know if she was pregnant? She wrote to say she thought she was."

"Yes, I'm sad to say she was, but not nearly far enough along for the fetus to survive the death of the mother. I'd let you speak directly to the technician who performed the autopsy and examined her clothes, but she's out sick with the flu. However, you may claim the clothes if you wish."

"Yes, doctor, it surely would be nice to have her effects."

"Please be seated. It will take a few minutes to locate the proper forms, and her clothes are locked in our evidence locker."

"What about her lunch and the radiation detector?"

"Of course, we disposed of the lunch after we analyzed the food. But you may claim the detector. Please be seated."

Zooey sat down in a chair next to the door as he trudged off toward the back of the lab. Virgil was lurking around the room, keeping a low profile, and Zooey motioned him over.

"Hello, sweetheart," he said with a smirk. "If you'll just remove your clothes, we'll run the necessary tests."

Zooey crossed her arms over her chest. "I don't take off this dress for just anyone, doctor."

"Very funny." He leaned over to whisper in her ear. "I hope you're satisfied now."

Zooey shrugged. "There's got to be something, Virgil. Otherwise, why all the trouble coming after us?"

"If there's anything suspicious about the things in Mary's car, they're long gone by now."

"Maybe. But it seemed worth a chance."

After ten minutes, the doctor returned, flustered. "Hmm, well, you see," he waved his hands weakly, "the clothes have disappeared from our evidence locker. I'm sure there's a good explanation, but the woman in charge is out with the flu, as I mentioned. They are probably stored somewhere else." He checked his watch. "It's almost quitting time. Can we call you tomorrow?"

"We're only in town for two days, doctor, and we haven't even reserved a hotel room yet. You don't suppose anyone took them?"

The doctor looked dismayed. "Now, Mrs. Wilson, why would anyone do that?"

"I don't know. Poor Mary. First, she's dead, and now her clothes have disappeared. The lieutenant assured us there was nothing wrong."

"The lieutenant was right. Now, you call us first thing tomorrow and we'll have the clothes for you, I promise. I assure you, this is just a bureaucratic matter that can be quickly rectified by a call to the sick woman. Please, don't you worry."

"Oh, I won't, doctor, and I'm sorry for causing such a fuss. I can see this case is in capable hands. Come on, Duane, let's leave this poor man to do his work. We'll call you tomorrow, Doctor. Thanks so much for all your valuable time."

"Don't mention it, please. This is my job." Doctor Kepler smiled reassuringly.

Zooey left the lab, Virgil trailing behind with his head lowered. As Zooey drove from the police headquarters to her apartment, Virgil watched the street.

"I can't understand why nobody's tailing us," he said. "Why is the heat off, all of a sudden?"

"You're complaining? Maybe if I start honking the horn like crazy we'll attract some attention."

"At least we'd know where our enemies are. They've got to be tailing us somehow. It makes me nervous."

"I wonder why Mary's clothes were missing from the lab."

"Odd, isn't it?"

Zooey parked her car in the alley behind her apartment building, and they climbed the back stairs.

"So I finally get to view the inner sanctum?" Virgil asked.

"I hope you appreciate it," she replied.

He walked through the front door and down the short hall to her tiny kitchen.

She poured herself a glass of water in the kitchen, and then followed Virgil into the living room. She found him examining her bookshelves. It made her uncomfortable, as though he was reading her private papers.

"No poetry?" he said.

"What do you mean?"

"Sensitive young ladies like yourself always read poetry, don't they? I know I do."

"You? Shut up."

"I'm just making it up to impress you," he said, picking up a volume of *The Complete Sherlock Holmes*. "I don't suppose the name 'James Merrill' means anything to you?"

"Listen, I stopped my formal education at high school and I'm not proud of it, so don't rub it in."

"Okay. Where's your bathroom? I want to wash up and get out of these ridiculous clothes."

"Down the hall."

He limped away, and soon splashing sounds came from the bathroom while Zooey poured them each a brandy. A few minutes later, Virgil appeared again in a white shirt and a pair of jeans, clothes he'd brought in a paper bag. They'd done the costuming at her office.

Zooey still wore her leopard-skin dress. "Hey, let me take you out for a drink in that outfit," Virgil said. "You're a hot number looking like that."

"Forget it, Virg. Help yourself to this brandy while I get changed."

"Happily." He lifted the snifter. "Classy broad, aren't you?"

"Yeah, and don't you forget it."

"I have an excellent memory."

She changed into a pair of jeans and blouse, returned and grabbed her brandy, and then found Virgil standing out on her balcony. It was the beginning of a long summer sunset, the sky a pale raspberry with tints of lemon, turning fiery red at the edges.

Three nights ago, I killed a man, Zooey thought, though her trip to New York already seemed far away.

"Now what's our next move, master detective?" Virgil said. "And I'm not putting on any more disguises."

Zooey was pleasantly surprised that Virgil was asking her advice. "Not even the back end of a horse costume?"

"No."

"Tomorrow morning, I think we should visit Mary's apartment. Joe gave me the address when I first met him. I'm sure any damning evidence is long gone, but I think we should take a look anyway."

"And I suppose I'll have to beg for a room at the Orchid tonight."

"I'm sure you don't have to beg. But no, you can stay here; we'll protect each other. But you sleep on the couch, right?" She sipped her brandy and looked at him.

"Of course. Listen, kid, it's been a long time since I've been involved with a woman for more than a scratch and a tickle. It's ridiculous to think of it now."

He raised his glass. "To the investigation." He drank. "And to honorable old drunks like me."

21

Late Tuesday morning, Zooey sat parked outside Mary Gentry's apartment with Virgil, scouting the area in an old Buick Francesca had lent them on the chance Zooey's Mustang might be recognized. Mary had lived in a small, box-shaped apartment house constructed of blonde brick on a quiet street shaded by oak trees. Every building on the block had a similar design and a similarly undistinguished look; all the two-story homes were about thirty years old.

Zooey drummed her fingers on the steering wheel. She was beginning to think that having Virgil spend the night at her apartment hadn't been such a shrewd step. She wasn't accustomed to constant companionship, though Virgil slipped into it easily. He'd gotten up early to plug in the coffee pot and then made French toast for breakfast while she took a shower and dressed. His bantering jokes at the kitchen table had put her on edge.

Virgil reached across the front seat of the car and pinched her arm. "Hey, what're you thinking about?"

She clenched her teeth. "Let's just keep our eye on Mary's place, okay?"

Virgil shook his head. "What's the matter with you?"

"It's nothing," she snapped. "I think we can go up to Mary's apartment now. We've been waiting an hour and I haven't seen anything suspicious."

Virgil dug at her again. "Come on, Zooey, talk to me."

She sank forward against the steering wheel, pushing her face into her arms, and in the process accidentally honked the car horn. She moaned. "Oh, crap! Virgil, we're getting on each other's nerves again. Just let it be."

"I suppose you think I'm too damn old to be fooling around like this."

"Argh!" Zooey grabbed his collar and played at strangling him. "Are you *trying* to drive me crazy? Just don't push at me so hard. I'm not used to it." She let go of him and sat back, sulking. "And let me tell you that you're not too old. In fact, you're more like a twelve-year-old."

Virgil laughed. "And you're more like one hundred and fifty. Come on, where's your sense of humor this morning? Someday you'll be dead with nobody to bother you."

"Someday could be today," she said, and then reached across and opened his door, shoving him out. "Let's get going."

She slid out from behind the steering wheel and they walked down the sidewalk to Mary's apartment, situated thirty feet back from the street. Before entering the building, they pulled on gloves.

In the tiny entryway, Mary's name was still taped underneath the buzzer for apartment 2B; there were four apartments on each floor. The steel security door leading to the inside hallway was unlocked, so they pushed through and climbed the red flowered carpet going up the stairs to the second floor. The carpet, like both the railing and the shiny beige wallpaper, was worn.

Mary's apartment door stood at the end of the hall to their left, facing the alley. As Virgil examined the lock on the door, Zooey said softly, "Move aside. I'll do that."

"I can do it."

Zooey whispered more loudly, "Move aside, Virgil. I've had more practice with this kind of thing."

Virgil stepped aside and watched for unwanted observers while Zooey jimmied the lock. In a few seconds, they were in.

It was a standard apartment layout, with a living room on the right, a kitchen on the left and a hallway to the left of the kitchen leading to a bathroom and the bedroom.

She went into the kitchen while Virgil walked to the living room. On the refrigerator, the picture of a hippopotamus was taped with a slogan: "Don't you dare." Opening the door, she inhaled the stench of moldy cottage cheese, bean sprouts, a few eggs and soured milk. She quickly shut it again. The kitchen itself was neat and clean, the stove and countertops lined with labeled spice canisters. A little plaque above the sink pictured a kitten hanging from a string, with the words: "Hang in there, Baby."

Zooey opened a cupboard door and found dishes, chipped and of different patterns, obviously a garage sale collection. Next to these were stacked dark brown earthenware plates with orange flowers, a matched pattern Mary must have used for parties. The drawers contained nothing of interest, just string, rubber bands, mismatched silverware and teabags.

"Zooey, come here," called Virgil from the living room. She found him stooped over the remains of a shelf built of white bricks and painted white boards. It was toppled over, books and stereo equipment spilled on the floor.

"And look at that," Virgil said, pointing behind the wicker couch. The wall was gashed; below it, on the floor, lay the shattered remains of a porcelain statue.

Zooey walked behind the couch and picked up a piece of the statue from the carpet. She held the head of a little girl with a large blue bonnet on her head. Pieces of the girl's pink flowered dress lay on the floor.

"They call this Holly Hobbie, don't they?" asked Zooey.

Virgil nodded. "My wife loved this stuff. Why?"

Zooey noticed small pink and blue flowers on another fragment of the statue. She picked it up. It was the doll's hand holding the flowers. She stooped again and looked through the record albums scattered on the floor. Old folk and pop songs, mostly lightweight and sentimental. Fleetwood Mac. Carole King. Gordon Lightfoot. Nothing rap or heavy metal. Zooey thought Mary would have fit in with an earlier generation.

"The drawers are open. It seems like someone was looking for something," said Virgil. "Not too surprising."

Zooey frowned. "You're right, but it looks more like wreckage than a search. Things are just thrown around and broken."

"Maybe a struggle?"

She scanned the room, thinking. Green cushions printed with a tree-leaf design padded the wicker furniture; the floor was gold carpeting. "Maybe, but why isn't the furniture disturbed? Would you look through the drawers in her desk? I'll check down the hall."

She walked down the hallway and peered into the bathroom: a white shower curtain and purple towels; a dead fern in a wicker basket on top of the toilet; one pink toothbrush on the sink. Very clean and orderly, even though everything was now coated with a thin layer of dust. In a drawer below the sink, she found the wand from a pregnancy test. The test read positive. Zooey remembered that Joe had said Mary was pregnant.

In the bedroom, things were again thrown about. The bed was a large mattress on a low base covered with a flowery South Asian spread. There were Union leaflets and Xeroxed articles about nuclear power on a bedside table, the only evidence so far of Mary's concern with politics. The pillows were thrown off the bed and the lamp from the bedside table lay broken on the floor.

Zooey shuddered and sat down. Until now, Mary Gentry had been little more than a name.

Item: woman.

Item: murdered.

Now, Zooey had the sense of the person, someone like herself but also worlds away. Zooey wouldn't be caught dead owning a statuette of Holly Hobbie or the box of lilac-scented writing paper sitting on a shelf of the nightstand. Gordon Lightfoot made her feel like she'd eaten too many chocolate bars. The misty framed photo of a long-haired woman playing the cello in a field of daisies, hanging askew on the wall, probably came from a Hallmark Card shop.

Mary was not some screaming anarchist; in fact, she'd probably been fresh and pleasing. Her photograph stared up from a cracked china frame on the floor at Zooey's feet. Zooey recognized Mary's face from the newspaper articles she'd read and picked up the frame to take a closer look. Mary was sitting at somebody's kitchen table, wearing a deep blue velour sweater; her face looked tired and thoughtful, her thick and slightly tousled dark hair falling loose around her shoulders. She was holding a book and had a coffee cup in the other hand. A coffee pot and an ashtray sat on the table in front of her.

She placed the photograph on the nightstand where she supposed it belonged, and absently gazed at the bed.

Mary was here: on the bed, the walls, even hanging on the door of the refrigerator, telling Zooey about who she'd been. It was a faint voice, Mary's voice, as it recited the fading list of a life. No doubt these belongings would soon be moved out and someone else's effects moved in, and the voice would grow fainter still. But to Zooey, at that moment, Mary's voice was clear and sad, and she knew that the voice would recite its list in her mind for a long time. "I like bean sprouts, 'nice' music, little girls in bonnets, beds low to the floor..."

And then there was the nuclear power plant. It was hard to fit a story about violence and organized crime into the scene around her, except that Mary's youthful ornaments had been tossed and broken.

Zooey found it difficult to believe that Mary had known who or what she was up against when she'd first contacted

Virgil Fitts. Maybe she'd found out the truth on that last day before she'd left the Blackstone Plant. Or maybe it was when she caught sight of a car in her rear-view mirror while she raced down County Road 5 to keep an appointment with a newspaper reporter from the *Spirit*.

Virgil walked in and sat down beside her on the bed. He picked up a torn book from the floor. "*The Joy of Sex*," he read aloud, and glanced at her. Zooey took the book from his hands with curiosity. She found its torn pages on the floor.

Zooey held the sections up, looking at Virgil.

So, she thought, Mary liked sex. For some reason it made her smile. "It wasn't a struggle, Virgil. Why would they choose this particular book to tear up?"

"A fight between lovers?"

"And the Holly Hobbie doll? No, it doesn't fit. I think Mary tore these things up herself…"

"And then she threw over the bookshelf and smashed her own stereo? That doesn't seem likely to me. She didn't have enough money to go trashing her own belongings like that."

Zooey shrugged. "I know there isn't much to go on. But I'm getting a feeling about who she was… Look at this stack of magazines. *People*—she must have had a subscription. Political radicals don't subscribe to *People Magazine*."

Virgil lit a cigarette and stared at the floor. "I never said she was a radical."

"Well, who was she then? Why did she come to you?"

"Something scared her."

Zooey picked up the photograph of Mary again and studied her face. "She must have felt betrayed. Joe wouldn't believe her, you didn't believe her, none of her friends believed her, and look what she tore up or smashed. A sex book. Her Holly Hobbie statue. She threw her music albums all over the floor."

Virgil reached for the photograph and looked at it for a minute, then threw it down again amid the torn-up sex book. "Yeah, maybe." He rubbed his face. "But it all sounds too much like *True Confessions* to me."

He raised his head, surveying the room. "The plain truth is, we're shooting in the dark. Take it from my experience, Zooey, you can't get so desperate for the facts that you start inventing them."

"If you've got any better ideas, I haven't heard them. And why are you so skeptical about the idea that Mary ripped up this apartment herself? Maybe it makes you feel guilty because you were one of the people who let her down."

Zooey paused and frowned. "And those clothes we picked up this morning from the lab. We don't know if they really belonged to her. If the lab lost or misplaced them, they wouldn't want to admit it." She stood up and pulled Virgil to his feet, then rearranged the sheets on the bed. They wandered slowly through the apartment again, Zooey photographing everything with her cellphone. Zooey felt sure they were on to something, and she wanted to be able to see the place again in pictures.

When she'd finished, Virgil opened the front door quietly. Zooey carefully closed it behind them. On the first floor, Zooey opened the steel fire door to the small lobby.

The gun she faced was small and efficient, with metal like royal blue velvet. But its owner was a fleshy skyscraper of a man wearing a lightweight sport coat over a red knit sport shirt. He stood well over six feet tall and probably outweighed Zooey by at least a hundred and fifty pounds.

"Back in," he ordered, pushing Zooey's shoulder with the snout of his gun. She jerked backward, bumping into Virgil.

"You too, Fitts. Back up the stairs."

"Karl Neibor," Virgil breathed.

"Shut up and go back upstairs," Neibor said. "Slowly, with your hands above your heads. No sudden moves."

Zooey climbed the stairs with Neibor's gun an inch behind her, feeling the skin on the back of her neck twitch. Her knees were weak and she forced herself to take slow, steady breaths to cover her panic.

In front of Mary's apartment door, Neibor said, "Open it."

Virgil immediately stepped forward to open the door and the three of them entered the apartment. Neibor made them stand with their hands in the air while he searched their clothes; he found both their guns and their cellphones and dumped them into a briefcase.

"What do you want?" Zooey practically shouted it in her attempt to sound tough, but the effect was of fright.

"Who is this?" Neibor asked Virgil.

"This is my girlfriend, Diane."

"The same girlfriend who was with you in New York? She must be the broad who capped Sakorski."

"Don't be ridiculous—look at her. She's just a kid. I gave her that gun for self-protection." Virgil looked calm, which helped Zooey to clear her thoughts.

"What I want to know, Fitts, is why you went to New York."

"You didn't think I'd take the bait?"

"I don't know what you're talking about."

"You don't know that Sakorski called from New York and offered to sell me the documents he found in Mary Gentry's car? Listen, can't I sit down? I hurt my knee."

"Sit over there on the couch. You too," he said to Zooey. "Sit beside him." He waved his gun at Zooey, and she sank down at Virgil's side.

"I knew you were following me," Virgil said, "but I couldn't figure out why until Vlad called about the documents. We all know that there was no evidence to support Mary's allegations about her Union and your involvement. In fact, I wrote a little story for the *Spirit* that said she might have been unstable and committed suicide. You must have read it."

"Cut the shit and tell me about Vlad in New York."

Zooey, feeling a little stronger, took a closer look at Neibor. Was this the man who'd set up the bombing at Mark's Bar? The man who'd destroyed Francesca's face? Neibor's face didn't mark him out as a killer; in fact, he had a perfectly ordinary look, the kind of man you'd pass on the street and then be unable to describe. Mid-fifties, ordinary features. A soft face, cheeks tugging downward into jowls; a small mouth and a thick, lumpy nose. Pale, inexpressive eyes. His hair was yellow-grey and thin at the top.

But he was tall, well over six feet, with long arms, broad shoulders and a heavy chest. He could have been an aging football player or a former furniture mover, maybe now pursuing a second career as a life insurance salesman. Somebody's husband or father. Francesca's lover.

"I told you," Virgil said, "Sakorski called me from New York after I winged him in the car chasing us that day."

"Shooting Vlad was a stupid move."

"He was shooting at me! What was I supposed to do, stop the car and let him finish the job?"

Zooey searched for an opening. If Neibor believed that she was only Virgil's girlfriend, he might not watch her closely. As far as she could tell, it was their only hope.

Neibor looked skeptical. "He said you opened up on him when you couldn't lose the tail."

"Couldn't lose the tail?" Virgil's voice was indignant. "Jesus Christ! Sakorski tried to gun me down on my way to a bar that night! Anyway, you know Francesca's driver Rashid—he can always lose a tail. So why did Sakorski start firing at our car, except on orders from you? Or maybe you don't have much control over your goons anymore."

"Shut up and tell me what Vlad said when he called from New York." Neibor pulled a plaid handkerchief out of his pocket to wipe his face. The man was dripping sweat.

"He said that he'd found evidence in Mary's car after he ran it off the road. Your work, right? A little job for the

Blackstone Plant executives, to get Mary out of their hair? He said that if I flew to New York he'd sell me the evidence she'd been carrying, some kind of documents, for $20,000. Naturally I was glad to oblige, except that when my girlfriend and I waited in a nightclub to keep our appointment with him, he didn't have any evidence. At least, not with him. It was a set-up and he intended to finish his contract to kill me."

Neibor's face stayed expressionless as he stood staring at Virgil's face, his gun still pointed at Virgil's chest. Zooey began to realize that something about this scene was very wrong. Not only did Neibor look genuinely surprised by Virgil's information about Sakorski, but he didn't seem to know who Zooey was.

"Don't tell me this is new information to you? Weren't you the one who put him up to it?" Virgil said.

Neibor stared at Virgil. "Okay, so you killed Vlad. Where are the documents?"

"I told you, man, if they exist, Vlad didn't bring them. But I don't think he had anything."

"Somebody set you up, but not me," Neibor said. "So maybe you can tell me what you're doing now, breaking into this apartment."

"Looking around, what do you think? We didn't find anything. You searched us, remember?"

Neibor pointed the gun at each of them in turn, thinking.

"I'll tell you what I think, and it's something I never suspected," Virgil said. "We've both been duped by Sakorski, and we'd both better find out now who really hired him to kill me."

"I've got only one thing to say, Fitts. There's no reason to leave you and your friend here alive unless you give me those Union documents."

"I told you, we don't have them!"

Zooey sat, quietly trying to figure out whether, if she jumped forward suddenly and grabbed at Neibor's legs, she could topple him over without getting shot. It was a weak plan, considering Neibor's size, but she was about to give it a try.

There was a soft click behind Neibor, and Rashid burst through the door, gun in hand. The minute she saw Rashid's face, Zooey knew it was time to act. As Neibor turned his head to the door, she threw herself at his knees, he went down on his back and Rashid kicked Neibor's gun from his hand. Virgil jumped from the couch and grabbed it off the floor.

"Jesus, that was close," he said. "Rashid, you saved our lives."

Rashid pressed his Magnum against Neibor's left ear. "Hold still, asshole," he said. "I don't need no excuse to cap your ass."

Virgil put his hands in Neibor's clothes and searched, unsuccessfully, for another weapon while Zooey picked herself up from the floor.

"Rashid, thanks," was all she could manage to say.

He grinned back at her.

"Get his briefcase," Virgil said to Zooey. "Our guns and phones are in there. Rashid, what are we going to do with him?"

"You know you're making a mistake, Fitts," Neibor said. "I won't forget this."

"Neither will we. Rashid, where should we take him?"

"The car's outside," Rashid said.

He got Neibor to his feet and pushed him forward. They descended the stairs again with Neibor leading the way this time and Zooey in the rear, her mind racing as the implications of Neibor's words began to settle in. If Neibor really didn't know who she was, then who had planted the bomb in Mark's Bar?

22

Rashid drove Francesca's car through a Washington suburb Zooey had never seen, and it was there that they released Karl Neibor. A long conversation had passed between Virgil and Neibor by then, though Zooey hadn't heard a word of it. Virgil had pulled Zooey aside before they climbed into the limousine with Neibor, and he'd insisted that they continue to pretend, for Zooey's sake, that she was his girlfriend Diane. "There's no harm in it," he'd said, "and you'll be safer that way. Just sit up front with Rashid. I'm going to have Rashid put up the privacy window between the front and back seats; I want Karl to feel that we're talking privately. I'll tell you later what he says."

Zooey felt almost ashamed for agreeing so readily, but right now she felt as she had in New York: namely, that she was in the center of events that made no sense. She couldn't understand Neibor's seeming failure to recognize her, or his ignorance of these damn mysterious "documents" that Sakorski had offered to sell. Maybe it had been a mistake for her to trust Virgil the way she had; why was he talking so intently with Neibor in the back seat? Hadn't Francesca said that Neibor was the person Virgil wanted to destroy?

Rashid hadn't said a word.

"How did you know where to find us?" she finally asked him. "For that matter, how did you know that Karl Neibor had a gun on us?"

"Nothing strange about that," he said. "Mr. Fitts called Miz Darmini this morning and told her that you two were making a visit to the apartment. She got worried and told me to go check it out. I heard your voices through the door and I figured out what was going down."

"Lucky for us you did."

"I didn't know if it was just Neibor with you. Guess we lucked out there."

Soon after that, Virgil tapped the glass by Rashid's head with his gun and signaled for him to pull over. Rashid slowed and then idled next to the curb in a residential neighborhood, and Neibor got out. He walked slowly down the sidewalk without looking back.

Zooey climbed out of the front seat and confronted Virgil in the rear. She'd barely closed the car door when Rashid stepped on the accelerator. "What's happening?" she asked. "Why did you let him go?"

"I found out what I wanted to know. We couldn't hold him indefinitely, Zooey, and I couldn't shoot the SOB, much as I wanted to." Virgil looked distracted; he was staring blankly ahead and tapping one fist on his knee.

"What did you find out?"

"He ordered Sakorski to kill Mary." He spoke without enthusiasm. It was confusing.

"Well, then you've got him. That's what you wanted, isn't it?"

"That's true." Virgil wasn't really listening; he pulled out his Camels and gazed thoughtfully out the window, lighting a cigarette.

"Wasn't it Neibor you were after? We can nail him now."

"Don't be so dense, Zooey. Didn't you hear what he said up in Mary's apartment? We're back to square one."

Zooey waited for more information, but Virgil sat quietly, smoking. "What do you mean?" she finally asked. "That he didn't set up the bomb at Mark's Bar?"

Virgil sighed. "Why don't you think he set up the bomb?"

"Because he didn't recognize me. How could he have someone follow me to the bar without any idea who I am? A short redhead, that's all he'd need to know even if he'd never seen me. I was with you, and I'm a short redhead. He doesn't look stupid enough not to add up those facts."

"I don't know. Why don't we sit quiet until we get to the Orchid? I want to think about it."

"Think about what? For God's sake, Virgil, what did Neibor say?"

"Shut up, will you? Let me think." It was the first time Zooey had seen Virgil this angry. He turned away and punched the car door.

"I can't believe that you let Neibor walk away from us," Zooey muttered.

"I've already said I couldn't just shoot him."

"Okay, okay."

Zooey sat puzzling it out, feeling more and more uneasy. Virgil had set Neibor up as the great villain in this case, but as far as she could tell, Neibor's position resembled theirs. It seemed he was involved in something he didn't understand either, with events that he couldn't explain. He'd obviously been watching Mary's apartment, though they'd seen no sign of him when they'd sat watching in the street. Or rather, she mused, someone else must have been watching the apartment building, since Neibor had only arrived at the scene just as they were leaving. Thinking about it again, he surely hadn't been waiting for them in the lobby all that time; if they'd left by a back entrance, he would have missed them.

Or had anyone been watching the apartment? Zooey found herself remembering the phone calls Virgil had made after they'd picked up the Buick that Francesca lent them. "It's nothing important," he'd said as he walked several feet away. "I'll be a minute." An hour later, Karl Neibor had just happened to arrive as they left Mary's apartment.

I'm losing my mind, Zooey thought. Why would Virgil call Neibor? Why would Neibor pretend not to know her? What was there to gain? She revived another, more likely theory: that Virgil was simply using her, and that he'd never told her the whole truth.

Although she wasn't convinced of that either, she decided to do the one thing she'd wanted since breakfast that morning: to dump Virgil, at least for a while. Even if he said more about his conversation with Neibor, she couldn't be completely sure that he'd be telling the truth.

"Virgil, I don't have time to go to the Orchid. I've got some appointments this afternoon and then something on for tonight. I'm going to have Rashid drop me off when I see a cab. I'll call you later."

"Zooey, are you all right?" There was concern in Virgil's voice; back to the old, prying Virgil. But even his annoying habit of probing her moods made her suspicious now.

"Sure, I'm fine."

She jumped into a cab shortly afterward, thinking, I'm going to find Mark's killer, with or without Virgil. And maybe I can do it through Joe Quigley.

23

Zooey went home tired and frustrated. She felt apprehensive, too, as she opened the door to her apartment and searched it until convinced that no one had been there.

She'd lied about her afternoon appointments. She did call Jason and warned him again to be careful, and she still had her evening dinner engagement at Joe Quigley's home.

Her irritation with Virgil subsided slightly, and she wished she'd questioned him more closely about his conversation with Karl Neibor.

She also had a lot of questions she wanted to ask Joe Quigley about the Blackstone Plant. For starters, she could ask him if he'd ever heard of Karl Neibor.

Though she wasn't much in the mood for dinner with Joe, she gave some thought to what she should wear. She put on a silky, sheer white blouse, a black leather vest and a tight pair of shiny black pants with black high-heeled sandals. Then she strolled to the bathroom, brushed out her hair and clipped on a pair of silver clamshell earrings.

Though she generally didn't give her appearance much thought, she figured this was the right look to draw Joe out for more information about his job and the Blackstone Plant.

She finished by putting on her makeup and then she stepped back one more time to evaluate the result in the mirror.

I'm not bad, Zooey thought, when I make the effort. Her flat, tomboyish body was exactly the kind of figure women's clothes designers made their creations for. She turned sideways, testing her profile. Sexy, despite the stitches in her chin.

Too bad, she thought, because she didn't generally care much for men, although her best friends had often been men. The women in her early life had been weak and dependent, just as she had been for much of her marriage, and unable to steer their lives with confidence. It was thirty years before she'd done anything alone.

She spritzed perfume on her wrists and neck and left.

She found Joe's house on a narrow street lined with expensive brick rowhouses. She parked the car and walked up to number 637 on Brook Street.

Joe greeted her at the door with a smile and his delicate handshake. He wore a white apron tied around his waist, and a grey pin-striped shirt with an expensive pair of black designer jeans.

"You look great!" Joe said. "Come in and make yourself comfortable. I'm making a soufflé in the kitchen—it's my standard 'first dinner-date at home' meal."

Thinking of this as a "date" brought a twinge to her stomach as she walked to the center of the living room and stood there, her hands on her hips.

Joe's house was a surprise. It looked as if an interior decorator had spent a fortune working on its casually comfortable style. The walls in the living room were painted a strong, unusual clay-red color she liked. The furniture was an interesting blend of patterns and styles, eclectic and complicated. An odd collection of art objects hung along one wall like a series of personal clues, including an old handmade straw broom, a delicately carved wooden fan and a wooden horse head painted in bright colors. An eighteenth-century landscape etching hung over the fireplace, and on the mantel stood a row of tiny primitive sculptures. In front of the fireplace lay a pile of large, soft and inviting pillows.

"Like a drink?" Joe called from where he had disappeared into the kitchen.

"You bet," she said, walking toward the sound of his voice. She passed a dining room table set with candles and into the kitchen where Joe stood chopping spinach at a massive butcher-block table set in the center of the room.

"Nice kitchen," she said. She stood across from him, striking what she hoped was an appealing pose. "And a beautiful house. Is it yours?"

"No, it belongs to my parents. I grew up in this house. When my father decided to practice law in New York, I moved out of my apartment and back here. I'm their only child, so the house will eventually belong to me anyway. My parents inherited it from my grandfather, my mother's father. He was a journalist who traveled overseas; he collected most of the unusual artwork in the living room."

He continued his chopping. "What about you, Zooey? Where did you grow up?"

"In North Carolina. I didn't care for it, though."

"What can I fix you to drink? Scotch? A beer? Wine?"

"Do you have the fixings for a gin and tonic?"

"Coming right up." Joe wiped his hands on his apron and opened the refrigerator. He filled a tall glass with ice and a slice of fresh lime before pouring a generous amount of gin topped off with tonic. He handed it to her, grinning. "Gin up."

"To your soufflé," she said, sipping.

"What shall we talk about while I continue with this dinner?"

Zooey shrugged. "Well, there's what everyone's talking about every time you turn on the television or read the papers: the Baltimore attack and the vigilante fighting shaking several cities. I just don't know what to make of it, and it scares me, Joe. Even here in Washington there've been some ugly confrontations between black and white neighborhoods, and between some white groups, as well. And I don't understand why the FBI can't find David Duke or Farrakhan. They just continue to release their inflammatory videos calling for us to murder each other. It feels like we're tearing ourselves apart. Then, of course, there's the president's latest tweet: 'White lives matter. We are all entitled to protect our families. Thank God for Second Amendment solutions to terrorist supporters!' None of that helps. Already the National Guard's on patrol in several cities, and even they're getting shot at by opposing sides." Zooey sighed.

"Let's not go there," said Joe. "It'll put us in a rotten mood. How about we talk about your detective work. Is Virgil Fitts still investigating the Blackstone Plant?"

"I guess so."

"You're not sure?"

"He doesn't tell me very much. But there was one name he mentioned once that I'd meant to ask you about. Virgil said something about a guy named Karl Neibor. Have you ever heard of him?"

Joe was reaching inside a bag of onions with his back turned, so she couldn't see his face. It seemed, though, that he hesitated before answering. "Well, the name sounds familiar for some reason. But I can't think of who it might be."

"Let me try one more name I heard. How about Vlad Sakorski?"

Joe turned around. "No, I don't think I know him. Who is he supposed to be?"

"Just another name that Virgil mentioned. Like I said, he doesn't tell me much. Have you got any new thoughts on what happened to Mary?"

"I haven't changed my original feelings much. That is, I still think her death was accidental. But the whole scandal has soured my job at the plant. I'm starting to look around for something else, maybe in a related field. It's a pity, because I once had great hopes for nuclear power. I think I explained this before, but the hybrid fission/fusion nuclear power we're experimenting with at Blackstone seems like the perfect way of providing unlimited cheap, no-carbon and climate-friendly unlimited energy worldwide, and it's been exciting to be part of its development despite all the misinformation and lies about it."

Joe chopped furiously at the onions for a few minutes, and when he started talking again, his tone changed. "I've been screwed over, and that's the bottom line. After all the years I've given to this project, after all the years I worked overtime and on weekends, the Personnel Director at the plant chose to smear my and Mary's reputations in order to discredit her allegations. I'll never forgive them for that; it's no wonder that my heart's just not in the work anymore. Everyone at work pretends that everything's back to normal, and that they've forgotten about Mary and the rumors about us. The truth is that nobody's forgotten a thing. There's a promotion coming up that was promised to me, but now they won't even consider me for the job. They think I'm a potential whistleblower. Of course, they don't want to let me go right away; that would be too obvious and I might make a stink. They'll just pass me over for promotions once or twice and they know I'll leave quietly on my own."

It looked like Joe was going to weep, but then Zooey smiled to herself as she realized it was just the onions he was chopping that had made him tear up. Zooey came over and wiped his face with a paper napkin.

"Wouldn't you like to get even with those guys?" she asked.

"There's no way of doing it, Zooey."

He sounded like Francesca.

"You're right," said Zooey, "there's not, if you assume that nothing wrong is happening at the plant. But if there is something wrong, you could expose it."

Joe shook his head and pulled out a mixing bowl. "Look, we've been over this territory before. Nothing illegal has happened or will happen at the Blackstone Plant. Nuclear power is far too controversial. There've been three large protests outside the plant already this year, and any proof of irregularity would be all that's needed to shut us down. The few big politicians and scientists who are convinced of the project's integrity have guaranteed funding until now. But even they'll back out immediately if there's any hint of a serious problem. You don't know the people I work for; if this plant goes down, their careers go down too. Most of those fat cats could never equal the salaries they're getting now anywhere else."

"But Joe, I was thinking about the conversation we had at the German restaurant. You gave me the impression then that you had more doubts about the whole situation."

Joe slid the soufflé carefully into the oven. He then pulled out a bottle of scotch and filled a glass with ice.

"Maybe I did, but I've been so confused and angry. I desperately wanted to wring somebody's neck for a while, and I didn't particularly care whose neck it was. I wasn't thinking straight."

"And now you have no doubts at all?"

"None. But Zooey, I also have to say that it doesn't matter much to me either way. My great hopes have gone down the drain. Don't you ever think about changing everything—like your job and where you live? I'd love to travel. What I'd like to do is to take maybe ten years, ten full years, and see as much of the world as I can. I could spend two years on each continent; maybe I'd spend three years in Asia. I'd hike and travel on foot, sleep under the stars in Greece, see the Taj Mahal by moonlight. Hike the Himalayas. Go to China, to Japan, Indonesia, the Philippines. All the places I've never seen, where I've never smelled the air or never tasted the food.

I want all of that, Zooey, and to hell with this stagnant life and nowhere job and the fat-cat-loving United States."

"You mean you really are going to quit your job?"

"Yes. And it's not just because of what happened to Mary. You have great ideas, great plans, and you work hard to make them real, but then they're shot down each and every time by petty bureaucrats and businessmen who are more interested in their public image and personal power than they are about the future of world energy. When I think about it now, I don't know why I've held on as long as I have. This project isn't any more important to me today than any other job that's available, except that I'd rather not work at the Blackstone Plant anymore."

Joe looked at her, smiling. "How about this? We'll get married and have ten kids and live happily ever after in a mansion in Peru."

She laughed. "Peru? Why the hell Peru? And besides, I never want to be married again."

"You've been married before?"

"Yes. I've been divorced for over three years now. I got married at age eighteen and it was a total disaster. But I never talk about it and it has nothing to do with what's happening now."

That wasn't quite true, but she didn't want to ruin the moment with her nightmare of a past.

"Maybe later," Joe said, "when we know each other better, you'll feel like talking about it."

She waved the possibility aside. "I seriously doubt it. Anyway, let's go back to your idea about living in Peru. Why did you choose Peru?"

"No special reason, except that it's far away from Washington. I've heard that there are beautiful mountain forests in that country. Wouldn't you like to live in a house built on top of a mountain?"

"I like the idea of it. But do they need private investigators in Peru? I doubt I could find a job there."

Joe took another sip of his scotch. "Tell me, Zooey, why did you ever become a detective, anyway? Are you any good at it?"

"No." She leaned one elbow on the counter. "Or, I don't know, sometimes I've done pretty well. It's just that I haven't been doing such a good job lately."

"What do you think about my travel plans? Want to come along?"

"Even if I wanted it, I don't have the money to do any of those things."

"Ah, yes, lack of money—the great destroyer of dreams. But tell me, what if we had a lot of money? I mean, what if a long-lost black-sheep uncle showed up and handed you a couple of million dollars, a respectable fortune? Would you run off with me then?"

"Are you trying to tell me that you're secretly wealthy?"

He shook his head. "No, I'm not, but I wish I were. But I do want a change."

"I don't even consider such things, Joe. It's never going to happen, so why think about it?"

"But you must have some dream about what you'd do if you had the freedom to do whatever you wanted, even if you know it will never happen."

"I don't know, Joe, I'm pretty hard-headed that way. I don't like to think too much about the future." She felt like saying the only dream she'd had recently involved finding Mark's killer, but decided against it. "Maybe it's just that I'm tired of being disappointed."

"Tell me, what's it really like being a detective? Hearing about people's problems, finding out their deepest secrets and their terrible lies. It must be a fascinating business."

"Oh, sometimes it is. Other times, I just find lost pets or investigate petty insurance claims."

"Is this something you plan to do for the rest of your life? I mean, if you're not planning to get married."

She thought about it, absently swirling the few drops left in her glass.

"Who knows? Maybe I'll end up going to law school, or maybe I'll wind up as a proofreader with a permanent squint in somebody's stuffy office. Maybe I'll join the Peace Corps and train people in Africa, teach them the detective trade and how to spy on their tribal bosses. The only thing I'm sure of is that I'm dropping the Gentry investigation. I'm done."

Joe grabbed his drink and directed Zooey back to the living room, his arm around her waist. "I'm glad to hear that, Zooey, but this is turning into a bummer. Let's change the subject."

"Sure." She sat close to him on the living room couch.

"Let's not talk about anything for a minute."

"Okay."

Joe sat silent, staring into the fire, and then he relaxed and leaned back. "I must sound like I'm obsessed with this thing."

"That's okay. I understand."

"I had a feeling you would. Anyway, I'd meant to tell you before that it's nice to have you here for dinner. I'm glad you called me." He traced the outline of her left hand with his index finger, and then reached up to stroke her arm.

His touch was disturbing, but at least it forced her thoughts from the subject of Karl Neibor. He stroked her shoulder and then gently took a handful of red hair, softly tugging her face up to his.

"You're lovely," he said. "You're the best thing that's happened to me since Mary died."

Zooey smiled. "But you hardly know me."

"I don't even know myself very well these days."

She pulled away slightly, pointing to the painted horse head that hung on the wall behind them. "What's that?" she asked. "I've never seen anything like it."

"It's from India," Joe said. "My grandfather loved India, and he spent three years living in Calcutta during British rule. He told me that the horse head comes from a state called Orissa, and it's a piece of folk or tribal art. Handsome, isn't it?"

"I know almost nothing about art or India, but I do like it. The horse has a funny expression. It makes me think that Indian artists must have a sense of humor."

"I've always wanted to go there because my grandfather talked so much about it."

Joe touched Zooey's hair again; she half-closed her eyes as he gently rubbed her scalp.

"That feels wonderful," she said. She was finding her interest in interrogating Joe slipping away.

After a while, a bell rang in the kitchen. "The soufflé!" Joe said. "Come into the kitchen and grab some plates, would you?"

"Sure."

The plates were off-white china with pink roses and green leaves. "Your mother must have picked these out," Zooey said.

"You're right."

Zooey lit the candles and they sat down at the dining room table for their meal, beginning with a salad of romaine lettuce sprinkled with blue cheese and walnuts, and continuing with crunchy French bread to accompany the soufflé. They both drank several glasses of a chilled white wine.

"I hope you're not disappointed that I didn't fix steaks," Joe said as Zooey finished the last of her dessert of chocolate truffles.

"Are you kidding? This was great. I can't cook at all."

"Come into the living room, then, and I'll show you my favorite way to finish off a meal."

Zooey smiled, wondering whether she should make her excuses and leave. She found that she didn't really want to leave, though, and her reasons didn't have anything to do with the Blackstone case. She was actually having a good time. Maybe it was the release of the stress of having been nearly killed by Karl Neibor that made her feel that way. She'd once read there was no finer aphrodisiac than a near-death experience.

She sat down on a pillow as he strolled in from the kitchen with a bottle of champagne and two tall, narrow glasses. "Do you like champagne?" he asked.

She laughed. "Are you kidding? It's perfect."

"I like the way you laugh," he said. "Especially since you're always so serious."

"So are you," she scoffed.

Zooey concluded that his wanting to know her didn't scare her the way it might have.

But then she forced her mind back to Mark, and back to the scene with Neibor that morning. "Was Mary a serious person? Or maybe I shouldn't ask."

Joe's smile faded, and he stopped in the act of prying off the champagne cork. "Oh, yes and no. Mostly no. She had a way of shaking me out of my morbid moods with her great sense of humor."

Zooey considered telling him that she'd visited Mary's apartment, but then decided against it.

"Here's another subject we can drop," said Joe. "I want to taste the champagne."

"Me too."

Joe pulled at the cork again, forcing it out with a pop, and then poured them each a glassful. He put their drinks on the floor and sat down on a pillow beside her.

"I'm sorry for bringing that subject up," Zooey said, picking up her champagne glass. "It's my habit, I guess, that I can't stop myself from saying what I'm thinking."

"Ah, yes. Habits are an opening to the soul, as a college professor of literature once told me. Quirks strike straight to the heart—in sensing these, one senses the heart." Joe gave a wry smile and toasted her with his glass. "But I don't think that you do always say what you're thinking. A good detective never would."

He reached over to touch her hair again. "Don't you think it's strange that I'd invite you over for dinner so soon after Mary's death?"

"I thought we weren't going to discuss that topic."

Joe sipped his champagne and sighed. "Good champagne, don't you think? It's French."

"I wouldn't know the difference, I'm afraid. But I love the way it makes my head float."

Joe took another sip. "I didn't mean to put you off before; I really don't want to avoid the subject of Mary. But I've gone from being sad to feeling numb lately, like the grief is passing. Do you think that's possible?"

"Of course."

"Or maybe I'm just going through another phase." He paused. "I'll never forget her, but I honestly can't say right now that we would have been happy together. I don't think I knew her as well as I thought I did, or as well as I should have, and I still feel guilty about letting her down. It makes me sad to think of it, but when we were together, I spent so much time working that I wasn't much good at being supportive. Or whatever it is you're supposed to be these days."

Zooey looked at him skeptically. "You don't strike me as an amateur with women."

He laughed.

"And," she continued, "I don't believe that you learned how to whip up these seduction dinners overnight."

"My mother taught me to cook," Joe said.

Zooey pushed on. "You always describe yourself as being inexperienced with women, but your style is so smooth and cool, I find it almost impossible to believe what you say."

"Smooth and cool?" Joe laughed. "You make me sound like a superior brand of scotch."

Zooey examined his eyes. "Tell me the truth, was Mary the first woman you loved?"

"Yes." Joe sat up quickly and poured them each more champagne. "But I never said that she was the first woman I slept with. Far from it, if you want to know the truth. But I've never been interested in the bar or the party scene. My preference is for something more serious."

"Like tonight."

"Oh, come on. You're just trying to trip me up. Things get more complicated when I start thinking about you."

"What do you mean?"

"Forget it. Never mind." He leaned close to her; she felt his breath on her cheek and then he delicately kissed her eyelids. He pulled back for a moment and looked at her, smiling his now-familiar ironic smile, and she experienced a strong, pleasurable sense of expectation. Then he kissed her slowly, sensuously, luxuriously, with his lips slightly parted and soft on hers. Every minute or so, he'd pull back again to look at her eyes. And she thought: this isn't part of the plan, but I can't remember when I've ever been kissed this well.

24

Zooey awoke at four o'clock in the morning, wondering for a moment where she was.

With Joe, of course. His arms were tight around her as he slept.

Oh God, what have I done? she thought. Feeling an urgent need to go home, she stretched her arms and legs so that Joe woke up.

"Zooey?" His eyes opened slightly.

"Joe, go back to sleep," she whispered. "I've got to get back to my apartment. I'll explain later."

He closed his eyes and reached for her shoulders, hugging her gently. "Are you sure you're all right?"

"Everything's great, really great. I'm sorry I have to leave, but I'll call you later."

"All right." He kissed her hair, but he was already falling asleep again.

She lay still for a moment, then pulled out of his arms and climbed from the bed. She dressed silently, groping for her clothes in the semi-dark. She paused at the doorway to look back at Joe. He breathed deeply. His face was delicate and calm; his hand lay across the dent in the bed where she'd been sleeping. For a moment, she felt a strong impulse to lie down beside him again.

But she tiptoed downstairs and found her shoes next to an empty champagne bottle. Quietly, she closed the front door behind her and walked to her car. When she turned on the engine, its firing sounded explosive on the quiet street.

As she drove home, she tried to figure out if she'd done something meaningful, or whether she'd simply drunk too much wine and made a fool of herself. If Joe had useful information, he'd thrown up the world's oldest smokescreen. But thinking about it that way didn't begin to explain what had happened between them.

She wasn't sure why she'd impulsively fled his home. Slowly, she allowed images from the evening to interrupt her thoughts: Joe's slim, lithe body and the warm smell of his skin.

It was odd to remember that while she'd been dressing up for Joe's dinner, she'd told herself that she didn't like men. Of course, she'd been naïvely planning to seduce information out of him. She'd pictured herself giving up a few kisses, at most, for the cause. She'd seen herself leaving his house early, saying something like, "Please, let's give ourselves time to know each other, Joe. It seems so important to do things that way."

She laughed out loud, thinking of that.

By the time she got home, she felt better about herself. Memories of the previous evening now left a sweet aftertaste, and it was obvious why she'd needed to leave before morning. The last time she'd awoken with a man's arms around her, the man had been her husband. It wasn't surprising that her first reaction had been confusion, especially since casual sex was a contradiction in terms for her. In some strange way she felt excited about what had happened with Joe, as if she'd lived out a fantasy that she hadn't been aware she had.

Another discovery was that her cellphone had died. She didn't discover it until she'd arrived home and finished a cup of yogurt and two cups of coffee. The moment she plugged it back in, Virgil called.

"Zooey! For Christ's sake, what's happened with you? Your phone's been unreachable since late yesterday afternoon."

She bristled. "Yes. I accidentally let it go dead."

"But where have you been? I sent Rashid over to your apartment last night to check it out, but you weren't there."

"Rashid got into my apartment? How did he get in? Who gave him permission to do that?"

"Permission? What in the hell are you talking about? If you'd been lying there shot, you would have been glad Rashid dropped by. Remember our encounter with Neibor?"

"All I remember is that you stuck me in the front seat of Francesca's limo where I couldn't hear anything you said to Neibor. And then you wouldn't tell me anything." She knew she sounded sulky and that this wasn't the way to get information from Virgil. "Look, I'm sorry you were worried. Let's get together and talk?"

"That's an excellent idea. I'm at the Orchid; do you want to meet me here?"

"Sure. Give me an hour."

She hung up, worried. Virgil's call felt like a bucket of cold water on the events of the night before.

25

When she arrived at the Orchid, the figure that greeted her at the front door was the most bizarre yet; Zooey burst out laughing the moment the door opened. Someone wearing a gorilla suit with the fur dyed pink waved her through when she asked for Virgil Fitts. The gorilla wore a red sun hat and red tennis shoes.

Francesca, Zooey thought, must be cracking up. The gorilla laughed as hard as Zooey did as it led her to another octagonal sitting room, this one shining in copper and gold. Virgil sat writing at a desk, and she sat in a chair next to him.

"Good morning, Fitts," she said. "Hard at work, I see."

He looked up with a worried expression. "So it's my lost companion, little Zooey Krause. I was beginning to think I'd never see you again."

"Little Zooey Krause? With an attitude like that, you could get rid of me quickly." She leaned back in her chair, annoyed.

"Listen, kid, we've got a lot to talk about, so let's not spend too much time fighting. I've got information and a brilliant plan."

"I wish you all the luck in the world, but you can count me out. I've decided to drop this investigation. The only reason I came here was to personally let you know my decision."

Virgil dropped the papers he'd been holding. "What?"

"And don't try to change my mind."

He clapped a hand to his forehead, shaking his head back and forth. "Is this because you're mad about what happened with Karl Neibor? Because I know you'll be interested in what I have to say. This situation is bigger than we imagined. I was pretty sure that Neibor killed Mary to keep her from ruining his little Union pension fund scam, and I know he really got worried when I visited the Blackstone Plant after her death asking questions. I figured I'd throw him off my ass by writing a story as if I believed all that nonsense about Mary's insanity. In a way, I wanted to believe it too—but that's another story. Then I went into hiding, and that's when I started making mistakes. When Vlad fired on our car the day I met you, I assumed that my unexplained disappearance had worried Neibor, and that he'd decided to get rid of me. But that's not true.

"Neibor told me it was Sakorski who had contacted him to say Mary had found proof of Neibor's meddling in the Union fund. He panicked and told Sakorski to intercept her and get whatever documents she had, so Sakorski ran her off the road. It was a 'lucky' break for Neibor that she died in the crash. It saved him from a suspicious murder if Sakorski had had to shoot her. But Neibor believes Sakorski kept the documents he found in her car. He knows Sakorski asked me for $20,000 to get them, and he thinks I paid it. Neibor offered me $40,000 in the car if I gave them back to him.

"But you see, while Neibor did order Sakorski to intercept Mary, he never ordered Sakorski to kill me. Neibor's as worried as we are about that. He wants to know who else is involved in this. Whoever it is, they were so serious about finishing me off that they set up that phony deal in New York, and found out enough about you to set off a bomb in Mark's Bar. And the bomb couldn't have been Neibor's work because he didn't know who the hell you were at Mary's apartment.

"And finally, Neibor doesn't know Sakorski's offer was a phony deal. He thinks I do have documents that Mary was carrying."

Zooey sighed. She'd only intended to stay long enough to cut off her involvement with Virgil, but now curiosity wouldn't let her leave just yet.

"Didn't you tell me in the beginning that you'd suspected some kind of cover-up involving Karl Neibor and some Blackstone Plant executives? You never said that Neibor was working alone."

Virgil nodded eagerly. "Exactly right! But Zooey, I assumed that Neibor had total responsibility for planning and carrying out all the dirty work. No fat-cat executive would ever get involved directly with a New York hitman like Sakorski who's wanted on a murder charge. They'd use Neibor to keep their names out of it. That way, if Vlad Sakorski got caught, he couldn't point the finger at anyone but Neibor. But in the end, whoever is working at Blackstone seems not to have trusted Neibor not to rat them out if he got caught. They wanted me, you and maybe even Neibor himself eliminated."

Virgil got up from his chair and paced the room.

"Okay, so what are you saying, Virgil? That a Blackstone executive contacted Sakorski directly? Is that your new information?"

He sat down again in a chair across from hers. "It's more than that, but yes, and that whoever that was also hired some other thug to blow up Mark's Bar. If we can prove all this..."

"You can be damn sure they've covered their tracks," Zooey interrupted. "After all, Sakorski's dead and he can't talk. So how can we prove anything at all? We're back to the beginning again—with nothing but a lot of Virgil Fitts's empty talk and wild conspiracy theories, with not a shred of evidence to back it up."

Virgil started to answer, but Zooey continued, "No—don't tell me about Karl Neibor again, because that's the weakest link I've heard from you yet. Why would you believe anything he said?"

Virgil stood up again and grimaced. "That's why you're mad at me, isn't it? Because I cut you out of the conversation."

Zooey rolled her eyes. "That's Virgil Fitts for you, always questioning my motives. Sure, I was mad at first. You and Neibor were chatting in the back seat of Francesca's car, and when I tried to ask you about it, you clammed up. I'm finished with your lies and secrets, Virgil, and I'm not going to risk my life, or any more of my friends' lives, on your paranoid fantasies. And I'm not going on any more of your wild goose chases for evidence that doesn't exist. I don't want to be involved in whatever little private war is going on between you and Neibor, which means that I'm not convinced that anything is wrong at the Blackstone Plant."

Virgil pulled at his hair and shouted, "Nothing wrong! Haven't you heard a word I've said?" He pounded his fist on the desk. "Shit, I hate dumb broads!"

"Dumb broads," Zooey mumbled. She'd been waiting for an opportunity like this. She grabbed her purse and made ready for a dash to the door. "You can go fuck yourself, Virgil, just go fuck yourself! I'm through with you!"

She was out the door before he could say a word. "Bastard," she mumbled to herself as she headed down the hall toward the star-shaped fountain in the entryway.

"Zooey!" Virgil ran after her.

She started running, but he caught her arm.

Zooey stood still for a minute, rigid with anger. "Haven't we played out this scene a little too often, Virgil? Now let me go and let's forget that we ever met."

"Zooey, what's happened to you? We're on the verge of cracking this case, I swear it! Don't give up when we're about to make sense of it all!"

She shook his hand from her arm and turned to him. "Then why do you need me? Crack the case and get the credit. That's what you really want, isn't it?"

Virgil stared at her for a minute, and then started to laugh. He sounded hysterical.

"What's wrong with you?" she asked.

He giggled weakly. "No, I don't want all the credit," he finally said. "Goddam, what in the world would make you say a thing like that? Go ahead and accuse me of cowardice, of hiding out and of failing Mary Gentry. I'm guilty of all those things. But no, I didn't get into this for the notoriety."

Zooey sighed and rubbed her eyes. "Just please let me go, Virgil. I don't want to talk about it anymore."

"Neither do I, but I'm begging you: please listen to what I have to say. There is another element I discovered that you don't know about. I promise that after you've heard everything, if you still want to quit this case, I won't say a word to stop you. You can walk right out the door and forget it ever happened. I promise that. But give me a chance to explain."

She stared at him, wondering again why she found this irritating, bull-headed journalist so impossible to hate.

"Why do you want my help, Virgil? You've never thought I was a good detective."

"That's not true and I have my reasons. Give me a chance to explain."

"Why do I have the feeling I'm going to regret this?" She looked down at her feet, figuring she had nothing to lose but maybe an hour. Then she'd be free of him. "Okay, you win. After all we've been through together, I suppose I owe you and Mark that much. But I warn you, I don't see how anything will change my mind."

"Fine, fine," he mumbled, turning back down the hallway.

"No, I don't want to hang around at the Orchid," Zooey said. "The bizarre features of this lust palace are starting to get on my nerves. Let's search out some sleazy bar and have a strong drink. I think I need one."

"Ah! I know just the place. It's right down the street."

Zooey let slip a tiny smile. "I figured you would."

They walked out to the street, passing the pink gorilla again. "By the way, what's the story with that fuzzy pink ape?" she asked.

"Oh, Francesca's always playing games. One of her richest clients gets powerfully aroused by children's toys; haven't you seen the room full of monster stuffed animals?"

"Yes, I saw it one day. But I didn't like the animals. They looked disturbing."

"All those animals are props for that one wealthy client," Virgil said.

"Just one more step in turning a whorehouse into a giant playpen?"

Virgil nodded. "Something like that." He pointed to a grimy sign: Joe's Bar.

"Here we are," he said.

The place was sleazy, smelled like garbage and looked like a dump. A perfect setting for her last meeting with Virgil, she thought. The buttons on the jukebox were coated with the sticky remains of spilled drinks and the grime of unwashed hands from thirty years of abuse, and the bartender, a swollen-faced man slumped behind the counter, was three sheets to the wind, as were the few other customers who stared blearily through red-rimmed eyes into space.

"Now tell me," she said when they'd settled at a table in the back, "the rest of what Neibor told you."

"Gin and tonic?" Virgil asked Zooey.

She nodded, and he ordered drinks.

"Listen," he said, "I pointed out to Neibor that he was the only direct link between whomever in Blackstone was working with him and Mary's death, and that they had all the information needed to blackmail him into taking the rap for her death, if necessary. He must have been thinking something similar. I told him that if his collaborators weren't sure that he could be trusted, they'd work to get rid of him too."

The tall, unshaven bartender stumbled to their table and plopped down their drinks. Virgil winked at Zooey as he took a long gulp of scotch.

"But that's one thing I don't understand," she said. "Wasn't it Karl Neibor that you wanted to get behind bars as a matter of revenge for what he did to Francesca?"

"Sure, I'd love to see that," he said.

Zooey sighed. "Let me try another theory, Virgil, just for the sake of argument. I talked to Joe Quigley—you remember him, right?—on the phone a few days ago. He told me more about the Blackstone Plant, about what an experimental project it is. Nuclear power almost died out after Chernobyl, the Three Mile Island accident and what happened in Japan, and this fission/fusion reactor, or whatever he calls it, that he's working on is supposed to solve the problems they had with the old nuclear plants.

"But according to Joe, public opinion has been so dead set against any kind of nuclear power that it was almost impossible to get funding for this new development. If a few prominent scientists hadn't convinced the government that this was a shining hope for the future, the Blackstone Plant would never have been built."

Virgil shifted his legs impatiently. "I know all of this, Zooey."

"I didn't, probably because I seldom read the newspapers. Anyway, Joe said that all these Blackstone executive types would do almost anything to keep the plant going. They need years of research to make this process work, but they're afraid that another wave of paranoia might shut them down by cutting off their funds."

"Sure, that fits right in."

"But they wouldn't do anything illegal, because if it were found out, they'd certainly lose the project. They might lie about Mary Gentry's sanity to avoid any adverse publicity, but they wouldn't hire a Russian hitman, even through Neibor, to run her off the road. What if she hadn't died in the crash? If Sakorski had had to shoot her, it could never have been ruled an accident. This whole scenario would have been too risky for them."

"There's sense in what you say, but how can you be sure? What about Mark?"

"I don't know, Virgil. But suppose that the arson squad was right and I was wrong, and that the explosion was a simple accident? The storage room just off the back entrance to the bar was a mess of half-empty cans of solvents, cleaners and who knows what else. There was gasoline stored back there too; I'm positive about that, because my car was running low once and Mark brought a gas can from the back to help me out. Besides, why would anyone want to kill me? I hadn't seen you for days when Mark's Bar blew up, and I'm sure that I've never been followed. No one's ever searched my apartment or visited my office. What does that say to you?"

"So this is all just a great big string of coincidences, is that what you're saying?"

Virgil's sarcastic tone stung. "Virgil, don't jump all over me," she said. "I'm trying to find another way of looking at the facts, that's all, and I think that's something we need to do right now. Think of how many people have died already. If you're wrong about all of this, then it's high time we quit."

They sat in silence, each staring down at the table.

"As I see it, we've got one chance to make sense of this thing," Virgil finally said. "We've got to get our hands on one piece of undisputed evidence that proves Mary's death wasn't an accident. Evidence I haven't yet told you about. Something that will be enough to rouse public suspicion and a demand for a detailed investigation by an impartial party. Not the local police this time, but maybe the FBI."

"Sure, great, that's what we've needed all along: one piece of solid evidence. But where do we find it?"

"There was one thing Neibor said; he said that running Mary off the road was a backup plan that he never intended."

"What does that mean?"

"He clammed up and wouldn't say. But think about two things. Mary had a radiation detector in her car that was smashed up in the 'accident.' Why did she have it with her when she was coming to see me? And why, when she called me, did she say, 'It's too late for me. They know, Virgil.' Why would she say that? What did 'they' know, who were 'they,' and why was it too late?"

Zooey shrugged. "Why would Sakorski say, 'Only you can do what we want. Only you.' What the hell did that mean?"

"Yeah, that's strange too. But don't forget, the original accusation Mary made to me wasn't about Union tampering with the pension fund. It was about cutting corners on safety regulations that might endanger employees. What if Mary discovered she'd been given a fatal dose of radiation poisoning? What if she was set up, so that someone at the plant could say she had a history of mental illness and poisoned herself to make it look like the plant was out of compliance? Or they could say that in her obsessive determination to discover something, she went into areas she wasn't supposed to be in, didn't know what she was handling and, because of that, she got in over her head and poisoned herself? Remember how her lab clothes were missing from the police lab, and how we weren't ever sure if the clothes they finally gave us belonged to Mary? And don't forget, according to what Joe said, Mary thought she was pregnant. What if what she thought was morning sickness was actually the early stages of radiation poisoning?"

"But..." Zooey found she couldn't finish the sentence.

"Neibor was the common denominator in all of this. The compromised executives working with him at the plant might have wanted insurance Mary wouldn't survive."

"But wouldn't somebody realize that she'd been poisoned after she died?"

"Funeral directors don't generally keep Geiger counters."

"But the police did an autopsy. What about that?"

"The cause of death was the accident. There wasn't time to die of radiation poisoning."

"This is all very suspicious, Virgil," Zooey said grudgingly. "So what's next? I suppose we'd have to convince the police to dig her up."

"No! They'll say the case is closed and blow us off. Besides, I think someone at Blackstone has connections with the police. Certainly, Neibor does. But if we get the evidence ourselves, the news will be so big that a cover-up will be impossible. If she's radioactive, we'll call in the Feds."

Zooey's stomach tightened as it dawned on her what Virgil planned. "You want to dig Mary up yourself?"

"It's the only way. I was hoping to convince you to help me."

"You're out of your mind! It's a felony if we're discovered. And what will we do if we're right? Take her corpse over to police headquarters? They'll say we contaminated it!"

"You've got a point there." Virgil waved for another round of drinks.

"I'm not saying that you've convinced me to do this, but, dammit, I have an idea about a way to do it. We'd have to ask your newspaper boss, Wallace Durnam, to come with us as a witness. He'd be our impartial observer. It'd be a big story for his paper."

"That's good! I'll get him on the phone right away."

Zooey grimaced. "Hold on a minute—I didn't say I'd do it. Do you know where the cemetery is?"

"Yes, but we'll have to get hold of a radiation detector."

He got up from his chair. "I'm calling Durnam. Whether you come with me or not is your decision, but I'm going ahead with this plan because it seems like our only chance. If you decide not to help, then just walk off and forget about everything I said." He left the table, sorting through his suit pocket for his phone.

Zooey sat with her elbows propped on the table, her chin in her hand. She stared absently out the smeared window at the front of the bar, watching young kids race home from summer school swinging their books and shouting.

It was hard to make sense of anything. She thought of Joe and their discussion of the night before, and her sense of relief this morning when she'd decided to drop the case. To be honest, part of the relief came from the idea of releasing herself from the oppressive feelings of guilt she had about Mark's death. If she could convince herself that his death had not been her fault, then there was no reason to continue this futile investigation.

She thought again about Mark—his pig stories, his tractor imitations and the way he'd helped get her established in Washington. True to his word, he'd never asked for anything in return outside of a return on his investment. She supposed that this last chance of getting evidence was something she should try for Mark's sake; if they succeeded, she'd be bringing Mark's killer to justice. If they failed, she'd drop the case.

Virgil returned. "He agreed. Now what about you?"

"Okay, I'll help you, but I'm considering this my last-ditch effort. If nothing turns up, I'm finished."

Virgil looked pleased, sipping his drink.

"There's one question you haven't answered, Virgil. Why were you so determined to make me help you? A strong man like Francesca's mammoth bodyguard would be so much more useful tonight."

Virgil fumbled for his cigarettes. "Maybe I like you."

"Very touching, I'm sure, but not too convincing. We fight like cornered rats."

"Great image," he laughed. "Look, like you said before, we've been through a lot, and besides, tonight I need someone I can trust. I don't want to involve Francesca any more deeply in this, especially if something goes wrong and Karl Neibor comes after me. I don't want to ask for help from someone who works for her either. But I don't know what you're complaining about. If my suspicions are correct, it'll help your career."

"Since when have you cared about my career?"

Virgil drained his drink. "This sounds like the start of another rat fight. Let's drop it and make some plans for tonight."

Zooey nodded, thinking that she'd have to ask Joe for a radiation detector and make up an excuse for not meeting him tonight. "You're a lunatic, Fitts, and don't think I've forgotten that fact for a moment."

He nodded sympathetically.

26

The Prospect Hill Cemetery lay behind a chain of oaks in a secluded Northwest Washington neighborhood. Mary's grave was not visible from the gate. The watchman, a frail retiree with emphysema, had trudged off with Gillie to get drunk in the toolshed.

Zooey and Virgil stumbled over a tree root in the shadows. It was a dark night, with only a narrow slice of moon for illumination. They didn't want to use their flashlights any more often than necessary. All they needed was to be noticed by some neighborhood insomniac taking a midnight stroll with his dog near the graveyard.

"Ouch!" Virgil picked himself up and rubbed his knee.

"Are you all right?"

"Yeah."

They walked on.

"What about the guard? Wouldn't it be easy for him to identify Gillie if someone discovers that the grave has been dug up?"

"Why would he know who Gillie is? Anyway, I gave Gillie a gallon jug of 101 proof Wild Turkey; he'll get that guard so sloshed he'll be lucky to remember his own name tomorrow. All of our faces will be nothing more than a blur."

"I hope you're right. The grave should be right around here somewhere..." Zooey flipped on the flashlight and shone it on a group of stone markers to their left. After a few minutes of searching, she spotted Mary's name. "That's it, the small one way at the back. See it?"

Virgil nodded and they walked over.

He dropped their shovels next to Mary's headstone, a simple stone marker engraved with her name, the dates "February 14, 1990 – July 2, 2019" and the standard "Rest in Peace." Several grander monuments loomed in the shadows around them; one tombstone's silhouette bore a scale model likeness of the Washington Monument.

Zooey set the radiation detector next to the shovels, and then directed the flashlight beam back to the feet of the two men who had followed them: Wallace Durnam and a young reporter he'd brought along. The reporter was a nervous kid with a pale face and short carrot-red hair. Durnam chewed his cigar.

"This better pay off, Virg, or the feds'll send you off on a long, happy holiday at the taxpayers' expense." Durnam chuckled, his bulky shadow looming in the dark.

Virgil scratched his head. "Hell, the feds will be shaking our hands by the time we've finished. Probably give us a gold medal."

"I wouldn't count on it," said Durnam. "Depends on who's on the payroll. Public funds wasted; a controversial federally funded project upended. It could even result in the termination of a few political careers. Besides, there are many environmental experts who really believe in the future of this fission-fusion process, and they won't be happy when you connect their pet project to a scandal. Matter of fact, I wouldn't be surprised if they tear you to shreds to cover the whole mess up."

"It's always nice to have an optimist in the crowd," Zooey muttered. "We'd better get on with this. Grab a shovel, Wally."

"We're only here to observe," said Durnam. "Call us when you uncover the corpse." He pulled out a flask and ambled heavily out of sight in the darkness with Wally trailing behind.

"Don't be too hard on Durnam," Virgil said. "He wouldn't have agreed to come here tonight if he didn't think we had a chance to prove something. But if he doesn't participate in the exhumation, he can't be charged if we're caught."

Zooey grabbed one shovel and tossed the other to Virgil. She hadn't thought about it while they'd been stumbling through the cemetery, but the idea of uncovering a decomposing corpse was starting to make her feel unsettled. Before, she'd only been concerned about the possibility of getting caught, and the location of the grave in this isolated corner was a lucky break. Still, they were taking a big chance on another one of Virgil's wild speculations.

"Worried?" said Virgil, seeming to read her mind.

"A little," she answered, poking her shovel into the soft black dirt. "I don't suppose you've ever done anything like this before, but how long do you think it will take?"

"Quite a while. A few hours, I'd guess."

"I figured as much."

They dug in. Despite the fact that the night was relatively cool, they were both sweating heavily after just a few minutes. Zooey was already panting, and she knew that it would take weeks for her shoulder muscles to recover from the unaccustomed strain. They dug in silence for a long time, Zooey stopping from time to time to listen for any suspicious noises. They made such a racket with the clank of shovels against dirt and stone that it seemed the whole neighborhood ought to have noticed their presence by now. But they were at least a hundred yards from the nearest house, and the only noises she heard were sporadic chirps from a tree full of restless birds.

"You know," Virgil said after a long while, "here we are, working together on a cool summer night under a sky lit by a thousand stars." He dropped his shovel and slowly straightened, gingerly stretching his arms and back. "Makes a guy feel like falling in love."

"You pick the weirdest times to get romantic," said Zooey, following his example and stretching too.

"It makes sense when you're in a cemetery; love and death—mortality and immortality—life's greatest themes. I couldn't think of a better time or place to talk about it."

Zooey watched his teeth gleam in a smile, and restrained the impulse to hit him with her shovel.

"I can't believe you're making jokes at a time like this," she said. "You liked Mary, and I figured that you'd be depressed tonight." It was a vindictive thing to say, but she couldn't help herself.

Virgil spat, wiping his forehead. Dirt mixed with sweat ran in long streaks across his dark brown face. "You have such a cheerful nature," he said.

For the next few minutes, she heard only the sound of his shoveling. Then he stopped again.

"Of course I liked Mary, and it's a punch in the gut to dig her up. Dead bodies always give me the creeps, anyway, and I've seen too many over the years in my job. The attempt at humor, as you very well know, is a way of easing the strain."

"No, I don't buy that," Zooey said. "You're a romantic at heart; a big teddy bear. You even think it's romantic to be poking around in a graveyard with me in the middle of the night."

"Did it ever occur to you that I might be reaching out for you?"

"No, and it's a good thing because I'm not a very good consoler. I'm just not very affectionate."

"Come on, Zooey, tell me something more about yourself. It'll take some time to finish this job."

Zooey rested her head against the shovel handle. "You're impossible."

"And you're an extreme case, Krause."

She resumed pitching the dirt with fervor. "Okay, Dr. Freud, what do you want to know this time? How about my earliest sexual fantasies?"

"That's a great idea. I'd love to hear about them."

"Well, you can forget it."

"Come on, tell me about where you grew up."

She shook her head, unbelieving. "You really want to hear this now?"

"It'll make the time pass faster; you'll see."

"All right, here it is: installment six in the life of Zooey Krause, as related to a lunatic in a graveyard during the thirtieth year of her life. If it hadn't been for the unlikely setting, she would never have revealed the truth."

"It has a snappy beginning…"

"Stop interrupting. I grew up in the tiny town of Smithfield, North Carolina, where nobody has any money and nobody hopes to ever see any money. Its great claim to fame is the Ava Gardner Museum. She was born near there, believe it or not. Visitors can also enjoy the annual Smithfield Ham and Yam Festival. We lived out among hills and forests, and I grew up as the older of two sisters. A lower-middle-class family; my dad worked at the post office. My mother used to clean people's homes until my dad died when I was ten.

"After he died, my mother basically cracked up. In fact, she cracked up the same day he died; she couldn't even go to the funeral. She lay in bed, crying, out of her mind and talking to God. They locked her up in the psych ward of a state hospital for a few months, and my sister Mary Ann and I stayed with neighbors until she finally came back home. They'd given her medications to control the hallucinations, but she only pretended to take them half the time and she was still crazy as a loon. She'd always been considered a little odd, but now she was almost helpless; I practically had to spoon-feed her. She walked around the house in a flannel bathrobe all day, smoking cigarettes and dropping ashes everywhere. She'd drop the butts and squash them out on the rug, if she remembered to put them out at all. The amazing thing is that she never burned down the house. I used to worry about it all the time while I was at school."

Zooey attacked the dirt with a fury. "Needless to say, I didn't do well at school. Sometimes I'd come home, and she'd be locked in her room, crying uncontrollably. I'd feel bad and shout her name, trying to get her to open the door. Sometimes she'd answer and let me in; other times, we wouldn't see her until the next morning at breakfast when she'd wander around the kitchen talking to herself, wearing too much makeup and looking like a zombie from lack of sleep. Then there were periods when she had great energy—she'd take us on picnics, cook us big meals, wash all our clothes and even iron our sheets and underwear.

"So I practically raised my sister, Mary Ann, by myself.

"Mary Ann's been gone for years, God knows where. Just like me, she left home as soon as she graduated from high school. Only she was smarter. She left for California, and I hope that maybe she did something good out there. Now me, I got married during the summer I turned eighteen. Alec had just graduated from Salem College with a degree in business, and gotten a job as a salesman at a new car lot in Chapel Hill, North Carolina, a college town. Boy, I thought I'd died and gone to heaven when he asked me to marry him; he was my salvation from that hell I grew up in. Mary Ann was old enough to handle herself by that time."

"Where did you get money during all those years?"

"My dad's pension. And both my sister and I had part-time jobs during the school year, and full-time jobs for the summers. We didn't mind; it was a way to get out of the house. But the best way to get out of the house was by marrying Alec, five years older than me. Later, he moved from cars to selling computer software and was quite successful. Anyway, it was the one escape nobody could blame me for."

Zooey laughed, shaking her head. "You should have seen me as a housewife, Virgil. I tried so hard at first to fit in. I had this *Good Housekeeping* idea about housewives, expecting that Alec and I would move into a perfect small house in a perfect neighborhood, and the neighbors would all welcome us. I'd have a close friend next door and we'd have coffee and go shopping together, and I could buy stylish clothes for a change.

"But it didn't work out that way at all. The truth was, I felt like a complete country bumpkin among all the intellectual professor-and student-types who lived near us in Chapel Hill. We had a tiny, crummy house, and the neighbors weren't friendly at all. I eventually made friends with a Japanese woman named Miko, but she moved away.

"I tried very hard to fit in. I fixed my hair and cleaned the house and tried cooking from recipes I read in magazines. They were usually disasters.

"Alec wanted children very badly, so after five years, after he'd changed jobs and was making more money and we'd moved into a nicer house, I got pregnant."

She felt the weight of anger and guilt press down on her.

"You don't like kids?" Virgil asked.

"You don't understand. I didn't get married because I loved Alec, and I wasn't a housewife because that's the job I wanted to do. It bored me. But I did desperately want a child. It was an ache. I wanted to become the happy mother that I'd never had. While I was pregnant, I did all the right things—ate the right foods, gave up smoking, took up knitting—the full disaster. And then, well along in the pregnancy, I miscarried.

"I was overcome with guilt and despair. It felt like it was somehow my fault. Alec said I had failed at even the most basic thing a woman can do. I believed him and hated myself. Alec was constantly rubbing it in my face. Me being small made him feel big.

"I'd had one solid chance to build a good life for myself, after I'd graduated from high school and was finally free to do what I wanted, but I'd blown it. By this time, I was getting suicidal.

"So I got a job as a clerk in a furniture warehouse. I ended up having an affair with a guy who worked there, and he was the one who convinced me that I deserved the chance to make the second half of my life better than the first. So, finally, I asked Alec for a divorce.

"At first, he was great about it; a martyr, in fact. I thought he was just being practical, recognizing that our marriage had been miserable for years. He was great to everyone. He was great to his friends and my mother. He was great to strangers on the street. Hell, I didn't have any friends, or he would have been great to them. In short, he was the worst son of a bitch imaginable. He drove the nail in every chance he got. There were screaming matches, and sometimes he hit me. I thought I deserved it.

"Finally, I got the courage to leave. The anger and the despair at losing the child I wanted so much were more than I could take. It was either leave him or kill myself. So I came to Washington. It was far away from all I had been and known. When I went to the train station, I saw Washington on the destinations board and decided since I knew nothing about the city and no one there, it was the perfect place to start my life over, if I could.

"Alec called me. Then my mother started calling, ranting over the phone, so I got an unlisted phone number. Alec finally flew to Washington and sat outside my rooming house all night, so I had to lay low for days until he finally gave up and flew back to North Carolina.

"Then I met Mark, and he set me up in the detective business. He saved my life…" She paused a moment, catching her breath. "I got a new apartment under a false name. The family writes to me at the office, but they don't know where I live. That's what makes my privacy so important. Sometimes I call them, but then I always wind up feeling like hell afterwards.

"I feel worst about losing the baby. I'd even picked out a name. Ralph, believe it or not. I don't know why. I just liked it. He'd be five now. I wanted him, and I feel that I failed him, but he'd probably have wound up a basket-case with a mother like me. I'd undoubtedly have taken out my whole rotten youth on him. Anyway, Alec isn't such a bad guy. He's making a lot of money now and must have a girlfriend, since he doesn't write those terrible letters to me anymore. I'm sure that he still hates me, though."

She leaned on her shovel. "So say what you want. Say that I'm scared and running away. Maybe what I've just said explains everything, or maybe it doesn't explain anything at all. It's not that 'discovering myself' bit at all. I'm always myself, always have been, and I'll never be anyone else. I just decided, for better or worse, to live with me. And I never want to explain myself to anything or to anyone ever again."

She paused. "And goddam you, Virgil, for making me do it."

She hadn't told this story to anyone, and she couldn't explain why she'd spoken about it now. She knew Virgil wanted to hug her, but he held back, and she was grateful for that. His restraint felt better than any embrace.

She began digging again, deep in thought, while Virgil took a rest. Finally, he said, "I hope you don't think you're the first."

"How's that?"

"Oh, you know—guilt about failed marriages, losing a kid. I got married young too, at nineteen, to my high school sweetheart. It's that deep-down romantic soul you were noticing earlier, the one that's lurking underneath this cold exterior."

"You can't fool me. You're a cream puff, Fitts."

"How kind of you to notice. Anyway, my wife was everything you weren't. She loved keeping house and raising children—and God, was she a terrific cook. We had three wonderful kids together, beautiful girls. I loved my wife and our marriage was good for many years… I just assumed that it would last forever, 'til death do us part,' like you say in the marriage vows. I honestly thought we were happy together.

"But looking back on it, I was a bastard from the start. I was just getting established in the newspaper business, and I started going out on all-night assignments without calling home. After a while, my wife stopped expecting me to come home for dinner or any other meal. And when I was home, I drank a lot. And I fooled around with other women sometimes, though it didn't mean anything important to me; it was always my wife that I loved. And besides, I always assumed that she got a little on the side too. My mistake. It seemed like we had an unspoken agreement about the things we wanted—I had my freedom; she had the house and the kids. She didn't seem unhappy.

"Then one day, right out of the blue, she told me she'd fallen in love with a lawyer whose wife had died. He made more money than I did, had a bigger house and…well, that's unfair. She said she wanted a full-time husband and father, someone who'd take her out to dinner sometimes and take the kids to the movies on the weekends. She said she knew I'd been fooling around and she was tired of my drinking. She wanted a divorce and she wanted the kids too. She wanted to start her life all over.

"My mistake was in fighting her. Suddenly, after all those years of being absent, I couldn't stand the idea of losing my daughters. My wife and her husband-to-be planned on moving to Texas, and I feared I'd never see my daughters again. So I fought back, and that was at the same time that Francesca's face got messed up. I helped run the Orchid while she was in the hospital and then later, while her face healed, I helped keep things going. It took a long time before Francesca got her strength back, and by that time, the private investigator my wife had hired had taken plenty of pictures of me going in and out of the Orchid every day for a month.

"I never should have fought for the kids, of course, and in the end, I didn't even win visitation rights. Francesca returned my help by getting me through that defeat."

He sighed, digging again. "My ex lives somewhere in Texas, now remarried. Like I said, I was gone a lot, drunk a lot, and I don't blame her. But I still feel bad. End of story."

They dug silently for another hour before they struck the coffin. Zooey was exhausted and soaked with sweat; she shone the flashlight as Virgil uncovered the pinewood box. She wasn't surprised at the coffin's simplicity. It fit with what she knew of Mary.

"Zooey, climb up and throw me the crowbar," Virgil said wearily. "Then climb back down here with the Geiger counter and we'll check Mary out before I call Durnam."

She scrambled up the steep hole and handed down the crowbar. Virgil wedged the tool under the coffin lid, and pushed heavily without result. She climbed carefully down to join him, set the Geiger counter down and added her weight to his on the crowbar. After a minute of tugging, the lid loosened; Virgil reached down to pull at it and the lid splintered. At that moment, Zooey looked up; a silhouette had appeared like a shadow above them—an ugly shadow that traced the form of Karl Neibor. Virgil saw him too.

"Shit..." Virgil mumbled. "We're finished."

"Put that crowbar down and climb out, Fitts, or I shoot Zooey."

Zooey crouched fearfully at the bottom of the hole, hoping that Durnam had already seen this complication and was calling the cops. She didn't relish explaining all this to the police, but it was better than dying in this hole next to Mary Gentry. Virgil climbed up quickly.

"Stand still, Fitts. This game is over. In the meantime, both of you—fill up this hole."

"Hey, Neibor, you shitfaced scumbag," said Zooey as she tossed her shovel up to Virgil.

Snarling, Neibor turned to look down at her as Virgil caught the handle and swung the shovel hard across Neibor's head. The blow sent him and his gun to the ground with a heavy thump.

Counting on Virgil to take care of Neibor, Zooey tugged again at the coffin lid. It opened easily now, and the decomposing corpse that faced her was her first look at Mary Gentry, the lovely young woman whom Karl Neibor and Vlad Sakorski had murdered. Zooey found herself remembering the photograph she'd seen in Mary's apartment. Feeling an unexpected wave of nausea, she steeled herself enough to grab the Geiger counter and pass it slowly over the pitiful form.

"Virgil!" she shouted. "I can't believe it! The Geiger counter doesn't register anything! Nothing!"

Zooey swept the body again.

"Virgil?" she shouted again and looked up. Neibor stirred but Virgil was nowhere in sight. "Virgil!"

In a panic, she dropped the Geiger counter and clambered out of the hole. She'd almost reached the top when she stepped on a loose clod of dirt and fell backward.

A flashlight beam illuminated her face from above, and a new voice shouted down to her: "Okay, you, get your butt out of that hole! Now!"

The police, she thought. Numbed by this latest dead end, she climbed out into a pair of handcuffs. The cop who held the light recognized her.

"Zooey Krause, so it's you? What the hell are you doing? Getting into some weird cult stuff? Or is there some cheating dead husband down there you're getting the dirt on?" He chuckled at his own joke.

A back-up cop grabbed the groggy Karl Neibor by the arm and pulled him up, but not before Neibor had surreptitiously picked up and pocketed his gun.

"Okay, Lieutenant Drummer," said Zooey. "I know how this looks. But I have a very good reason for digging up this body. Ask Karl Neibor, this goon beside me."

"That's enough," Drummer said. "We'll talk about it back at the station."

"No, that's not enough! Arrest this man too! I'm not going to move until you…"

"Shut up!" Drummer jerked her cuffs toward the squad car. "Vinny, find out who this guy is."

Durnam materialized out of the darkness as Vinny, the back-up cop, began chatting with Neibor, who persuasively argued that he was a neighbor who'd heard strange digging sounds in the graveyard. Durnam pointed a finger at Neibor.

"Officer, I know who this man is, and he doesn't live in the neighborhood. If you'll take a minute and search him, you'll find his name is Karl Neibor, if that rings a bell. And I doubt that gun he's carrying is registered."

"What kind of circus is this?" the cop said. "Who the hell are you?"

Durnam lost patience. "Wallace Durnam is who the hell I am, and I'm the editor of the *Washington Spirit*, if you know how to read. I'm the one who called the station and tipped you off."

"And you're another neighbor who just happened to notice a digging sound?"

"I came here to cover a story, you ass. Now search Neibor before he decides to shoot you and run off."

The cop glared at Durnam, but he reached for the bulge in Neibor's breast suit pocket and pulled out a gun as Lieutenant Drummer reappeared.

"What's the problem now?" he asked Vinny.

"The problem is cops, when they're too stupid to conduct a simple search," Durnam spat out. "Your buddy here was going to let a prominent local thug waltz away carrying a sidearm like Cinderella at the ball."

226

"Christ," said Drummer. "Durnam, that you? I've got no patience with weirdoes, detectives and newspaper editors built like grand pianos. We're all taking a trip to the station."

Durnam eyed him, standing his ground. "You going to arrest the man who tipped you off? Me, Wallace Durnam, editor-in-chief of the *Washington Spirit*?"

Drummer grabbed his arm. "I don't give a damn if you're Jesus Christ. Come on, or do I have to hire a tow truck to haul you off, you fat bastard?"

Durnam and Neibor joined Zooey in the back of the squad car, all of them handcuffed. Another car was called for the well-lubed Gillie.

Virgil had apparently slipped away in the dark.

27

The next morning, Zooey sat slumped on a chair in the visiting room of the downtown city jail. Her clothes were stained and filthy, she reeked of stale sweat and she felt like she'd really hit rock bottom this time. She pictured Joe reading the newspaper this morning and wondered whether her ghoulish grave-digging adventure would rate a front-page headline. Probably not, but he'd be sure to hear about it soon. Any attempt to dig up Mary Gentry's body wouldn't go unnoticed too long at the Blackstone Plant. She knew she'd be charged with a felony; she wondered how the safe, conventional side of Joe's character would feel about that. She couldn't visualize him visiting a girlfriend in jail, especially after she'd promised him that she'd quit the case.

The police had questioned her for over an hour the night before. It was hard to remember all the things they'd asked about as she sat in a stubborn fury, angry at herself, feeling that anything she said would only add to her troubles. A young attorney, apparently sent by Francesca, had mysteriously appeared during the proceedings and advised her not to talk. But then he'd sat quietly in the corner while the police asked repeatedly why she'd been digging up Mary Gentry's grave. They kept asking whether she'd been hired to investigate Mary's death and, if so, who had hired her. They wanted to know what she'd found out. When she'd refused to answer their questions, they threatened her with an additional charge of obstructing justice. Since Mary's case was officially closed, Zooey thought they might be bluffing, although the young attorney looked pensive.

She was also angry with the police, who'd been happy with the official verdict on Mary's death and the explosion at Mark's Bar. And then there was Virgil, the deserter, who'd run from the graveyard, leaving her to take the rap. The most charitable interpretation was that he figured he'd be more use to her if he wasn't locked up. But even if he did plan to help, what could he do for her now? The possibility that Mary had been poisoned had been their last chance to get the evidence to force a federal investigation into the case.

Zooey faced a smeared window through which she saw another yellowed room with a far door. After five minutes, the door opened and, to Zooey's surprise, a woman with a heavily bandaged face walked in. Zooey had expected her lawyer, but this was Francesca. She wore a tightly cut chocolate-brown business suit with a silky white blouse and a fat string of pearls. It was the first time Zooey had seen her in street clothes, and her broad, six-foot frame was even more imposing in ordinary dress with two-inch high-heeled pumps.

"Dear Zooey," Francesca said as she gracefully slid into the stained plastic chair on the opposite side of the glass barrier, "I'm so sorry that this had to happen."

"So am I." Zooey shook her head ruefully. "Well, I've sure made a mess of this."

"The situation is not as bad as it seems. I have been in contact with our journalist friend."

Zooey found it irritating, as usual, that she couldn't search Francesca's face for the meaning behind those words. "What happened to him last night?"

"Let's not talk about it now, as we don't know who may be listening. But there is reason to hope that this matter will soon be resolved."

Zooey nodded slowly, unable to hope for much. "So what else is happening?" she said casually. "Where's my lawyer?"

"Talking to court officials. He assures me that you will be released in a couple of hours. You need bail money, and Wallace Durnam has already guaranteed the necessary funds."

"Durnam? Are you kidding? I'm surprised he hasn't hired a lawyer to make sure I never get out of here. He must have been thrilled to spend the night in jail."

"Wallace and your friend Gillie were released last night after questioning."

"And how about Karl Neibor?"

"He, too, was released."

"That's great. Maybe he'll be waiting for me back at my apartment."

"He knows where you live?"

"By now, he might." A horrible thought suddenly occurred to her. "Has anyone talked to Jason?"

"Yes, he's safe, and no one visited your office. He was advised to take your important files and move into a hotel for the time being."

"Good. Thanks for calling him."

"It was the least I could do."

"I'm sure my detective days are over; if I'm convicted of a felony, they'll take my license away."

"Wallace Durnam might consider employing you. I believe that he rather enjoyed his little adventure last night. Probably it reminded him of his own early days as a reporter, and he does believe that you may have uncovered something important."

Another reference to possible good news. It was heartening.

"This is the first time I've seen you in public without your mask," Zooey said.

"I do find it useful, sometimes, not to identify myself in that way."

"But you still don't avoid the stares."

"No. But I have become accustomed to the stares; they have not bothered me for years. It is a matter of acceptance."

"I hope you won't mind if I say this, but I sometimes think that you accept too much, Francesca. For instance, that you let someone like Karl Neibor totally escape responsibility for what he did to you."

"My only regret is that Virgil feels it necessary to avenge Karl's actions. Besides, the total escape you describe for Karl Neibor does not exist."

Francesca shook her head. "My life is stalked by shadows. Karl Neibor is an ugly man, but I knew what kind of man he was, and I wasn't forced to take him into my life. I can't escape this knowledge, which makes me more accepting of what happened. What transpired wasn't just bad luck. Surely you don't believe that women choose their unions with men by chance?"

Zooey smiled. "There's always ignorance, remember." She recognized some truth in Francesca's philosophical outlook, which was a mixture of resignation and hard-headedness, with a hint of the mystic thrown in for color. "But wasn't it an accident that you met me?"

"No, I don't think so."

"So you believe in fate?"

"I've never believed in sheer coincidence. It wasn't an accident that we met. Perhaps, if I am deserving of vengeance, which I doubt, you and Virgil will provide it. In any case, I admire your courage."

This was a surprise, and a compliment that Zooey doubted she deserved. But she welcomed the warmth she heard in Francesca's voice. Then a guard in the corner behind Francesca signaled that their time was up.

"Thanks for everything," Zooey said, rising from her chair.

"I'll talk to you again in a couple of hours. Please try and relax until then."

"I will."

"We're doing everything possible to expedite your release."

"I know." Zooey smiled, touching her hand to the glass. "Take care of yourself too, Francesca."

She turned to follow the guard back to her cell, where she found a new roommate named Hannah Banana, a name, she said, she had chosen for herself. Hannah was short and plump with pale eyes and a soft baby face framed by long brown hair. Zooey guessed her age to be twenty, at most. They sat side by side on the lower bunkbed in their cell while Hannah played with her hair.

"Hannah, ya see, is like hands. So my name is like hands. Hands do things. I mean, what would we be without hands?"

"Cripples with handicapped parking permits?"

"Far out!"

Zooey moved away from her on the bed.

"And banana is a fruit. Fruits are good, you know."

"That makes you a kind of handy fruit," Zooey said drily.

"Yes, yes, a handy fruit! Awesome!"

Zooey shook her head. "Why were you arrested?"

"I guess they're charging me with attempted murder. I'm not sure. I belong to this behavioral institute and spiritual community called Vishnu Doothas, and like we had to punish this lawyer who kept kidnapping our members to take them back to their parents. So, me and this other guy, we put a tarantula in this lawyer's mailbox. God, it was hard getting hold of that spider; like, we had to order it from a special pet store and it cost twenty dollars or something like that.

"So we put the tarantula in his mailbox after the mail was delivered, and then we hid in the bushes to see what would happen. The lawyer came outside to get the mail, and it was creepy. I mean, you could picture that big, hairy spider crawling around inside the mailbox. We were so scared, but it was hard not to laugh. So he put his hand in the mailbox and he screamed and then, like, it bit him and all, but he didn't die. I guess tarantulas aren't all that poisonous. Who knew?"

"Hey, you don't have any of those bugs with you?" asked Zooey. The image of an enormous spider in their cell made her arm hairs stand straight up.

"No, like they took it away when I got arrested."

Afterwards, Zooey discreetly lifted the blanket on her upper bunk to check for bugs and then shook out her shoes. Hannah sang a country western music tune so loud it made Zooey cringe, but she didn't complain, thinking Hannah might be sensitive to criticism. Zooey lay on the top bunk counting cracks in the ceiling and idly digesting country western sentiment when the television mounted on the wall outside their cell announced a breaking news story.

"Another drone mounted attack, this time over Detroit," announced an anchor Zooey believed to be Chris Wallace on FOX News. "Three drones were seen simultaneously exploding above the city, causing mass panic. It is not yet known if these drones were carrying radioactive contaminants, as in Baltimore, but authorities are taking no chances. The group calling itself the *White Power Second Amendment Nationalists Front* has issued another David Duke video claiming responsibility, and promising more attacks against what Duke called African American and white traitor communities across the country. He further claimed the attack to be in retaliation for the recent murder of seven more white policemen, this time in Dallas, Texas, by a group claiming to be allied with Louis Farrakhan's *Black Lives Matter Armed Brigade*. Duke demanded that the government deport all African Americans to whatever, and I quote, 'shithole countries,' they came from. Whites, he said, will reclaim this nation, which will be purged of the inferior races that have corrupted and polluted what Duke calls 'our shinning white heritage.'"

As Zooey watched, the screen switched to scenes of mass panic in downtown Detroit. Just as in Baltimore, traffic was gridlocked. On camera, a white mob pulled a black family from a car and beat them. Police were nowhere to be seen.

"The President has tweeted his support for every loyal patriot to take to the streets in protest. Terrorists, he said, deserve swift community justice. There is no time for politically correct delay."

Wallace shook his head. "Neighborhoods in Chicago, Baltimore and other cities have become war zones. The National Guard, already active in several cities, is being deployed to additional locations. Several guardsmen have been killed in riots by snipers."

Hannah had stopped singing and was listening too. "Hey, dig that. I wish I was black. Then I could have shot those cops who arrested me."

"Opportunity lost," sighed Zooey.

The newscast continued: "The FBI continues its manhunt for both Duke and Farrakhan, with many in Congress sharply critical of their inability to bring both of these men into custody. Top officials also refused to comment today on the rumor that Washington, D.C., is the next city targeted by Duke's group. It is believed that the CIA is also now engaged in the manhunt, and is leading the investigation to determine the source of the radioactive material used in the Baltimore and Detroit attacks, although easily obtained radioactive medical waste is suspected. More on this breaking story in just a minute."

A thought struck Zooey so hard that she jumped in her bunk, startling Hannah. Sources of nuclear waste? She slapped the bunk in frustration. Why didn't she pay more attention to the news? "I can't believe it," she said out loud.

"What?"

"I can't believe I'm so stupid." She shook her head.

"Stupid?"

"It's nothing, Hannah, just something I thought of while I was lying here. Something I should have realized long before this."

An hour later, a guard came to Zooey's cell and released her. As she left the jail, she found Rashid Sharps and Virgil Fitts waiting for her outside.

28

"Your first trip to the joint, Miz Krause?" said Rashid, chuckling, as he settled Zooey next to Virgil in the back seat of his limo. Virgil squeezed her shoulders.

"Yeah, and I never want another. My cellmate was a young religious freak who thought her father was a reincarnation of a heretic seventeenth-century philosopher by the name of Spinoza. She also thought that all good human beings are the descendants of fruit, and that the dark side of the moon is inhabited by demons she called the 'green cheesies.'"

"I'm sorry about running off last night," said Virgil as he loosened his grip on Zooey's shoulders. "But when I saw the cops arrive, I thought our only chance was for me to slip away."

"Drop dead."

Virgil sighed. "What good would it have been for both of us to be locked up? We got you out, didn't we?"

Zooey shrugged. "I don't have to be happy about it, since the whole thing was your idea in the first place. I panicked when I was down in that stupid hole alone, keeping company with Mary's body, and then Neibor started to come around again. Fortunately, that's when Lieutenant Drummer yelled down at me."

"I should have hit Neibor harder, but it all happened so fast. Quick work of yours, by the way, throwing me that shovel."

"Desperation is the mother of invention." Zooey looked out the window. "By the way, where are we going?"

"To the Orchid. Francesca's guys are keeping watch outside. We'll be safe."

"I thought we weren't going to let her get more deeply involved. Karl Neibor must really be gunning for us now, after he caught us digging up Mary."

"Yeah, but you haven't heard the good news. Durnam thinks we have enough information to write a story for tomorrow's paper. He thinks we can raise enough questions to get the public riled up, and that's the first step in forcing a new investigation."

"What?" said Zooey. "What evidence do we have, Virgil?"

"We have enough to get people wondering what's going on at the Blackstone Plant. And, by the way, you'd better think twice about your friend Joe Quigley. I found out early this morning that the Geiger counter he gave us doesn't work."

"How do you know that?"

"Let me tell you what happened, from the beginning. After the cops showed up last night, I did hear you shout that Mary was not radioactive. I ran like hell and climbed over the fence that circles the cemetery. I kept running until I hit the first nearby houses, and then hid in some neighbor's garage for half the night. When I couldn't hear anyone searching for me at about five o'clock in the morning, I got up and, deciding to take a chance, I crawled back over the fence into the cemetery and crept around until I found Mary's grave. It was nearly dawn by then, and I figured that once it got light, I'd lose any chance to check Mary out before the cops had her buried again. There was only the night watchman at the gravesite, still drunk as a skunk and passed out from sharing that bottle with Gillie."

"Virgil, you're lucky the police didn't post a guard."

"Yeah, well, the main thing was to finish the job and to work quickly, before the night watchman came to. I wanted to double check the results you got, just to be sure that, in the confusion of Neibor and the police arriving, you didn't do something wrong with the Geiger counter."

"Yeah," said Zooey. "How could a dumb broad manage to use a radiation detector correctly? You're such a jackass, you know."

Virgil sighed. "It's hard to be a hero around here. But no, you didn't use it incorrectly, as I'll explain in a moment.

"Anyway, the detector you used was gone, so I crawled back into the grave and opened Mary's coffin. Mary was wearing white lacy gloves, so I grabbed one of those and got the hell out of there and over the fence again. I walked through blocks of suburban backyards until I reached a small shopping mall where I could safely hail a cab. I knocked on Francesca's door at about seven o'clock this morning."

"And the glove was radioactive?"

"Right!" Virgil laughed and shook her shoulders. "Francesca arranged to get hold of another Geiger counter this morning, and when we put the glove next to it, it rattled like a china closet in an earthquake."

Rashid parked in front of the smoke-colored glass of the Orchid's entrance.

"Come on, let's go inside," Virgil said. "We've got a lot of work to do tonight."

Zooey thought again about Joe; had he already found out about her arrest? He must have been wondering why she hadn't called him. She also realized that she might have to tell Virgil more about him if he continued to question the seemingly broken Geiger counter.

"What about my apartment?" she asked.

"What do you mean?" He waved Zooey through the front door. An attendant, a delicately featured woman with long black hair, stood just inside the door in a coral-colored kimono. She smiled warmly at Zooey.

"I was wondering if Neibor had searched it, looking for the evidence he thinks we have."

"I don't know. To tell you the truth, I haven't had time to think about it. You know we called Jason?"

"Francesca told me."

"Good. Ah, here she is."

Francesca glided toward them in her mask and kimono.

"Thanks for springing me," said Zooey.

"I was glad to be able to help. Now, come and have something to eat. We have much to discuss."

Zooey nodded, falling in step behind her and said, "I have some big news for you too."

They walked left past the star-shaped fountain to the end of the hall, where Francesca unlocked the door to a dining/living room. Zooey wondered if this room was part of Francesca's private living quarters. The couches and chairs were covered with soft velvet the color of polished brass; the carpet and walls were the same warm tone. It was another hexagonal windowless chamber; Zooey pictured these rooms lined up side by side like combs in a beehive. This one had a door in the rear, and a yellow lacquer table laid with two place settings of bronze-colored china. A tiny Asian woman wearing an apron over her kimono opened the door behind the table.

"Zooey," said Francesca, "would you like to wash and change clothes? The cook will show you the bathroom. I hung a fresh kimono just inside the door."

"I'd love it." She followed the cook to a small bathroom behind the dining room. Francesca was right; she couldn't remember when she'd craved a shower more intensely. She stripped, throwing her filthy clothes in a heap outside the bathroom door, and turned on the water. A fresh bar of black soap on the rack inside the shower stall smelled of sandalwood and was imprinted with the words "Made in Mysore, India." She lost herself in its exotic scent as she rubbed all traces of grime and sweat from her skin and hair.

When her bruised and stitched-up body was clean again, she turned off the water and wrapped herself in a thick towel. She stared into the mirror as she worked the snarls out of her tangled hair. Traces of strain showed under her eyes; her face looked gaunt and tired. "Krause, you're a mess," she said out loud.

A tiny bottle next to the sink held a delicate jasmine perfume; she smoothed tiny drops of it on her breasts, neck and arms before slipping into the loose black kimono that Francesca had left for her. She tied the kimono loosely with a red satin sash and slid into a pair of red sandals.

She returned to a heavy silence in the living room; Virgil and Francesca both turned to stare at her.

"Nice to see you again," Zooey said.

"Sit down," Francesca said, motioning to a chair. Virgil poured her a glass of wine from a decanter on the table. Zooey took it, and then sank back into the surprisingly soft chair cushions.

"It's my turn to give you something to think about," Zooey said. "I was watching the jail's television this afternoon and heard a report about David Duke's group that attacked Baltimore and now Detroit."

"Then you haven't heard. Just minutes ago, drones also exploded over San Francisco," said Francesca. "Duke again took responsibility, saying that, you'll excuse the language, liberal faggots and traitors to the white race were getting what they deserved."

Zooey shook her head. "Some people seem to think Washington, D.C., is next. Evidently, the CIA is investigating the source of the contaminants used in the attacks. The trouble is that I never pay attention to current events. Mark was the one who handled that department.

"This is the disturbing thing: that all this time we've been trying to figure out what's going wrong at a nuclear plant and wondering what the hell these Blackstone Plant officials are trying to cover up, while the CIA has been wondering where this white nationalist terror group got the radioactive material for their attacks. They think it's discarded medical waste, but what if it's not?"

Virgil's nodded. "Goddam it, Zooey, maybe…"

"But Mary was suspicious about the safety regulations at the Blackstone Plant," said Francesca. "And now you're talking about an illegal sale of radioactive material. Could Karl Neibor possibly be involved in a transaction with terrorists?"

"Possibly him, but he would need cooperation with someone in the plant." Zooey said.

"I don't believe that Karl is bright or well-connected enough to handle such a transaction," said Francesca.

"But he was the one who killed Mary," Zooey said.

"If such a deal happened," Virgil said, "then any attention Mary drew to the plant would be a threat. But if Karl Neibor got rid of Mary, the problem was solved."

"So Karl Neibor got rid of Mary, and that was the end of any unwanted investigation," said Zooey.

Virgil nodded, thinking. "Right. Maybe Neibor was just involved in pension fund fraud, and the Blackstone officials who made the deal to sell radioactive waste could have simply used Neibor as a tool to silence Mary by convincing Neibor that Mary Gentry had enough proof to expose Neibor's pension fund activities. That allowed those involved at Blackstone to stay clear of the matter.

"I also think somebody was using Neibor as a tool," Virgil continued. "What I couldn't figure out was why, after Mary was dead, someone at the plant was so desperate to get rid of Zooey and me that they'd use a hitman like Vlad Sakorski for the job."

"Because whoever is behind this illegal sale of waste knew that Mary found out about it," Zooey said. "Someone was afraid that we'd make a connection between her death and these attacks."

Francesca shook her head. "Eventually," she said, "the CIA or FBI will discover the source of the radioactive material used in these attacks. I cannot believe wealthy executives at the Blackstone Plant would take such risks, when the odds of being found out are almost certain. Even if there was a such a deal, given the risks involved, how could Mary have found out about it?"

"She could have been searching through someone's files," Zooey said, "looking for proof of her suspicions about Union and Corporate collusion to cut safety corners. Maybe she accidentally stumbled across something important about the handling of waste at the plant. What do you think, Virgil?"

He nodded. "Possible, I guess, though it's hard to understand how she could just stumble on to such information. But if she did..."

"And she called to tell you about it..." Zooey said.

"Her phone might have been tapped," Francesca said.

"And if someone at the plant found out what she'd discovered," Virgil said, "they had an easy way of stopping her. All they had to do was tell Neibor that Mary had just stolen incriminating documents that were very damaging to him, and that she was carrying them to a newspaper reporter for immediate publication. Wouldn't Karl want to stop her any way he could? So he okayed Sakorski to run down her car."

They considered the idea while the cook served their meal.

"Let me get this idea straight," Virgil said. "Someone sold nuclear plant waste. It wouldn't take more than a maybe ten or twenty kilos for these terrorists to weaponize using drones. The sale itself could have occurred as early as last year, but when Mary started drawing media attention to the Blackstone Plant this spring, someone got upset."

"Neibor worked with Sakorski, but so did someone else, someone who ordered Sakorski to kill both of us," Zooey said.

241

"Damn, I've been an idiot," Virgil said. He poured himself another glass of wine.

"I don't know," said Francesca. "What proof do you have to back up these allegations?"

"That brings us back to our new evidence about Mary," Zooey said. "And another puzzle: why was she poisoned?"

"Maybe they'd planned to kill her that way all along; to make it look like she'd accidently poisoned herself by poking around in unauthorized areas," Virgil said, jumping up and pacing. "I remember a similar case forty years ago, a case where a woman was supposedly killed bringing evidence against a nuclear plant to a newspaper reporter, and that her friends claimed that she'd been poisoned for the same reasons. This might have been true in Mary's case, as well. But if she'd found out about the nuclear waste deal, the plant officials would've had to get rid of her immediately. They couldn't wait for a slower death by radiation poisoning."

"That's possible," Zooey said. "But what if Francesca is right, and this is just another one of our wild conspiracy theories, Virgil? I'm already up on a felony charge."

Virgil grimaced. "It's a chance we've got to take, because our only defense is to justify our actions with what we've found out. If the FBI identifies and stops this terrorist group by following our leads, I don't think we'll have too much to worry about."

Francesca stood up. "For your sake, I hope you're right. But again, I cannot imagine Blackstone executives taking such foolish risks. What could they possibly receive in return to make such a gamble worthwhile?"

"We've got to get to work right away," Virgil said. "We've got to write a concise story detailing what we've found out and what we suspect, and it's got to be finished in a couple of hours. Durnam's holding a blank space on the front page, but he'll need the finished copy by midnight, at the latest.

After that, it's out of our hands."

"But maybe we should call someone now," Zooey said. "If we're right, the authorities might be able to go to Blackstone and find the people responsible."

"Who'd believe us," said Virgil, "if we called the FBI with a story like this now?"

"Oh, I think they would listen," Francesca said, "considering all the lives at stake. Why would an article in tomorrow's paper give your theories more validity?"

"Because we'd be putting our story before the public," Virgil said, "and that will make a cover-up impossible. Covering-up will be the Blackstone group's first move."

"No," said Francesca. "By printing a newspaper article, you will give the Blackstone culprits advance warning to take action."

"That's a chance we'll have to take," Virgil said. "But we can't spend any more time discussing it. We've got a deadline to meet if we want the story to feature in tomorrow's paper."

"Virgil, you're not listening to me," Francesca said. "By printing the story, you'll give advance warning to the instigators. They'll have more time to possibly leave the country."

"But Francesca, it's been two weeks since the attack on Baltimore. I'll bet the CIA and the FBI are besieged with calls from psychos, seers, psychics, cultists and God knows who else. A million false leads to sniff out."

Francesca shrugged. "I'm afraid that your instincts as a journalist are interfering with your responsibility to the people who live in the city targeted for the next attack, possibly our city. Many lives are at stake, if you're right. Your ideas are a bit far-fetched, but I must insist that you give them to the authorities. Even if they will not listen…"

"I agree," Zooey said.

Virgil threw up his arms. "All right, all right, I give up. We'll have it both ways. Francesca, you call anyone you like and give them the news. Meanwhile, we'll write the story. Okay?"

"I will provide a computer if you'd like to start writing. Wait here."

Francesca left the room

"Are we out of our minds, Virgil?" said Zooey.

"It's possible. But there is one more thing we should discuss."

"Shoot."

"Why did Joe Quigley give you a dummy Geiger counter? If I hadn't escaped from the police, we'd have thought that Mary's body wasn't poisoned. According to the people I spoke to, the level I detected indicated that she would've been dead in a few days. We'd have missed out on this evidence entirely, and then where would we be?"

"I confess I don't understand this thing about the Geiger counter. I waved it over Mary's body, and the needle registered a normal level."

"I'm not saying that the Geiger counter was broken, but it was rigged, somehow. It wouldn't register the body as being radioactive."

"Look, you don't have to worry about Joe Quigley. I've gotten to know him pretty well, and he's straight."

"Are you sure?"

"Very sure."

"I thought you didn't know him very well."

"We've talked a few times." A thought occurred to Zooey. "You don't think, Virgil, that someone at the plant knows about the connection between Joe and me? That would put Joe in danger."

"You mean someone might know that Joe hired you?"

"It's possible. He got the Geiger counter for me from work; I told him that I needed it for another case, something I was going to use as a prop for an investigation of a phony insurance claim."

244

"If you said you only needed a prop, then maybe he didn't think you needed a live machine?"

"That's possible." She thought about it. "But what if someone had been listening in on our call…"

"They might have made sure that he gave you a rigged machine?" Virgil finished.

"God, I hate to think it's true. Neibor might be after Joe right now! I've got to call him!"

"Hold on, Zooey. We should talk about this."

"No time! I've already lost Mark because of this."

The thought of a repetition of the explosion at Mark's Bar made her panic; she punched out Joe's telephone number on her cellphone. There was no signal.

"Damn, Virgil. What are we going to do? I'd better go to his house right away!"

"We'll send Rashid and Francesca's bodyguard," Virgil said. "They'll be able to handle any trouble better than we could. Anyway, I need you to help me write this story. When it's published tomorrow, we'll be safe."

"Safe?"

"Because everything we know will be public knowledge, and any attempt to quiet us will be pointless. Finishing this story will help all of us."

"All right," Zooey grudgingly agreed. But she couldn't quiet the fear that she'd succeeded in getting another close friend into serious trouble.

29

They finished the story just before midnight, and Virgil lay down on Francesca's couch, immediately falling asleep. He'd attacked the story with the intensity of an aging athlete, as if he thought that this one winning performance would justify a career of near-misses. Zooey had never fully realized the importance of this case to Virgil. She supposed that Durnam might not have taken Virgil back at the *Spirit* if he hadn't promised such a spectacular story. Virgil, maybe, had saved himself a job.

He'd written the story as straight first-person: "the kind of sensational style people expect from the *Spirit*, but it's the best way I know how to tell a story," was how he'd described it. He beat the computer keys with two fingers, and chain-smoked Camels while he brooded over the facts. Zooey worked out their movements on a calendar while they argued over details and suppositions. But their different, irreconcilable opinions over matters of style and substance only slowed them down, and in the end, Virgil consulted her only when his memory failed. Reading the final manuscript, Zooey recognized a forceful tone that Virgil's usual reports for the *Spirit* had lacked.

In the bathroom, she changed back into her own clothes, which had reappeared clean and pressed.

There had been no word from Joe.

Zooey had called his house frequently, but received no answer. Rashid called her to say he had found no one at home, and nothing was amiss. His absence worried Zooey, and she decided to visit his house again when Rashid returned from an errand Francesca had sent him on. Virgil would never miss her.

Zooey sipped a cup of strong coffee, thinking about Virgil as she watched him sleep, when a knock at the door informed her that Rashid and the car were ready outside. She scribbled a note for Virgil and then walked out to the Orchid lobby, where she spotted Francesca and a French maid attendant greeting a group of affluent, middle-aged drunks. Their Southern accents identified them as out-of-towners; they looked like the soggy remnants of a high-rollers lobbyist convention.

Francesca saw Zooey try to sneak through the lobby without being noticed, and excused herself from the cheerful group surrounding her. "Zooey, I hear that you requested the limousine. Where are you going?"

"I won't be long, Francesca. I've got to run over to Joe Quigley's house and find out if everything's all right there. Using one of your phones, Joe hasn't answered his phone all evening, and I'm worried."

"That's not a good idea. I hired extra security for the Orchid tonight, so you will be safe here. Why not wait until morning?"

"Please don't argue with me, Francesca. I've already succeeded in putting one friend of mine in danger, and I've got no intention of letting this one wander around without a warning. If I find him, maybe I could bring him back here."

The loud, laughing group of men behind them grew impatient; one of them called out Francesca's name.

"I haven't got time to argue with you," Francesca said irritably. "Do as you please. I know you will, anyway."

"I'm sorry." Zooey backed away toward the door. "But this is something I've got to do."

"Do what you must."

Francesca wheeled in the opposite direction, joining the crowd of men again with a gay voice. "Gentlemen, if you'll follow me? We've got quite a party planned." The men catcalled and whistled, following ecstatically behind Francesca.

"What a lousy job she has," Zooey muttered as she headed out to the limo at the curb. It was easy to see that Francesca was getting tired and impatient. She'd been keeping long hours, helping Zooey and Virgil in addition to running the Orchid. Zooey hoped that this sleepless ordeal would end with the publication of the newspaper article they'd written.

It was one o'clock in the morning and Rashid, too, looked weary. "Rashid," she said, climbing into the back seat of the car, "when was the last time you got a decent night's sleep?"

"Caught a cat nap this afternoon," Rashid answered. "Where to?"

"Back to Joe Quigley's house."

He pulled out from the curb.

"You're sure you didn't see anything suspicious when you visited his house before? No one watching the place, no cars loitering outside?"

"If they was a flea on the sidewalk, I would've spotted them. But I didn't see nothing."

"Good job." She leaned back. "And stop at an all-night store on the way, all right? I need a bite to eat."

"I know a place around the corner." Rashid swung around in front of a tiny, brightly-lit 24/7 delicatessen. "What do you want? I'll go in."

Having a chauffeur was a luxury she could learn to live with. "Cream cheese bagel."

He jumped out and looked up and down the empty street. Zooey looked too. There was nobody outside but a street dog, sniffing the curb for a tasty bit of garbage.

In a moment, Rashid returned. "Here you go." Rashid opened the car door and handed her a small paper bag.

"Thanks."

They headed south down Fremont Avenue in another endless zigzag route across the city. But with the streets so empty, any attempt to follow them would have been obvious. As they neared their destination, Zooey asked, "Why don't you park down the block from Joe's house? That way, we can sneak up on the place to see if anyone's watching."

"Figured on that," said Rashid as he pulled into the first empty space he found down the block.

But there was nothing awry, except for the fact that Joe still wasn't home. Zooey had no idea where he might be, and she didn't know where else to look for him or who else to call. The front door of his house was locked; one light burned in the hallway beyond, but the rest of the house was dark. The doorway and windows were protected with locked iron grates, so a break-in would be difficult. The only thing left was to write him a note. She reached into her bag for a pen and paper.

"Joe: I need to talk to you. Please call me as soon as you get home, no matter what time it is. Love, Z."

She stuck the note through the iron grate and under the door. Returning to the car, she said, "Rashid, I'm sorry for making you drive all over the city, but I'd like for us to go back to my apartment. I want to know if Karl Neibor searched it."

When they were stopped at a red light, Rashid turned around to look at her. "I wouldn't be surprised to find some guys waiting for you there."

"I know. But let's have a look anyway."

Rashid sighed. "Whatever you say."

The car turned left on Calvert Street and sped up until they neared Zooey's apartment.

"Park this heap about three blocks away in an alley," Zooey said. "Then you can escort me up the back stairs of my apartment house."

Rashid swung right and parked illegally in an alley behind a clump of trees.

"This is as hidden as we're gonna get in this neighborhood," he said. "Get out and I'll lock the doors."

The back entrance to Zooey's apartment house faced an alley three blocks further down. They walked quickly toward it, Rashid's head rotating slowly from side to side like a bird; his left hand caressed him Magnum under the blazer he always wore. Zooey knew she ought to be scared, but she felt a defiant calm settle in as she unlocked the steel fire door at the back of her apartment house.

Rashid climbed the stairs in front of her, a smooth and soundless crawl that was remarkable considering his damaged knee. When Zooey examined the lock on her front door for signs of forced entry, she found nothing. She took out her keys and unlocked it. Rashid motioned her silently to stand aside, and then he threw the door open, entering aggressively with his gun drawn.

Zooey pulled out her gun and peeked in behind him.

She saw nothing unusual in the hallway, so they crept into the kitchen. Seeing no sign of a search, they walked through to the living room at the end of the hall. The apartment appeared untouched. A familiar half-full glass of brandy sat next to her laptop on her desk. She stepped cautiously toward it.

"I'll check the bedroom. You stay back here." Rashid stalked through each room, pulling open closet doors and peering under the bed. Nothing. Meanwhile, Zooey checked her books and papers. A thin film of dust covered everything and it was obvious that nothing had been disturbed.

"It's clean, Rashid."

He limped back into the living room. "Then let's go back to the Orchid."

"No, I want to change clothes and lie down for a while. Why don't you take the limo back to the Orchid and grab some sleep? I think we both could use some of that."

"Miz Darmini gave strict instructions to stick with you."

"I know, but in a few hours the morning papers will be out and Neibor won't dare touch me. He'll be the first one arrested if anything happens. Besides, I don't think he really knows where I live, or he would have come here."

Rashid shrugged, looking tired. "It's your choice. But keep this front door bolted, your gun close and call the Orchid when you're ready to leave."

"Sure thing."

He walked to the front door and opened it, looking both ways down the hall before pulling the door shut behind him. Zooey heard him wait until she fixed the bolt; then the sound of his curious gait faded as he rambled off down the hallway toward the back stairs. She leaned up against the door for a minute, and then walked back to the living room. She picked up the snifter of leftover brandy as she dialed Joe's house again. Her cellphone finally had a signal. No answer. She couldn't imagine where he was. Walking into the bedroom, she pulled off her clothes and stretched out full-length on the bed. At least no one had sacked her apartment; she was asleep before another thought had time to form.

She had been sleeping soundly for several hours when she awoke with a start. It was her cellphone, and she was fuzzily aware that it had been ringing for several minutes from the living room. She jumped up and made a clumsy dash for the phone, banging her knee on a chair, but she was too late. The caller had given up.

She dragged herself to the bathroom and rinsed her face, arms and chest with cold water. She felt dull and stunned; there were leftover pieces of dream interrupting her thoughts. Something about a train rushing by, and she'd been yelling at a man above the roar. There was a strange awareness, too, of a huge, skinny dog.

The phone rang again, and it was Virgil. "Zooey! Are you all right? Your voice sounds funny."

"I just woke up, but sure, I'm fine. Did you call a few minutes ago?"

"Yeah. Where were you, in the shower?"

"You woke me up, but I couldn't get to the phone in time."

He insisted that she return to the Orchid. "Rashid should be back here any minute, and I'll send him for you. Did you know he was watching your house until about fifteen minutes ago?"

"Oh, no. I should have guessed. What time is it, anyway?"

"Eight thirty-five."

"Poor Rashid. If I'd thought of it, he could have slept on the couch in here."

"Francesca would have killed him if he'd come back here without you."

"I should have known. I owe him an apology."

They talked for a few more minutes, Virgil telling her that the *Spirit* was already on the newsstands. Then Zooey hung up the phone and wandered into the kitchen. She'd just buttered a piece of toast when she remembered again about Joe. She went back to the living room and called his house; no answer. Then she tried the Blackstone Plant again, and this time finally got an answer. "Quigley here."

"Joe, it's Zooey."

"At last! I've been wondering what happened to you. I was worried."

"I've been worried about you too. I called your house all night; I even left a note under your front door. Didn't you find it?"

"No, I worked all night at the plant. I left a message yesterday with the answering machine at your office—I don't suppose you checked it."

"No, dammit, I didn't. Well, anyway, I suppose you know about my arrest by now."

"I read about it in the *Spirit*."

"I'm sure you wonder what the hell I was doing."

"I was shocked. I thought you said you were quitting the case."

"I know. Are you angry about it?"

A silence. "Not so much now. But I was angry when I first heard about it. Maybe I was wrong to ask you to change your life because of me. But the point is, you said that you'd quit the case, and I believed what you said. I felt relieved that I didn't have to worry about your connection with the Blackstone Plant, and I gave you that Geiger counter trusting that you only needed it as a prop for a demonstration. I never could have guessed that you and Virgil were going to dig up Mary's grave. Maybe the fact of it doesn't matter so much now... but I believed you."

"I know."

"But let's forget about it for right now. I was more worried than anything else. I also called the police department several times, but the bastards there wouldn't tell me a thing. You're out of jail now? Everything's okay?"

"Everything's fine. I was worried about you."

"Why worry about me?"

"It's a long story and I don't want to explain it over the phone... but you remember what happened to my partner, Mark? I was afraid something like that would happen to you."

"That makes two of us. So what are we going to do?"

"It's already done. I don't suppose you've read the paper this morning?"

"Haven't had time."

"You'll understand when you read the headlines. Virgil and I wrote a front-page article last night. It's an exposé of the Blackstone Plant."

"What are you talking about?"

"Mary's body was radioactive, Joe. Virgil had guessed it, so we had to dig her body up to see if it was true. There's something very spooky going on at that plant, Joe. I wish you weren't working there now."

"This is my last day, Zooey, and then I'm out. I'm done with them. I was just finishing up last-minute details last night." Joe sounded worried. "But what's this about Mary being radioactive? I don't understand."

"We don't understand it either, but at least I'm really off the case now. We're hoping that somebody more powerful than us will investigate her death; the authorities have known about our discoveries since last night."

"Really? Who did you call?"

"It was Francesca who called. I'm not sure who she contacted, but with her connections, I'm sure she got hold of someone important. The wheels should roll very rapidly from now on."

"I'm sure they will. That's good." The buzzer rang from downstairs; Rashid had arrived. "Joe, can I call you later? I'm going over to the Orchid."

"I'll call you there. I've got a few last meetings to attend here. Okay?"

"You sure you're not mad at me?"

"Why should I be?"

"I'm going to get the Blackstone Plant in a lot of trouble."

"Hey, I don't care about that anymore. A bunch of morons run it anyway; they don't give a damn about the project. I can't get out of here soon enough."

The buzzer rang again. "Well, I've got to go, Joe. I'll talk to you soon."

She hung up and ran into the bedroom to put on fresh clothes. Her short conversation with Joe had been a relief; not only was he safe, but she'd been nervous about his reaction to her arrest. Not to mention the fact that she had continued to work on the case when she'd told him she was done.

30

Zooey returned to the Orchid with Rashid, who seemed to watch the rear-view mirror more closely than the road ahead as they crept down Beach Drive in heavy traffic. Every other car looked ready to explode from the heat, and an overheated blue Plymouth blocked traffic in the opposite direction. They turned left to Q Street and sped up until they neared the Orchid.

"Rashid, if you don't get some sleep, I'll ask Francesca to fire you. You're falling asleep at the wheel."

Rashid smiled drowsily as he dropped her off at the curb.

"Don't worry, Miz Krause. Miz Darmini already told me."

It was a now-familiar kimono-clad hostess who greeted Zooey at the Orchid door. "Virgil is in Francesca's room down the hall," she said.

"Thanks. I know where that is."

When she pushed open the unlocked door to Francesca's living room, Zooey spotted Virgil still asleep on Francesca's couch. Francesca, her mask off, sat opposite him at her dining room table, drinking tea. Zooey entered the room and stopped, then held her breath and steeled herself as Francesca turned toward her; it was only the second time she'd seen the grotesque scaring that savaged Francesca's face. The two women stared at one another for a quiet moment, then Zooey strolled over to pat Francesca's shoulder.

"Have some tea?" Francesca asked.

"Sure."

Francesca poured.

"I see that Virgil's still catching up on his beauty rest," Zooey said. "I couldn't sleep for more than a few hours myself."

"And I have been up all night." Francesca paused. "You shouldn't have gone back to your apartment. But it hardly matters now. I heard this morning that Karl Neibor left the country yesterday."

"Free as a bird? I suppose he'll surface again as a plantation owner in Paraguay, with a name like Carlos Neiboros. But at least he won't bother you again."

Francesca fingered her mask, which stood propped up on the chair beside her. "Yet I have been sitting here thinking about how uneasy I feel. I am not convinced that you and Virgil have discovered the cause of the events surrounding the death of Mary Gentry. Your reasoning has produced a good solution, yes, and one which fits the facts, but it is not the only possible solution and I doubt that it is the correct solution."

"It doesn't matter, though, does it?" said Zooey. "It's out of our hands. What agency did you notify last night?"

"I used my professional contacts with certain public officials; they will ensure that the FBI and CIA take your story seriously."

"So the truth will surface. We don't have to worry."

Francesca's manner was unusually subdued. "I suppose."

Zooey stirred a drop of cream into her tea. "Okay, Francesca. What's bothering you?"

Francesca leaned back and crossed her arms on her chest. "The faulty Geiger counter. And the fact that I don't know how or why Karl Neibor was able to find you at the graveyard the other night. I am certain that nobody followed your car because, unknown to Virgil, I had hired a security man to follow your car at a distance. You wouldn't have seen his car; I'd ordered this man to stay out of sight, but to watch for anyone who might follow you. At the cemetery, he was told to hide near the front gates and to watch for any unexpected events where he might assist. His call was the reason the police arrived so promptly after Karl Neibor's arrival; Wallace Durnam's call to the police station wasn't placed until five minutes later."

"I wondered how the police appeared so quickly."

"My security man saw Karl Neibor arrive. Karl hadn't been following you and Virgil; otherwise, he would have interrupted your work earlier. No, he arrived at a high speed and hurriedly parked his car outside the cemetery gates. He walked toward the location of Mary Gentry's grave as if he knew exactly what he was doing, and exactly what to expect. That's when my security man called the police."

"It looks like you saved our skins again, and I didn't even know it. Thanks."

"I did what I felt necessary." Francesca's voice was tired. "Still, I cannot understand how Karl Neibor knew where to find you. I believe that someone must have told him of your plans."

"No one could have known. I didn't tell anyone."

"What about this man who gave you the Geiger counter?"

Zooey shook her head. "I didn't tell him what we were going to do."

"But a knowledgeable man might have guessed."

Zooey sipped her tea. "Maybe you should be the detective. So you're wondering whether the man—Joe Quigley—who gave me the Geiger counter, figured out what we'd use it for and then tipped off Karl Neibor as to where we'd be that night."

"Something like that," Francesca said with a nod, watching Zooey.

"That would be fine, except for a bit of personal bias on my part. I think I'm falling in love with this man, Joe Quigley, and that's a highly unusual occurrence for me. If I believed that Joe Quigley tipped Neibor off, I'd have to admit that he's completely fooled me. Besides, he hasn't asked for information about our investigation; he hasn't even wanted to talk much about it. I originally agreed to have dinner with him in order to find out if he knew anything that might interest us. In the end, he was trying to convince me to drop this case. And he's quitting his job at the Blackstone Plant; in fact, this is his last day. I talked to him this morning."

"Did you ask why he'd given you a faulty Geiger counter?"

"I told him it was for a prop for a presentation I wanted to give, so he thought it didn't have to work. I was afraid he'd be upset because I'd dug up the grave of his former girlfriend. Not to mention I was afraid of how he'd feel about me being arrested, and that I was writing an article that condemned the management at the Blackstone Plant. All of this was after I'd told him that I'd given the case up. But he was really calm about it all. I don't think we have to worry about him."

Francesca nodded. "Perhaps you are right, Zooey." She stood and refastened the mask around her face, then straightened the folds in her kimono. "I will return in a few minutes."

She disappeared through the door at the rear of the room.

Zooey decided that it was time to wake up Virgil. She crossed the room and shook his shoulder gently. When he didn't stir, she slapped his cheek lightly.

He opened his eyes and stared at her abstractly, still dreaming and not seeing her. Then he blinked and closed his eyes again, drifting back into sleep.

I suppose there's no reason to wake him, Zooey thought. She'd just wanted someone to talk to. It was hard to figure out what she was going to do all day at the Orchid. She hadn't seen any shelves of detective fiction that could help pass the time. The only reason for staying at all was to reassure Francesca, who seemed convinced that Zooey was still in danger.

Francesca returned carrying a small television. "Virgil's favorite toy," she said, placing it on a table next to Zooey.

"Thanks," Zooey said as Francesca left. She turned the television on to a breaking news story from CNN.

"More news out of Detroit," announced Chris Cuomo. "The three drones that exploded over the city are confirmed to have been carrying radioactive material. It has spread throughout the downtown area."

On the television screen, figures in HAZMAT suits walked down empty streets waving radiation detectors over the sidewalks.

"Two people are hospitalized from breathing radioactive dust," Cuomo continued. "But twenty-two were killed and dozens hospitalized in the panic to evacuate the city. Apparently, terrified drivers just drove through crowds of people. In fact, in Baltimore, Detroit and San Francisco, the majority of casualties from these attacks are the result of mass panic.

"Another video from David Duke, the purported leader of the group calling itself the *White Power Second Amendment Nationalists*, has warned of new attacks.

"Supporters of Duke are organizing marches across the Midwest, many participants openly displaying military-grade assault weapons. Counter-protesters have been beaten by some of the marchers."

A video box showed several counter-protesters savagely beaten as enraged bystanders cheered the assailants.

"Elsewhere, we have reports of cars packed with heavily armed whites cruising African American communities, randomly firing on black men they find on the street. In one case in Chicago, blacks returned fire, killing all four white men in the SUV they were driving.

"A new video counter-posting by Louis Farrakhan of the *Black Lives Matter Armed Brigade* threatens new attacks on white communities. Already more than a dozen white police officers have been shot by snipers in several neighborhoods across America."

Chris Cuomo was abruptly interrupted on the television by a local news bulletin and an announcer Zooey didn't recognize.

"Breaking local news. The National Terrorism Advisory System has just raised the national threat level to 'Imminent.' Drone attacks are already reported in another fifteen major metropolitan cities and more are expected. Washington, D.C., is included in this alert. We repeat, Washington is at risk of attack. If an imminent attack is confirmed, you are advised to stay in your homes and seal all windows and doors to prevent possibly contaminated dust from entering. Duct tape is advised for use in this regard. Stay tuned for additional information. We repeat, drone attacks are already reported in twelve major metropolitan centers and Washington is included in this alert. A statement from the mayor is expected momentarily, and rumors from sources at the Mayor's Office report the possibility that a plan to evacuate the city of Washington will be announced at any moment."

Zooey's cellphone beeped, making her jump. She picked up the phone to hear Joe's voice on the other end of the line.

"Zooey?"

"Joe! I just heard about these ongoing drone attacks."

"I've heard about it too. But that isn't what I called you about. I've just had a long talk with my lawyer downtown, and I've discovered some very important information that concerns your investigation. I need to see you here, alone, and right away. I have only a minute to talk, so listen carefully. Meet me at the Karney Law Firm; that's on the seventh floor at 1545 Wisconsin Avenue Northwest. That's in Georgetown. Got it?"

"Why do I have to come alone? Are you in some kind of trouble?"

"No, but please do as I ask, Zooey, and you'll find all your questions answered."

"But is this about the Blackstone Plant?"

"Don't worry about that now."

She hesitated. "I'm afraid I don't understand."

"Zooey, please trust me. I don't have time to explain right now on the phone. I'll meet you at the Karney office as soon as possible, all right? It's important that you hurry."

She hesitated again. "All right, I'll be there."

He hung up.

Zooey opened the door to find Francesca in the hallway.

"Zooey," she said, "can I have something brought to your room?"

Zooey shook her head. "I've got to be going."

"I don't think that's wise. Why do you need to leave?"

"I need to meet someone."

Francesca paused, obviously considering Zooey from behind her mask. "Would this have something to do with your new friend, Joseph?"

Zooey rolled her eyes. "Nothing gets by you, Francesca."

"Let me send Rashid with you."

"No, I need to go alone. I promised."

"Why alone?"

"Francesca, I just do. Please leave it at that. It's between Joe and me."

"Where are you going?"

"I don't want to say."

"I insist."

Zooey had never heard Francesca sound so firm, and she frowned. "Why does it matter?"

"I need to know where you are, in case."

"In case of what?" Zooey said, exasperated.

"I don't like what is happening and who it is happening to. I want to know where to find you, in case."

Turning to the large man standing discreetly behind her, she said, "So you are going nowhere unless you tell me where it is you intend to go. I can have Charles here see that you do not leave unless you tell me."

Zooey sighed, and gave her the address.

31

Zooey decided to hail a cab. Despite his denial, she feared Joe was in trouble. Karl Neibor might have been out of the country, but he wasn't the only person to worry about; it was possible that the CIA or FBI had already started investigating the Blackstone Plant. She didn't want to believe it, but she had to consider the possibility that Joe's visit to his lawyer meant that he was worried about how an investigation might drag him in. Or he might have been bringing a wrongful death suit against the company because he'd discovered how Mary was exposed to toxic levels of radiation.

After several full cabs passed, an empty cab raced toward her at a high speed. Certain the driver didn't intend to stop, Zooey desperately jumped into the street to flag it down. The cab screeched to a halt inches from her, the driver yelling, "Get in, goddammit!"

She ran to open the cab door, flinging herself into the rear seat. "1545 Wisconsin Avenue Northwest," she said.

"Are you crazy, jumping in front of me?" the cabbie snarled. He did a quick U-turn and barreled off as horns honked all around.

"I was afraid you wouldn't stop, and this is an emergency."

"Hell, all Washington's gonna be an emergency in about ten minutes. Everybody's gonna head out 'cause of the possibility of one of them damn drone attacks."

"What have you heard?"

"The count's up to fifteen cities with them drone explosions, is what I hear."

His radio blared a local reporter interviewing random members of a crowd in front of the Mayor's Office.

"The Mayor hasn't made a decision yet to evacuate Washington?" said Zooey.

"Nope. But this city ain't gonna wait for no word. I'm headed out myself, and I'll take any paying customer along, if you're interested."

"Thanks, but no. I've got an emergency visit to make."

Five minutes later, the driver slammed on his brakes at Wisconsin Avenue so hard Zooey flew like a doll against the front seat.

"Here we are," he said. "No charge. I'm headed right out, and if I was you, I'd do the same. Ain't gonna be safe here."

"Thanks. Good luck." Zooey pushed out of the cab and spotted the building, a tall brick office complex. She bolted across the street and then down sidewalks crowded with people all talking about leaving the city. The edgy fear she heard in their voices was contagious; it made Zooey's heart pound faster, wondering what would happen when this city's anxiety turned to panic.

In the lawyer's building, the descending elevators were jammed with people leaving work. She was the only person who entered an elevator car going up.

The sign on the door at the end of the hall on the seventh floor read "Karney Law Firm" in raised gold letters.

Zooey pulled the door open slowly. Peering cautiously inside, she saw a corner office with a stunning view of the city and the Potomac River in the distance. In the center of the room stood an elephantine oak desk, and Joe stood beside it, securing the top of a large canvas sack.

He looked up with his familiar confident smile. She was surprised to see him wearing blue jeans, a brown suede jacket and a casual blue shirt rather than his standard business attire.

"Zooey! Thank God you came quickly. We've got to get out of Washington right now."

"I'm afraid you're right. Everyone's leaving this building and the crowds outside look scared."

"You came alone?"

"Yes, but where's your lawyer?"

"He left a few minutes ago."

"Why didn't you want anyone to come with me?"

"We're going to escape this little disaster together. And alone. I have plans."

A television in the corner of the room flashed a breaking news bulletin, a local announcer reading from a paper he clutched. "It is just reported that three drones have exploded over metropolitan Washington. I repeat, three drones were observed simultaneously exploding over Washington. The National Terrorism Advisory System advises people not to panic, but to stay in their homes. Close your windows and seal your doors. Collect water in your bathtubs immediately. Washington is now the nineteenth city to be attacked today. We will provide further instructions shortly."

"Oh, crap," said Zooey, watching crowds below her window scattering in all directions. She turned back to Joe, standing next to her.

"It'll be a madhouse for a while," he said. "We've got to get going."

"Where do you plan to go?"

"There's a boat waiting for us at the Georgetown Ferry Terminal on the Potomac River. It'll take us out to the Chesapeake Bay and then to a ship waiting for us off the coast."

"We're leaving the country?"

"There's not much time to explain right now, Zooey, but we're going to Russia. I can't wait for you to see the house

265

they've built for us. It's on a beautiful lake far up in the mountains. I'll show you the photos when there's time. It will feel a bit isolated at first, I'm sure, but the peace and quiet will be a relief after all this. But don't worry about getting stuck there permanently, because that's just our first stop. After we get things set up, and the heat is off, we can travel just about anywhere we like on the new identities they'll give us.

"Joe, I swear to God, I don't understand a word you're saying."

"The payoff." He smiled, patting the canvas bag beside him. "There's twenty million dollars in currency, diamonds and four gold bars in this bag. Zooey, we're free! Take a look if you don't believe me. On the other hand, I don't want to untie the sack again. There's plenty of time for you to luxuriate in the sight of it later, when we're safely out of Washington."

The sack was fitted with straps, which Joe pulled to shorten.

Zooey felt like she'd just stepped into quick-drying cement. "You've got the payoff for attacking Baltimore and Detroit and all those other cities?"

"Don't be silly. I hatched a plan with Herb Calcut, the Human Resources Director at the Blackstone Plant, to sell radioactive waste. It was his plan, really. Frankly, I didn't care who bought it. You can't imagine how much the Russians and ISIS were willing to pay for stuff we just wanted to bury. I had no idea how they planned to use it.

"It all was Herb's idea. The Russians contacted him, but he didn't have any way to get his hands on what they wanted. He came to me because he knew I did, and he knew how unhappy I had become with the job."

"You sold nuclear waste to ISIS? They paid with Russian money? It wasn't to some white nationalist group?"

"No, no, no. The white and black nationalist things are a red herring. And all those videos? Herb told me the Russians kidnapped and disappeared both Duke and Farrakhan. All those videos were high-tech fakes created by the Russians. Apparently, they are so good at it you can't tell the real thing from the fakes."

Joe shifted the weight of the pack on his back experimentally. "Man, this is heavy."

"You sold them nuclear waste?" Zooey repeated, stunned.

Joe sighed. "Don't be naïve, Zooey. As a president of ours said, this country has killed lots of people too. What difference does it make what SOB or what country is in charge? It's always the same old shit. In the end, only a fool doesn't look out for himself in this crumby world."

"But why did the Russians want nuclear waste from Blackstone?"

Joe chuckled. "It had to be from an American source. They knew the CIA or FBI would be able to identify the source of any foreign material. It had to come from here."

A horrific thought occurred on Zooey. "You killed Mary Gentry?"

Joe frowned at her, surprised. "Of course not! I loved her! She was pregnant with my child, for God's sake. Herb Calcut and Neibor did that, with help from Herb's Russian partners. I would never have hurt Mary any more than I could hurt you. I want us to be together. We have enough to live like royalty for the rest of our lives."

He patted the sack.

"But Joe, what about all the people in the cities attacked?"

Joe shrugged. "Nobody was actually killed by nuclear waste. It's the panic that kills. People are stupid, panicky and violent, Zooey. You know that. A drowning man will always pull down the person next to him."

"But people lost their homes and their lives…"

"Zooey, I didn't plan or have anything to do with the attacks. I didn't know what they'd do with the waste, and I didn't care, frankly. Why should we?

"Herb told me ISIS didn't have the money or expertise to carry this off. The Russians backed it, funded it and advised them, but they didn't want to get caught attacking the U.S., so they seized on ISIS as a front. The drones are all from ISIS. You can buy the damn things anywhere now.

"The whole plan was to spark a civil war in the United States, and it looks like it's working. But even if the truth comes out, who does the U.S. attack? ISIS isn't a country. You've got to give the Russians credit, it's pretty damn clever."

"So that's the connection to Sakorski and the Russian mob. But what about Herb Calcut? Is he going with you?"

"He's in the hospital and won't last a day. I slipped toxic levels of nuclear waste into a lunch we shared to celebrate our success. It was my revenge for what he did to Mary and my baby, the stupid son of a bitch. He thought I was a fool to trust her, but he shouldn't have gone around me with Neibor to have her killed. So he's paying for it with his life, and we get to keep all the payoff ourselves."

He patted the sack on his back.

"Look, there'll be plenty of time to explain, but we need to leave, and I mean leave now. I know we haven't known each other long, but I want you to come with me.

"I always thought you were someone who wanted a better chance in life, and I'm offering it to you. I used to have ideals too, about nuclear power and justice and all the rest of that crap. But I learned the corruption in this country is a terminal cancer; besides, what the Russians and ISIS did was just taking advantage of how divided this country has become. I didn't plan it—I just fell into it—someone was going to sell them this stuff, so why don't we reap the benefit and let the idiots in this country fight it out? They deserve each other. I give up on America. In fact, the whole world is going to hell in a handbasket, but we can leave all that behind. What matters is us."

"Jesus, Mark's dead, Mary and her baby are dead—and you're going to take this fortune and go to Russia?"

"Pay attention," Joe said, exasperated. "All I did was make a sale. I had nothing to do with the rest of it. My involvement was a business transaction, pure and simple. Supply and demand. Capitalism at its finest. We, you and I, have the means to live well for the rest of our lives. We deserve it.

"Zooey, let's just think about us and to hell with the rest of them. This planet could be paradise, but look at how we've fucked it up. 'Greed is good' is the modern religion, Zooey. Let's take care of ourselves."

"Just tell me one thing," Zooey said. "What about the explosion that killed Mark?"

"That was the Russians and ISIS. I had nothing to do with that. They saw you snooping around as a threat. You can blame Herb Calcut for that. You weren't going to stop investigating. The Russians and ISIS thought you needed to be taken care of."

"So they tried to kill me, and instead killed Mark."

"They did it, not me. I would never have agreed to that."

"Then why did you hire me in the first place?"

Adjusting the shoulder straps tighter on the pack again, he said, "I wanted to find out what Fitts knew. I needed to know if Mary's death was really an accident or if the Russians were behind it. Calcut was lying to me, and I needed to know if Calcut killed my child. I didn't know you wouldn't drop the case after you found him. Please, there isn't time. We need to leave. I want you to come with me. Let's spend the rest of our lives figuring out how to spend this fortune."

"And Mary found out what was going on?"

Joe heaved a frustrated sigh. "First, she found out Karl Neibor had an illegal connection with her Union's pension fund. Then, she not only made her way into a top security area, but she managed to open Herb's private safe. How she managed it, I'll never know, but she discovered evidence of the sale of the nuclear waste. She saw mentions of my name in connection with it, and thought that I'd been involved with the plan from the beginning. So she wrote a weird note, like, 'Finally I understand,' put it on my desk, and then she called Virgil Fitts. Snooping around got her accidently poisoned, and then calling Virgil was what got her killed. What I found out later was that her little detective work at the plant was immediately discovered by Herb. An hour later, she was dead. Like I said, Herb convinced Karl Neibor she was a threat, and Karl used Sakorski to get rid of her. If she had just left well enough alone, none of it would have happened."

Zooey nodded, finally understanding what she'd seen at Mary's apartment. "Mary thought you'd betrayed her. That's why she sacked her own apartment..."

"Herb also found out that I gave you the Geiger counter, and figured out why you wanted it. I didn't tell him that you'd be in the cemetery, believe me. But the bastard is cooked. So you have your revenge."

He grabbed and kissed her; she knew she should have pulled away, but recognized that she had to play along. She forced herself to kiss him back, hard.

"I'll come with you," she said. "You're right about everything."

She hated herself for saying it.

Joe looked down at her and caressed her face. "I'm glad, Zooey. I think we'll be very happy. I'm glad you chose us."

Joe straightened and walked to the window. "Oh my God!" he whispered.

She stood beside him and gasped. Every street was jammed with cars, and desperate waves of people flooded the sidewalks.

"We haven't got much time," Joe said. "Let's go."

They ran through the office and into the hallway.

Zooey formed a quick plan; she could pull out her gun and stop Joe as they tried to fight the crowds on their way to the Georgetown ferry. She wondered how Joe planned to get there; she doubted he'd be able to carry the heavy sack that far.

When they'd gone halfway down the corridor, a bell rang announcing the arrival of one of the six elevators. Joe pushed the down button calling for another lift, and then he withdrew a gun from his coat pocket. To Zooey's horror, when the doors opened Rashid stepped out. Virgil, Francesca and her bodyguard followed behind.

"Get back!" Zooey shrieked.

The elevator next to Joe opened as Joe fired his gun three times. Everyone threw themselves to the ground, including Zooey, who pulled out her own weapon as Joe stepped into the elevator. She fired but missed.

Joe's face registered shock and rage, realizing that he'd been betrayed. He cursed as the elevator doors closed.

Virgil was the first to leap to his feet, and he ran to Francesca. Zooey joined him.

"Virgil, oh God! Francesca's shot!" A red stain spread across her shoulder

"I will be all right," said Francesca, clutching her shoulder.

Rashid was down too, with a slight wound to the head.

The bodyguard knelt next to him but Rashid waved him to Francesca.

"What are you doing here?" said Zooey to Virgil.

"After the drone attack, Francesca decided we should leave Washington, and we came to get you."

Zooey decided Virgil and the bodyguard could take care of Rashid and Francesca, but there was only one thing she wanted now, and she wanted it like religion: to stop Joe.

She jumped up and ran for the open elevator.

Zooey fell flat on her face, with Virgil wrapped around her legs.

"What the hell are you doing?" she screamed.

Virgil struggled to grab Zooey's shoulders, and he shook her. "Zooey, what the hell are *you* doing?"

"Look, I don't have time to explain it, but you stay behind and call the authorities. I'm going to stop Joe! He's behind this, and he's headed to the Georgetown Ferry Terminal."

Virgil looked stunned. His hands fell and he shook his head. Zooey jumped up and ran into the elevator.

She reached the front lobby just in time to see Joe take off up the sidewalk on a motorcycle.

32

Zooey found gridlocked cars, honking, many piled high with valuables strapped to their roofs. Zooey saw several drivers locked in fistfights.

Joe, she realized, had planned well. Not only did the chaos cover his escape, but she couldn't fire her gun in his direction because of the crowds. She wanted to cry but was too angry to manage it.

Virgil ran past her, spotting a motorcycle that slowly forced its way toward them through the crowds jammed on the sidewalk. The driver was a young man wearing a red helmet.

Virgil jumped forward, grabbed the bike and dragged the kid off of it, his fists flailing desperately. Zooey raced over and pointed her gun in his face. He went pale.

"Sorry, kid," Zooey said, "but this is a real emergency. We've got to take your bike."

"No!" the kid shouted, but he was afraid to move.

Virgil climbed on the bike and turned to Zooey. "Jump on!"

As Zooey climbed on behind him, a bullet zinged past her. She turned to see a man in a car down the street shooting at them.

"Goddam looters!" he screamed.

Zooey fired a shot above his head, and he ducked for cover. Virgil gunned the bike, and they flew after Joe.

Zooey squeezed her left arm tighter around Virgil's waist as he swerved to avoid a child on the sidewalk; the bike struck a garbage can and sent it crashing into a car behind them. Zooey turned to see the passengers giving them the finger, shouting profanities. They rounded a corner to see Joe clear a packed intersection at the end of the next block and disappear down the sidewalk and out of sight. Virgil raced down the boulevard and tried to pick his way between honking cars when he reached the intersection. The drivers, seeing their efforts, perversely closed up the gaps.

"This is an emergency! Let us through!" yelled Zooey.

The driver of a Cadillac, an old man in a cowboy hat, yelled, "What makes you bikers so special? You can wait with the rest of us!"

Zooey raised her gun. "Move your damn car or I'll cap your ass!"

He threw it into reverse so hard that he smacked into the car behind him, those drivers screaming bloody murder.

Virgil shouted repeatedly, "We've got to get through," but it was Zooey's gun that cleared a path. Again, she heard gunfire from somewhere down the street behind them, and a bullet shattered the back window of the car in front of them.

"Jesus Christ! Virgil, get us out of here before someone gets killed!" She fired across the tops of the cars as Virgil sped after Joe, until she found the gun was empty. She dropped the empty clip and slid in the spare from her holster.

"He's headed in an opposite direction from everyone else!" yelled Virgil.

"He's headed for the ferry terminal on the Potomac River! Everyone else it trying to get to the highway out of town."

Up ahead, Joe was caught in the middle of another closed intersection, and they were half a block away when he saw them. He fired his gun twice above his head, and the cars surrounding him backed away, letting him through. Virgil hit the opening at full tilt, but Zooey found she still couldn't get a clear shot at Joe.

As they began closing on him, Joe aimed and fired in their direction, nearly losing control of his bike.

The bullet struck Virgil in the left arm. He faltered, and they fell behind.

"I'm hit! Grab the clutch," he called. "If I yell 'clutch,' pull it in so I can shift! Don't try to steer."

She grabbed the clutch handle and tried to keep an aim on Joe with her other hand.

Ahead of them, Joe approached another intersection jammed solid. He threw down the bike and jumped up on the hood of the nearest car, leaping from car to car across the intersection. Zooey slid off the bike and stood up, firing twice as he widened the distance between them. She missed, and Joe disappeared on the other side of the intersection.

"Damn!" She climbed on the nearest hood and followed Joe's route, hopping from car to car past rows of hostile and frightened faces.

"Hey! What the hell're you doing? You're denting my car!"

She jumped from the last car as Joe turned and fired at her again. She heard glass shatter and turned to see he'd hit the storefront at her back.

Suddenly, Virgil was beside her, and she pushed him down for cover. "You've been hit, Virg. Stay back."

"I'm all right. Let's go." He sounded breathless.

They jumped up and ran after Joe, ducking into doorways or behind cars as he turned to fire.

"I can't shoot, Virg! Every bullet's sure to hit some car!"

"Just keep him in sight till we chase him into the open. That bag he's carrying looks heavy; it's bound to slow him down."

Virgil was panting and his left arm hung limp, his shirtsleeve blood-soaked below the elbow.

"Take it easy, Virgil. You could bleed out."

Joe was now a full block ahead. Zooey couldn't believe his speed despite the heavy bag strapped to his back.

He'd completely fooled her. Now, more than anything, she wanted to stop him; she only wished Virgil would stay behind. She didn't want to lose any more friends.

The streets cleared as they approached the river. She was out of breath and each inhalation cut through her chest, yet Joe still jogged steadily ahead of them.

Virgil grabbed her. Panting, he stammered, "Can't…" as Joe ducked behind the corner of the last building before the river.

The roads here had nearly cleared out of cars headed for the highways out of town. Zooey darted out and pointed her gun at the driver of the only approaching vehicle. When the driver braked and raised his hands, she opened his door and pulled him out. She slammed shut the car door and stepped on the accelerator, spinning 180 degrees and burning rubber before Virgil could get in.

Just before the river, she slammed on the brakes and, the tires screaming, the car slid sideways, facing Joe running for the empty pier.

Jumping from the car, Zooey shot wildly as Joe approached a boat moored at the end of the dock. He reached down to untie the ropes holding the boat to the dock while calling to someone.

She steadied herself and knelt down. Taking slow and careful aim, she fired at the hand untying the ropes. Joe threw up his arms and she knew he'd been hit. The gun he held flew spinning through the air and dropped into the water.

She fired again, but found the clip was empty and she didn't have another. Without thinking, she threw the gun down and hurled herself after Joe.

A man appeared on the deck of the boat and stood a moment, surveying the situation. He pulled a gun from his waistband and waved it at Zooey, beckoning her to come closer. She was near enough that she doubted he would miss if she tried to run.

She walked up and stood next to Joe, who smirked at her, holding his wounded hand.

"Idiot traitor," he mumbled.

Looking up at the man with the gun, Joe said, "Shoot her, Mohammed. She knows too much. Then let's get out of here to that Russian ship."

Mohammed looked at Joe, and then laughed. "What Russian ship?"

He fired once and Joe buckled, his face twisted in shock. "What?" he gasped.

"Joe, Joe, Joe." Mohammed smiled. "If your own people can't trust you, how in the name of Allah can we? Eliminating you ties up our last few loose ends."

He fired once more, and Joe crumpled forward, falling against the side of the boat and then into the river. He struggled in the water for a moment, his eyes wide, gasping for air, but the weight of the pack on his back pulled him down like a rock, his agonized face disappearing from sight beneath the dark water.

Zooey stood limp, staring into the river where Joe had disappeared. Despite knowing she was sure to be next, she laughed. "That's a waste of a lot of money. I'm surprised you didn't make him drop the sack first."

Mohammed chuckled. "Eh, not really. Joe was an idiot. The money was all counterfeit, the jewels fake and the gold bars were gold-plated lead. Worth about 200 bucks altogether."

He looked at Zooey and she at him. "Sorry, Miss, but Joe is right. You know too much."

He raised his gun and a shot rang out. Zooey flinched, but to her amazement, it was Mohammed who staggered back. Zooey heard five more shots, and Mohammed fell to the deck of the boat, twitching for a moment, and then he lay still.

Zooey turned. Virgil stood a short distance away, panting, and in the act of lowering his gun.

EPILOGUE

Zooey sat in Francesca's living room, sipping green tea. Francesca, seated across from her, did the same, her mask propped up on the table staring blankly at Zooey.

"How's your shoulder?" Zooey asked.

Francesca shrugged painfully. "I shall survive. I always do. And you, my dear Zooey, how are you?"

"I was thinking of what Sakorski said after I shot him and he was dying. He said, 'Only you can do what we want.' I think he meant only we can destroy ourselves. Russia and ISIS will never be strong enough to do it to us. But they got clever, didn't they? No more suicide bombers. No more flying planes into buildings. No more random attacks. Instead, they pitted us against ourselves. It nearly succeeded, didn't it?"

Francesca sighed. "Who says it won't? The tribal violence they inspired is still wracking the country. Many don't believe the government's claim that the Russians and ISIS were behind all this. They believe the fake videos of Duke and Farrakhan, as well as the new Russian media propaganda proclaiming that they had nothing to do with the attacks. They point to the fact that the nuclear waste was from an American source, which the FBI admits. There is so much hate, Zooey. I do not know where it will end.

"Still, if not for you and Virgil, we might never have discovered the truth. We can only hope the truth will, in the end, prevail. The

FBI and the nation owe you a great debt for exposing who was behind the drone attacks, even if conspiracy enthusiasts will no doubt continue to say it was Duke and Farrakhan, or even that our own government was responsible." Francesca sighed.

"What's stunning," she continued, "is that most of the rest of the drones, after Baltimore and Detroit, weren't even armed with nuclear waste. The panic and fear they produced were far more effective than the actual damage done by nuclear waste dropped on those cites. They are still counting the dead and injured, as well as the financial losses caused by the panic and looting in the targeted cities."

Zooey thought for a moment. "You know," she finally said with some bitterness, "I fell in love with the wrong man. Again. We may destroy ourselves as a nation, but each of us is also better than anyone else at destroying ourselves."

"If choosing the wrong man were a crime, there would hardly be a woman left who would not be in jail, my dear."

"You know," Zooey said wistfully, "Mark loved me. I cared for him, but I didn't love him. I should have. But I never could have."

"Oh, Zooey, the heart wants what the heart wants. What does it matter? Love and obsession, perhaps it is all the same thing. I, of all people, am not the one to judge." She shrugged. "Look around here. Obsession is what I cater to. But you are a good person, Zooey, and I know you will find your way."

"How do you know that? Why would you think that?"

"Because, unlike me, you wear no mask. You want to believe, and love will find a way."

Finishing her tea, Francesca placed the mask on her face again.

"But let us get down to business, my dear. What is it you intend to do with yourself now that this is thankfully over?"

Zooey shrugged. "I don't know. I have come to the conclusion I'm not much of a detective. I'm certainly no Philip Marlowe."

"I disagree, but what about Mark's Bar? What will happen with that?"

"Well, I did learn Mark left it to me, along with what money he had. Like I said, the poor sap loved me, and I certainly didn't deserve it. But even with his inheritance, I don't have the cash needed to rebuild. I'm not sure I want to."

"Well, I have a proposal. Money is the one thing I have in abundance. Why don't I become your silent partner and fund the reconstruction of the bar? You could run your detective agency from it. The Mark's Memorial Soft Shoulder Bar and Detective Agency."

"Seriously?"

"Completely. I know Virgil will be your most loyal bar customer."

Zooey thought for a moment. "I think Mark would like that. There's just one problem. Virgil will never pay his tab because he saved my life and he'll drink on that for the rest of his Godforsaken days."

"Send me his tab. I'll consider it a cost of doing business."

Made in the USA
Middletown, DE
22 September 2020